THE ANNIHILATION OF
FOREVERLAND

THE ANNIHILATION OF
FOREVERLAND

Tony Bertauski

ISBN-13: 978-0982845288
ISBN-10: 0982845286

See more about the author and forthcoming books at
http://www.bertauski.com

Novels by Tony Bertauski

Claus: Legend of the Fat Man
The Discovery of Socket Greeny
The Training of Socket Greeny
The Legend of Socket Greeny

Novellas by Tony Bertauski

Drayton (The Taker)
Bearing the Cross (Drayton #2)
Swift is the Current (Drayton #3)
Yellow (Drayton #4)

Dedicated to things that matter.
You know who you are.

Where there's needles, there's pain.
The Needle's Prick by The Zin

ROUND
1

Local Computer Genius Arrested on Federal Charges

SUMMERVILLE, South Carolina. – Tyler Ballard, 37, was apprehended by authorities of the Federal Bureau of Investigation for practicing federally banned computer technology.

Ballard is best known for inventing the controversial technique of Computer-Assisted Alternate Reality (CAAR) that induces lucid dream states. The program requires a direct connection with the user's frontal lobe by means of a needle-probe piercing the forehead that results in a realistic computer-generated environment. Users reported no difference between their CAAR experience and flesh-body experience.

The controversial technology was later banned in most countries when all users began to suffer irreparable psychological damage that resulted in vegetative states.

Ballard was practicing CAAR in his basement with his wife, Patricia Ballard, 36. Patricia suffers from bipolar disorder and, Tyler Ballard claims, was responding well to CAAR treatments. Authorities dispute this claim since Patricia has been unresponsive to physical stimuli since the arrest.

Harold Ballard, 12, their only son, was placed in the custody of his grandparents.

1

Click-click-click-click.

The walls inched closer. Reed gripped the bars of his shrinking cell.

His legs, shaking.

The cold seeped through his bare feet. The soles were numb, his ankles ached. He lifted his feet one at a time, alternating back and forth to keep the bitter chill from reaching his groin, but he couldn't waste strength anymore. He let go of the bars to shake the numbness from his fingers.

He'd been standing for quite some time. *Has it been hours?* Occasionally he would sit to rest his aching legs, but soon the cell would be too narrow for that. He'd have to stand up. And when the top of his cage started moving down – and it would – he'd be forced to not-quite stand, not-quite sit.

He knew how things worked.

Although he couldn't measure time in the near-blackout room, this round felt longer than previous ones. Perhaps it would never end. Maybe he'd have to stand until his knees crumbled under his dead weight. His frigid bones would shatter like frozen glass when he hit the ground. He'd fall like a boneless bag, his muscles liquefied in a soupy mix of lactic acid and calcium, his nerves firing randomly, his eyes bulging, teeth chattering—

Don't think. No thoughts.

Reed learned that his suffering was only compounded by thoughts, that the false suffering of what he *thought* would happen would crush him before the true suffering did. He learned to be present with the burning, the cold, and the aches. *The agony.*

He couldn't think. He had to be present, no matter what.

Sprinklers dripped from the ribs of the domed ceiling that met at the apex where an enormous ceiling fan still moved from the momentum of its last cycle. Eventually, the sprinklers would hiss another cloud and the fan would churn again and the damp air would sift through the bars and over Reed's wet skin, heightening the aches in his joints like clamps. For now, there was just the drip of the sprinklers and the soft snoring of his cellmates.

Six individual cells were inside the building, three on each side of a concrete aisle. Each one contained a boy about Reed's age. They were all in their teens, the youngest being fourteen. Their cells were spacious; only Reed's had gotten smaller. Despite the concrete, they all lay on the floor, completely unaware of the anguish inside the domed building.

They weren't sleeping, though. Sleep is when you close your eyes and drift off to unconsciousness. No, they were somewhere else. The black strap around each of their heads took them away from the pain. They had a choice to stay awake like Reed, but they chose to lay down, strap on, and go wherever it took them. They didn't care where.

In fact, they wanted to go.

To escape.

Reed couldn't blame them. They were kids. They were scared and alone. Reed was all those things, too. But he didn't have a strap around his head. He stayed in his flesh.

He took a deep breath, let it out slowly. Started counting, again.

1, 2, 3, 4, 5, 6, 7, 8, 9...10.

And then he did it again. Again.

And again.

He didn't measure time with his breathing. He only breathed. His life was in his breath. It ebbed and flowed like the tides. It came and went like the lunar phases. When he could be here and now, the suffering was tolerable. He counted, and counted and counted.

Distracted, he looked up at the fan. The blades had come to a complete stop. The air was humid and stagnant and cold. Around the domed ceiling were circular skylights that stared down with unforgiving blackness, indifferent to suffering. Reed tried not to look with the hopes of seeing light pour through them, signaling an end. Regardless if it was day or night, the skylights were closed until the round of suffering was over, so looking, hoping and wishing for light was no help. It only slowed time when he did. And time had nearly stopped where he was at.

1, 2, 3—

A door opened at the far right; light knifed across the room, followed by a metallic snap and darkness again. Hard shoes clicked unevenly across the floor. Reed smelled the old man before he limped in front of his cell, a fragrance that smelled more like deodorant than cologne. Mr. Smith looked over his rectangular glasses.

"Reed, why do you resist?"

Reed met his gaze but didn't reply. Mr. Smith wasn't interested in a discussion. It was always a lecture. No point to prolong it.

"Don't be afraid." The dark covered his wrinkles and dyed-black hair, but it couldn't hide his false tone. "I promise, you try it once, you'll see. You don't have to do it again if you don't like it. We're here to help, my boy. Here to help. You don't have to go through this suffering."

Did he forget they were the ones that put him in there? Did he forget they made the rules and called the shots and forced him to play? Reed knew he – himself – he had gone mad but IS EVERYONE CRAZY?

Reed let his thoughts play in his eyes. Mr. Smith crossed his arms, unmoved.

"We don't want to hurt you, I promise. We're just here to prepare you for a better life, that's all. Just take the lucid gear, the pain will go away. I promise."

He reached through the bars and batted the black strap hanging above Reed's head. It turned like a seductive mobile. Reed turned his back on him. Mr. Smith sighed. A pencil scratched on a clipboard.

"Have it your way, Reed," he said, before limp-shuffling along. "The Director wants to see you after this round is over."

He listened to the incessant lead-scribbled notes and click-clack of shiny shoes. When Mr. Smith was gone, Reed was left with only the occasional drip of the dormant sprinklers. He began to breathe again, all the way to ten and over. And over. And over. No thoughts. Just 1, 2, 3… 1, 2, 3… 1, 2—

Click-click-click-click.

Reed locked his knees and leaned back as the cell walls moved closer. Soon the fan would turn again and the mist would drift down to bead on his shoulders. Reed couldn't stop the thoughts from telling him what the near future would feel like. How bad it was going to get.

He looked up at the lucid gear dangling above his head.

He took a breath.

And began counting again.

2

"Danny Boy!"

Danny's aunt's voice was muffled. She was calling from his bedroom with that thick Irish accent, obviously thought he was still in bed. Eventually, she'd come up to the attic where Danny was hunched over the keyboard, eyes on the screen. His mother had cleared a space out of the corner just for him, no one else, and even when the weather was too hot or too cold, Danny would sit up there all day.

"Danny Boy! Where are you, darling?"

He couldn't be interrupted now. He'd been acting sick for two weeks and got behind in school work. His mother trusted he was getting the homework done but he'd spent all his time modding the computer to do exactly what he was doing now.

People are stupid.

They used easy passwords and repeated the same one over and over. *Who thinks the word* password *is a password? Morons.*

It wasn't difficult to get past the school's firewall. Danny broke the encrypted password – using a program *he* wrote, thank you very much. In two seconds, he'd be a second grade, straight-A student. Once again.

Thank you very much.

Wait. I'm 13, not 7.

"Danny Boy?" The steps creaked. "Are you up here all ready? It's not even six o'clock in the morning, sonny boy."

Danny's fingers danced over the keys.

"Danny Boy… what are you doing?"

One more stroke and—

CRRUNNCH!

Danny fell out of the chair. The sound was deafening, like a metal pole plunging through the roof, smashing wood and shingles. Dust swirled in the new light. The steps creaked again, but something had changed. There wasn't insulation hanging from the ceiling anymore and there was a pile of boxes that wasn't there before.

The house changed.

"What are you doing in the attic?" A man was on the top step holding a golf club.

Danny blinked but it wasn't his aunt. And he wasn't in front of a computer anymore. He was lying in a crib. He was a thirteen-year-old kid in a baby's crib. In someone else's house.

The man's golf shoes sounded funny on the wood floor. He stopped short of the crib with his hands on his hips, the club teetering in his left hand. "Son, what in the hell are you doing? You think you're still a baby?"

Danny didn't move. Then the man smiled like a proud father.

"Well, if you want to do the baby thing again, let's give it a try."

He dropped the club and started tickling Danny's ribs. His fingers hit the funny spot and Danny gave out a chuckle. The man was all smiles, making happy-daddy sounds as he tortured him with loving grabs. Danny tried to knock him away but the man was too strong. Danny was about to piss his pants he was laughing so hard.

"Come here, you." The man snatched Danny up by the arms with a strong grip, but it wasn't strong enough. Danny slipped out of his clutches. He heard the man gasp as Danny fell out of the rickety crib, thought he'd land on his feet but the drop was farther than he expected. He crashed, all right; not on the floor, but on grass.

The sun was over him. The house was gone.

A crowd cheered. Danny was wearing a baseball uniform with a glove on his left hand. He'd never played baseball in his life, but there he was in center field with a cap pulled down just above his eyes.

Somewhere, an aluminum bat went *ting*.

The players on the infield turned around. The ball was high in the sky. The sun was in his eyes. He lifted the glove but couldn't see it. He tried squinting, tried covering the sun with his right hand but it was blinding. And the ball was going to hit him smack in the face. But he couldn't let the team down. He had to catch it. He had to—

And then he was swimming in the ocean. The waves crashed around him. There were other kids, too. Danny had never been to the beach, but there he was, swimming in water that churned at his waist—

And then he was coloring Easter eggs. There was a lady at the sink with an apron and some little girl across the table. He'd never seen her before—

Opening birthday presents and people were singing. People he'd never—

Playing Hide and Seek. He was hiding behind a bush with someone he'd—

Baking cookies—

School bus—

The scenes stacked on top of each other until he couldn't tell where one began and the next ended. It was all a blur. All a blur.

All a blur.

The throbbing.

That was the first thing Danny noticed before he cracked the seal of his sleep-crusted eyelashes. The head-splitting throb. His forehead felt like it had been punched with a dental tool.

"Don't sit up just yet, young man." A soft hand was on his arm. "Give it a few seconds."

He did what the man said.

When he opened his eyes, the light seemed bright. It took a minute of rapid blinking to adjust. He was in a doctor's office, on a patient's table. The paper that covered the table was bunched up under him, crinkling when he moved. There was an old man sitting on a stool next to him. His face was plenty wrinkled and his hair as white as the coat he wore.

"I'm Mr. Jones." The man broke out in grin worthy of a father looking at his newborn.

"Wa…" Danny's tongue was gummy. "Water, please."

"Sit up first, all right?"

When Danny was up, Mr. Jones passed him a paper cup and watched him chug it.

"More, please."

"Let that settle for a moment, okay. There's more when you're ready."

He wrapped a band around Danny's arm and took his blood pressure. Then took his temperature and pulse. He did some scribbling on a clipboard, occasionally looking up and humming.

The room, now that Danny had a chance to focus, was less like a doctor's office and more like a lab. There seemed to be large equipment attached to the wall that could be pulled out and centered on hinged arms. And behind him, the room went back another twenty feet with a treadmill and monitors and more machines.

"You go by Danny Boy?" the man asked.

"I'm sorry?"

"You were dreaming before you woke up and mumbled Danny Boy. I thought maybe that was what you preferred to be called. Danny Boy."

"My aunt… she called me that…"

"Ah, yes. Aunts are special, aren't they?" He grinned, again.

Danny reached for his head that felt so full of… stuff. But Mr. Jones caught him by the wrist. "Just relax a second, Danny Boy."

"I was having this weird dream… like it was a bunch of dreams all crammed into one."

"Dreams are like that." Mr. Jones quickly looked at his clipboard.

"Where am I?"

"You've had an accident, but you're okay now. Would you like some more water?"

"Yes, please."

He downed a second paper cup and wadded it before handing it back.

"Um, Doctor…"

"You can call me Mr. Jones."

"Mr. Jones, am I in a hospital?"

"You're somewhere much better than a hospital, my boy. You're in a special rehabilitation center that is unique for your condition. You'll have the best care that money can buy while you're here and you'll get to do things no other kid on this planet has ever tried. You'll also… ah, ah, ah… don't touch."

Danny reached for his forehead. There was a round band-aid the size of a Bull's eye right in the middle where it hurt. He tried to remember an accident, anything that he would've been doing that would've knocked him on the head, but all the memories were gibberish. He couldn't remember his home address or phone number. If his aunt hadn't been calling for him, he wouldn't remember his name.

"Is this why I'm here?" He tried to touch the bandage again.

"In some ways, yes."

"Did I fall on an ice pick?"

"No." Mr. Jones snorted. "You've been asleep for a long time while you've undergone treatment, so you may feel a bit woozy when you stand up. Be careful, all right? I want you to lean forward and let your toes touch the ground… good. Now stay just like that a second." Mr. Jones spun on the stool and coasted to the computer behind him. "And don't touch your forehead."

Danny's toes were tingly. Just the little weight that was on them, he could tell standing wasn't going to go well. He left his forehead alone, reached for his stiff neck, instead. It was sore, too. And there was a knot between the vertebrae. It felt like a band had been inserted just under the skin about the width of a wedding ring that made it seem like one large neck bone. Mr. Jones had one bulging on his neck, too.

"What's this?"

"That's part of your treatment," Mr. Jones said without looking. "It's new technology meant to stay in touch with your nervous system. We'll talk more about that later."

"Okay," was all Danny could think to say. He was thirteen. When an adult said something, he listened and that was that. But nothing was making sense, not the strange lab or Mr. Jones and his proud grin like everything was normal. His head was just so full.

"Where are my parents?"

Mr. Jones took several moments at the computer before he stood up with the clipboard over his stomach. "They want you to get better, Danny Boy. And that's what you're going to be… better."

Smile.

"When will I see them?"

"Can you put all your weight forward?"

He held out his hand and Danny took it. His weight was a little wobbly, but he felt better on his feet than he thought he would.

"Where are we?" Danny asked.

"Take a step for me and I'll tell you."

He took one step, then two. They reached the door and Mr. Jones opened it without letting go. The hallway was long and white.

"We're going that way." He pointed to the left. At that end was a glass wall.

Danny dragged his feet the first couple of steps. He was already breathing a little hard. Mr. Jones was slightly hunched over next to him. Danny put his hand on the wall and traced it with his fingers. His knees were weak but Mr. Jones watched him with a smile like everything was just okie-dokie. His touch became lighter as Danny's footsteps became more confident. When he let go, Danny still touched the wall but was walking closer to normal when they reached the end.

The glass wall was slightly curved like the building was a giant cylinder. They were a few stories above ground. A little ways away was the back of a horseshoe-shaped building. Beyond that was a large green field with people.

"You're going to love it here, Danny Boy," he whispered.

The field looked like a college campus lined with tropical trees and palms with giant white birds. Danny was smart but he wasn't college-smart. Unless something happened to his brain. He reached for his forehead. Mr. Jones gently caught his arm before he could graze the band-aid with his fingertips.

"I'm going to be your Investor while you're here. I'm invested in your future, Danny Boy. If you ever need anything or have any questions, I'm the one that will help, all right?"

Danny nodded.

Mr. Jones smacked a sticker on Danny's shirt. *Hello, I'm Danny Boy.*

"I'll be by your side the whole way, Danny Boy. That you can trust. We have a deal?"

They shook hands and watched the activity below. It looked like one big summer camp on a tropical island. Danny's parents weren't rich, they couldn't afford something like this. At least he didn't think so. He couldn't remember them at the moment. But he wasn't going to ask questions, even though Mr. Jones said he could.

"Let's go down to the Yard," Mr. Jones said, gesturing to the wide-open field, "and meet your fellow campers."

By the time they reached the elevator and selected the ground floor, Danny had already forgotten about the doctor's office and the dream and the confusion. He stared at the doors inside the elevator; the reflection of a red-headed kid with a slight body and freckles looked back. He looked like a stranger with a name tag stuck on his t-shirt.

"I'm Danny Boy," he whispered.

3

They walked through the woods for ten minutes. The path was mulched and the trees thick above them with dangling vines and scrubby palms. Mr. Jones was sweating through his shirt and had to stop midway to catch his breath and wipe his face. He was all hunched over. Danny found a stick and Mr. Jones said thank you.

They came out of the trees at the back of the horseshoe-shaped building that had no windows. It was a huge blank wall tinted green with algae and one door right in the middle. They went inside.

Danny's room was smack in the middle of the building. Unlike the back wall, this side of the building faced the Yard with plenty of windows. Danny could see to the other side. It was big enough to hold five or six football fields.

Mr. Jones sat on the bed wiping the sweat from the folds of his neck. He gave Danny a feeble smile and pointed to things. "There's your sink and the bathroom is next to the closet. Your drawers already have clothes folded in them. The hamper chute is down the hall." He took a few wheezy breaths. "You can get new sheets once a week."

Danny opened the closet and thumbed through the shirts and pants that were all brand new and all pressed and ready to wear. All exactly his size. Mr. Jones attempted to stand but the mattress drew him back down. Danny offered a hand but he ignored it, doing sort of a side roll to one buttock before throwing himself onto his feet. He nodded with a pained grin.

"Out there, Danny Boy," he said, sweeping his hand at the window, "that's where most of the boys hang out in their spare time. The Yard is where you'll find them."

The Yard sounds like a prison.

The area near the dorm was crisscrossed with sidewalks forming an X with – from what Danny could tell – a giant sun dial in the middle. Tables were in between the sidewalks but the Yard beyond was grassy.

"But you're not limited to the Yard. You can go wherever you want, I mean it. You're free here, Danny Boy. Go climb a tree, hike the trails, fishing… whatever. Well, you can go anywhere," he lifted a finger, "except where I live. None of the campers are allowed in the Investors' quarters."

"Where's that?"

"We have accommodations back where we came from, only a little further. Besides that, the sky's the limit, my boy."

"Can I go home?"

Chuckle. "Not unless you're a real good swimmer. We're on an island, Danny Boy. It's about five square miles or so, but there's nothing but water as far as the eye can see. Even if you're a good swimmer, I don't recommend it. Sharks and ship-eating coral and the like will tear you up."

He wanted to call them, but there wasn't a phone in the room and Mr. Jones didn't have one on his belt, either. There wasn't even a clock. Besides, Danny was having a hard time remembering what his folks looked like and that disturbed him, so he tried to forget it.

"Where are we?"

"Let's just say we're plenty isolated." Mr. Jones shuffled closer to the window. "Now, this isn't all recess, just so you know. You see over there on the left is the library where you'll be taking classes, but don't get nervous. They're not like high school. You don't get grades, they're just fun classes to keep your brain active and strong. And next to the library is the gym to keep your body active and strong." Mr. Jones flexed his biceps and said with his best Russian accent, "Strong like bull!"

He lifted Danny's arm, smacked his bicep like he was trying to wake it up.

"Listen, Danny Boy. We just want you of sound body and mind when you're ready to graduate. Only the best, only the best, my boy."

The cafeteria, Mr. Jones said, was on the west wing of the dormitory. As long as Danny was here, everything was free. Games, food, classes, all of it paid for. By who, he didn't say. He might have some limitations on food because, Mr. Jones said with a chuckle, "I don't want you getting fat on me."

"They're all boys," Danny Boy said.

"Pardon me?"

Danny pointed at the field. "This is a boys' camp, right?"

"Well, it's easier that way, Danny Boy. Girls can be a distraction and we want all your attention on improving your body and mind. But just between you and me," Mr. Jones winked and nudged him with an elbow, "you'll have plenty of chances to meet girls when you're ready. Nothing wrong with that, if you ask me. Nothing wrong, indeed. By the way, see those boys down there?"

He pointed at a group sitting at one of the many picnic tables.

"That's your group. You ready to go meet some of your fellow campers?"

Danny didn't know what to say. Didn't seem like he had much of a choice. Mr. Jones walked a little easier to the door this time. He stood a little taller and started to open the door.

"What's that building over there?"

Mr. Jones answered without looking. "We'll talk about that later."

It was past the far end of the field buried in the trees. Its dome-shaped roof was just above the forest canopy. Sunlight reflected off the circular skylights.

"Come along, Danny Boy. There's nothing to worry about."

Danny followed him, reluctantly. He was thirteen years old. When an adult says there's nothing to worry about, there's usually plenty.

4

Everyone stared.

Mr. Jones walked damn near zero miles an hour. Danny kept his eyes straight ahead. They cut across the grass. Everyone seemed pretty tan, but the sun bit into Danny's fair skin. They were aimed at the group at a picnic table near the sun dial. Four of them were playing cards. The fifth was watching. When they got close, the game stopped and they watched the painfully slow approach of Mr. Jones and his sidekick.

"Well, lookie there," one of them mumbled. "We got ourselves a new poke."

Mr. Jones leaned one hand on the table.

"Boys." He took a long breath. "This is your new camper. I'd like you to meet Danny Boy."

"Hey, *Danny Boy,*" one of them said.

Most gave a head nod. Danny sort of smiled, waiting for Mr. Jones to either leave or die.

"This is your group, or camp," Mr. Jones finally said. "You'll be going through your work with them for the next couple months, so you'll get to know them pretty well."

"We love pokes," someone said.

"Now be nice, boys. You remember what it was like when you first got here, extend some courtesy to this young man. I don't want to hear about any funny business. You remember that, now. I've got my eye on you. Anything happens to my Danny Boy I'll come down here and tan your hides, you understand?"

My Danny Boy?

The card dealer with a shag of black hair waggled his bushy eyebrows and those around the table smirked.

"I'm not kidding, boys. You try me and see how fast I can reach into my pocket."

Danny wondered what was in the pocket. A notepad or a laser beam?

A golf cart silently pulled up while Mr. Jones eyeballed each of them. The driver was older than Mr. Jones. His gray hair looked wet and parted on the right. The white line of his scalp showed through the part as straight as a razor. He set the brake and made an attempt to get out but his belly was rubbing against the steering wheel. He got it on the second try.

"Mr. Miller," Mr. Jones said.

Mr. Miller acknowledged Mr. Jones with a nod but ignored the rest of them. He walked to the other side of the table to speak with a gangly kid with an Adam's apple the size of a walnut. His cheeks were pasty and he stared vacantly at the table while Mr. Miller spoke quietly into his ear, occasionally nodding. The walnut bobbed up and down. Mr. Miller patted him on the back and waddled back to the cart without making eye contact with anyone, again.

"Remember, I'm watching, boys." Mr. Jones pointed two fingers at his eyes, then at the rest of them. Danny needed him to leave for a whole lot of reasons. If the rest of the Investors were as decrepit as Mr. Jones, they would be as much help as a box of kittens.

And when he thought it couldn't get any worse.

Mr. Jones waved him over to the cart. He stopped a couple steps away. Mr. Jones pulled him closer and put his hand – soft with lotion – on Danny's cheek, lovingly. "You call if you need me. All right, my boy?"

He did not.

Do.

That.

Danny jumped back and shook like a wet dog. Mr. Jones looked a little hurt, but then nodded like maybe he realized and understood that you just don't do that TO A THIRTEEN YEAR OLD BOY!

Unless you wanted him to die of embarrassment, of shame and humiliation.

The entire world would have to be on fire before he called Mr. Jones for help.

The card game was more important than Danny. That was a good thing.

He walked away to get some space. If he was going to hang out with them, he needed to make a new first impression. He shoved his hands in his pockets and turned his back, looked around the Yard. There were maybe a couple dozen boys out there, but they were a mix of race and nationality. He heard someone speaking French. Regardless, they were all boys. Every last one of them.

But you'll get your chance.

There was only one loner. He had his shirt over his shoulder. His long hair was dark. He walked slowly, one foot in front of the other, like he was just soaking in the sun with nowhere to go. Even from where Danny was standing – about fifty feet away – he bet he could count the kid's ribs.

"Hey, I'm Zin." A kid about Danny's height stepped next to him. He was plump, brown skinned with a shaved head and a mean looking zit in the middle of his forehead. "You're Danny Boy, huh right."

"Oh. Yeah." Danny peeled off the nametag.

"Ain't much of a welcome wagon, but that's the way it goes around here. You'll figure it out soon enough."

"How soon is that?"

"It'll feel like home in a day. Two, tops."

Danny had transferred to a new school when he was ten (or was it five?). His dad was a teacher (or was he an engineer?) and got transferred to the mountains (or was it the beach?). Danny got in a fight the first day (or did he run away?). The biggest of the bunch got up right in the middle of class and slapped him while the teacher had her back turned. They duked it out after school.

(Or was it lunch?)

"How long you been here?" Danny asked.

"Long enough. I can tell you one thing, I didn't get a welcome half as warm as you got. As soon as the Investors left they threw me in a trash can."

Yep, there it is. This was prison because he was standing in the Yard and there were no girls, just boys. No need for barbed wire when you were surrounded by "sharks and ship eating coral and the like".

He remembered a time he got in trouble, something about a computer. Danny knew that if he was right – that this really was some sort of prison enclosed by water – then there had to be rape. He'd watched enough *Locked Up* episodes to know the weak got it good and these guys were going to bust into his room for a little midnight snack and who was going to stop them? Mr. Jones and his team of geriatric superheroes?

"Listen, it's a little intimidating the first day," Zin said, picking up on Danny's expression or the pale color of his cheeks, "but you get used to it in no time. And these guys aren't going to do anything to you, so don't worry. We all look out for each other."

"How'd you end up here?"

"Same way as everyone else." He shrugged. "Woke up with my Investor staring at me and couldn't remember a damn thing. I take that back, I remembered too many things and nothing made sense. You?"

Danny wanted to just forget about the dream and the weird feeling in his head and Mr. Jones touching his cheek.

"That's what I thought. Listen, don't sweat it." Zin lightly punched his shoulder. "This place has its ups and downs, but it ain't so bad… look, that's the library over there… and the game room is behind the gym…"

Another orientation, but this one felt better coming from Zin without the creepy grin Mr. Jones was wearing when he did it. The buildings were all dome-shaped besides the horseshoe-shaped dormitory. Zin pointed everything out and then named everyone in their camp.

"And if you want to know what time it is, there you go." He pointed at the sun dial. "It's never wrong."

"What's that?" Danny pointed at the round building across the Yard, the same one he'd seen from his room.

"That's the Haystack. You'll find out about that in a few weeks when we start a new round. I don't want to spoil the surprise."

"That much fun?"

Zin thought about it. "Yes and no."

"He looks like he had a blast." Danny nodded to Mr. Miller's kid, still staring. Saliva glistened on his lip.

The kid with a mop of black hair dealing the cards had been listening. "Yeah, old Parker here is about to get smoked, ya'll." He smacked zombie-Parker on the back and rattled his head. Parker didn't seem to notice so much. Or care.

"Sid means that Parker's about to graduate," Zin said. "We all graduate at some point."

"From what?"

"From the island. You're here because you got problems, Danny Boy. You'll learn that problems start with your mind, that we assign concepts and requirements to life that create friction and chaos. If we want to heal, we start with the mind. Or at least, that's what the Investors tell us. Who the hell knows."

Zin's smile was infectious.

"You believe that?" Danny asked.

"Sure, why not? Don't you see, Danny Boy, the universe is perfectly imperfect." Zin wiggled his hands in mysterious-fashion. "There are no problems, you just think there are. And you believe what you think, and that's why you're here. We're going to fix you."

Zin jabbed at Danny's forehead.

"And once you're fixed, you get smoked. And once you're smoke, you're out of here."

Zin pointed at the cylindrical building rising up from behind the dorms. Bands of glass windows alternated with bands of metal. Five floors. One of those glass floors was where Danny woke up and walked down the hall. The top floor was black glass. At the very top was a long chimney.

"That's right," Zin added. "Once you go to the Chimney, you leave the island. It's graduation time, kind of like how they pick a new pope, when someone graduates the Chimney puffs and then it's sayonara, baby."

"Where do we go?"

"Home, I guess. Where else?"

The thought of going home wasn't as comforting as it should've been, mainly because Danny couldn't quite remember it.

"Come on." Sid slung his arm around Parker's shoulders. "Let's have some fun before they smoke you, pal. What'd you say, huh? Old times?"

Parker was glassy-eyed.

"That's the spirit. Let's go, ya'll." They chucked the cards on the table and left the mess behind. "Zinski, bring the new poke. We'll need him to take Parker's spot on the team so let's get him to the game room. We got a match in an hour."

Zin pulled Danny along. Sid walked with his arm around Parker. It didn't look like he was going to make it unless someone kept him propped up. A cold feeling crept into Danny's stomach. He had a feeling what happened to him.

"What's a poke?"

"That means you're a rookie, a virgin that just got popped." Zin pointed at the round band-aid on Danny's head. "You got poked, Danny Boy."

Danny touched the bandage. He felt a little guilty after Mr. Jones told him not to, then he noticed the zit on Zin's forehead. When he first saw it, it looked like a deep blackhead. It was a little red and puffy around the edges, like maybe he was squeezing it. *Is that a hole?*

A cold feeling trickled into his legs.

Danny noticed the loner kid with the shirt over his shoulder. He was hardly a kid, looked like he was nineteen or twenty. Easily the oldest one around. An old man (there seemed to be an endless supply of them) limped toward him. There were a few words exchanged.

"Yo, Danny Boy!" Zin was calling. "Don't get lost on day one, hurry up!"

Danny watched the long-haired kid follow the limping old man. Maybe he was going to get smoked.

5

Mr. Smith didn't talk much. Reed expected that.

The old man limped along with a small grunt whenever he heaved his bum leg forward.

The elevator was in the center of the first floor. The inside was curved like a big tin can. There were only buttons for four floors. Nothing for the fifth. The doors remained opened while Mr. Smith looked at the numbers and the small camera staring back. A few seconds later, they closed and the elevator made the gut-dropping rise to the top of the Chimney.

Mr. Smith put his hand on Reed's chest. "Wait here."

The elevator opened. There were no walls on the top floor. Just one big room. One section had bedroom furniture, another office furniture; there was a bar with liquor bottles. But nothing in-between.

On the far side, by the dim windows, a large man wearing a flowery shirt was looking through an oversized telescope. Mr. Smith limped over. His words murmured across the room. The Director never looked up from the eyepiece but occasionally muttered back.

There had been other boys that failed in the Haystack for whatever reason and they just disappeared. No graduation or farewell just *poof* – they were gone. Didn't matter if they went mental or the needle lobotomized them, it was game over.

Move on to the next contestant.

But they had been patient with Reed. He was nineteen. He'd be twenty in a couple months. And twenty – for whatever reason – was a magic number. *Poof.*

Mr. Smith didn't look happy.

He was trying to hold his voice in check and kept stealing glances at Reed when he got too loud. The Director never bothered to pull off his telescope while Mr. Smith waved his arms and smacked his fist. And then he was dismissed. Mr. Smith came back like a peg-legged pirate that dipped his hair in a bucket of ink.

His cheeks were flush.

"The Director would like a word."

"Reed, my boy, come here." The Director was still hunched over the telescope when Reed approached. "You don't want to miss this, take a look."

Reed hesitated. The Director stood up and stretched his back. "Well, do I need to mail you an invitation? Come on, you must see this," he said, happily. "Nature is happening, son."

The Director was a large man with a scraggly beard and squinty, smiling eyes. He was wearing baggy shorts and flip-flops. Reed stopped short of the telescope, peering out the window at the back side of the island – a view rarely seen by any of the teenage campers. Rarely was one of them brought up to the Director's office. The Investors' living quarters hundred yards away, right on the edge of the island – the Mansion with stately palms. Beyond that was endless water.

"Reed, unless you can stretch your eyeball out of your head, you're going to have to bend over to see what I'm talking about." The Director smiled. "Take a look."

Reed did so. Slowly. He adjusted his eye around the lens. It was focused far out into the ocean. Everything shimmered blue.

"You see it?" the Director asked. "Don't touch the scope, just look with your eye. Just stay open and you'll see it."

There was nothing. Suddenly, there was a spray of water. A humpback whale broke the surface, its slick body rolled over and the white speckled tail slapped the water. He wanted to see it again.

"Magnificent, right?" The Director slapped him on the back. "Nature."

Reed stayed perched over the telescope. Moments later, another one came up for a breath and disappeared beneath the waves, free to go as deep and as far away as it wished.

"How many rounds have you been through, Reed?"

Reed stood.

The Director was at the bar near a section of plush furniture. Ice rattled in a couple of tumblers and the Director poured drinks. One with Coke, the other whiskey. He brought the Coke to Reed, handed it to him with a stiff smile, the eyes still crinkled.

"I've lost count," the Director said. "Twenty-five, would you say?"

"Sounds a little high."

"Math wasn't my strong suit, but twenty-five times you've been through the Haystack, Reed." The Director took a drink and grimaced. "You like punishment?"

"I've discovered my inner masochist."

"Well, then, how about I punch you in the face and we'll have a ball." He smiled wide and laughed loud. Reed joined him. They were both in on the joke for several moments, although the Director laughed a little hard.

The Director leisurely strolled away. He swirled the glass. He stopped at a large cage behind the expansive mahogany desk. It reached up to the ceiling, inside were a pair of large white parrots. He looked up at them, said, "Why won't you take the lucid gear, Reed?"

"I'm not crazy about getting punched in the head with a needle."

"It's not a needle, Reed. It's lucid gear, and it doesn't hurt, you know that. The other boys have told you so. Hell, I'm telling you." He pointed at the neat little hole in his forehead.

"Forgive me," Reed said. "The *needle-like* lucid gear goes through the skull. It can't feel good."

The ice rattled. The Director sipped, nodding. He looked over, head cocked. A grim smile. He jerked his head, signaling Reed to come over. The glass of Coke was still full, soaking in his hand. *Sweat or condensation?*

Together, they watched the birds.

"This is my island, Reed. It's my program, my vision that happens here. These…" He waved his drink toward the Mansion. "These Investors fund it, but it's my vision to use cutting edge technology – revolutionary ideas – to help people like you, Reed."

"I didn't ask for help."

"Yes, you did. You just don't know it."

"I don't know much of anything, thanks to you."

The Director ignored the insult. "You're a kid, Reed. You don't know anything about life and your place in it. And it's a damn shame to see a kid like you with so much potential just waste away to nothing. I can't accept a world that turns its back on people that need help, Reed. I can't. I won't."

Reed realized the floor was slowly rotating. His view of the Mansion was slightly askew from when he arrived. Eventually, they'd be turning back towards the dormitory and the Yard.

"Why do you think I brought you here, Reed?"

"You know I don't know that."

The Director was nodding. He knew that Reed couldn't make sense of the multitude of memories that crowded his mind; memories they both knew were implanted in Reed's head to keep him confused, to keep him from remembering his past.

The Director put his drink on a small table and opened the doors beneath it. He pulled out a small cage squirming with oversized cockroaches. The parrots flapped madly, squawking. Feathers floated out of the cage.

"You think I brought you here to torture, mmm?"

"It's crossed my mind."

"You think I get my jollies by filling an island with young boys to torture?" He popped the lid and reached inside. The cockroaches hissed. "You think that's me?"

"I don't know who you are, Director. Like you said, I don't even know who I am."

A wingless cockroach clung to the Director's finger, blowing air from the spiracles on its abdomen to hiss loudly. He held it close to his face. The cockroach hunched over and went quiet.

"I like you, Reed. You remind me of myself, all full of piss and vinegar. For all I know, you're refusing the lucid gear just to spite me, to spite Mr. Smith. And I can respect that. I mean, Jesus lord, you've withstood some discomfort, son. I don't think I could've done it when I was your age and I was one tough son of a bitch. You believe that?"

There was a long pause. The Director turned his hand over; the cockroach clung to it upside-down.

Reed answered, "Believe what?"

"That I was a tough S-O-B?"

"Again, I don't know you, sir."

"Yes, you do, Reed." The Director glared, intensely. "You know me."

Reed turned away. He didn't know the Director, but that look told him everything he needed to. *You know what I do.*

The Director plucked the cockroach off his hand. It threw a fit, hissing and scratching for a grip. He pinched it by the abdomen. The birds jumped to the branch nearest the cage, their beaks jawing open and close, open and close. The Director dangled the cockroach just out of their reach. Feathers flew.

The cockroach hissed and hissed, and then it ended with its exoskeleton crunching loudly in the curved beak of the larger bird. The Director took a sip of his drink, watching the bird pull half the insect's body, legs flailing, out of its mouth with its claw, chewing on it like popcorn.

"What makes you so tough, Reed?"

"I don't know, sir. Maybe my father was a Navy SEAL."

The Director stepped directly in front of Reed. They were eye to eye, only inches apart. Scotch was on his breath. "Every single boy that's been to the island has taken the lucid gear the very first time they go to the Haystack. Not one has resisted, and you've done it… how many times, Reed?"

Shrug.

"Twenty-five," the Director said. "You get it wrong again, I'll slap you."

He stayed uncomfortably closer, staring. The bird grinding the insect into bite-sized pieces.

Reed knew how he resisted, but how did he tell the man responsible for all the misery around him that it was a dream that told him not to take the needle? *Sounds crazy, but what doesn't?*

It happened when he woke up in the lab with Mr. Smith staring at him. He clung to a memory as he opened his eyes. It was a girl with long red hair. She told him – as if she was talking to him – to resist. She told him that if he did, they would be together again, one day. It wouldn't be easy, but he had to resist. If anyone could do it, he could.

He didn't know what resisting meant until he entered the Haystack.

And when his resolve faded, when he considered reaching for the needle because he just couldn't take it anymore, when he just wanted it to end, he would have another dream.

Resist.

The Director, looking as far into Reed's eyes as he could and seeing nothing, stepped away. He sipped, thinking. Reed noticed the lump on the back of his neck when he bent over for another cockroach, the tracker imbedded between the C4 and C5 vertebrae. No one went unchecked on the island, not even the man at the top.

"I can't accept watching you piss away an opportunity, Reed. Do you know what's right in front of you? The effort Mr. Smith and I made to bring you here, to offer you freedom from your problems, to give you a nobler life. Do you know what it costs every day we keep you here and watch you deny the healing we offer?"

He squeezed the cockroach in his palm, crunching inside his closed fist.

"Do you know how hard we work TO GIVE YOU A BETTER LIFE?"

The birds jumped. So did Reed.

"We're pioneers, Reed," he said, softly. "We're forging into new ground of healing the world. You're a pioneer, do you understand that?"

Reed nodded, slowly.

The Director held his gaze, then offered his hand to the unfed bird. It pushed its beak between the bars and snatched the cockroach out of his palm. The Director flicked the slimy remains on the bottom of the cage and walked away wiping his hands with a paper towel.

The Director went to another telescope at the perimeter of the room, this one aimed over the Mansion. The floor had rotated. Reed was looking at the dorm and the Yard beyond.

"You have a shot at a second life, but I can't make you take it. All I can do is offer you healing. No one can make you go lucid, you have to want it. Don't you see, that's why we make you uncomfortable before it's offered? Your mind detaches from the body when it's in pain, yet you continue to stay. You won't take what I offer, Reed. And I can't understand that."

The Director spent a few minutes focusing on a new target. He stood up, hands on his hips. Staring out, pensive. Struggling with a thought. A decision. "Five more rounds, Reed." The Director looked at Reed over the couches and tables and space in between. "I'm giving you an opportunity to help me help you. This is your last chance to take my outstretched hand. I can't help the unwilling, son. You understand?"

The Director smiled, eyes squinting.

"If you don't, then I've failed you, son. And I'm sorry for that."

The Director went back to the telescope. The birds licked their beaks. Reed looked at the Yard below, wiping his slick forehead where the needle hole had long since healed.

6

Danny remembered going to summer camp… or something like that. The more he thought about it, maybe it was just camping. They went fishing. It seemed like a really fun time in his life.

The island was even better.

No one assaulted him in his sleep. No one dumped him in a trash can or even so much as gave him a wedgie. It was ten days of non-stop fun.

It started in the game room which turned out to be a game *building*. Flat screen monitors were positioned around the perimeter showing on-going games or flashing team standings of various competitions. Most of them were small capsules where campers could experience three-dimensional action while some were simple screen games for one or two people.

On the first day, Sid led them through the crowd. There were about twenty-five people – all boys, no old men – watching or playing. They made their way to center stage: a twenty-foot wide circular platform enclosed by a clear dome. Inside was a small scale layout of a war-torn city with smoldered buildings and overturned cars. Digital troops strategically stalked the cityscape and miniature helicopters rained bullets and missiles into clouds of smoke and fire.

There was a group on each side that controlled the tiny figures and with each explosion and each death, numbers changed on the four-side scoreboard hanging from the ceiling. Names repositioned in the standings. An hour later, one team stood victorious.

Zin smacked Danny in the chest. “We’re up.”

The taunting started when they stepped onto the small stage vacated by the losers, a group of Middle Eastern boys in their early teens. Danny saw the other team on the opposite side of the dome – they were Russian, maybe – pulling on black gloves. Sid was trading insults with the crowd, pointing at the scoreboard and thumping his chest. Zin gave Danny a pair of gloves and knee pads.

"No time for instruction. You'll figure it out."

The gloves slid on like silk embedded with fine wire mesh. The knee pads strapped on without anything special. Sid passed out yellow-tinted goggles with embedded earbuds and miniature microphones. Danny was still playing with the goggles when he was assigned to a tower and told to keep his head down.

"Watch and learn." That was the only time Sid addressed Danny. "And try not to get killed, poke."

The game started.

Instead of watching the action like the spectators, Danny saw it inside the goggles. The view was first person, like he was inside the dome, shrunk down to size. The goggles absorbed his vision. When he turned his head, the view changed.

He was in a tower with a two-ton bell. For the first twenty minutes, he did what he was told, experimenting with the controls and not getting killed. He learned his movements were controlled by bending his knees. The gloves controlled his hands and weapons. After that, he watched half of his crew get slaughtered on one of Sid's stupid ambushes.

When there was nothing to lose, he went to the ground.

He felt the rubble under his feet, the heat of burning automobiles. He ran from building to building and by the time he neared the action, Zin was the only one left. He was hiding inside a bunker that was about to be flamed.

When Danny was later asked how he slaughtered the opposing team, he didn't have a good answer. He just said that it made sense, that he didn't realize he was intuiting the enemy's moves and shot them with effortless accuracy and moved with the grace of a veteran assassin. He just did it.

He sniped the last enemy from three hundreds. After that, everyone in the game room knew his name.

There were classes, too.

Although, like Mr. Jones said, it wasn't really class. They talked about economics and geology and philosophy, but it was just talk. There was no homework, no tests. The instructors were the old men, of course, that insisted they exercise their whole brains when they thought about various topics, so they kept the discussion lively. The boys debated loudly, acted out their passion and shook hands when it was all over. It wasn't bad, Danny had to admit. Without the busy-work of homework, he was interested in class.

Sort of. Kind of.

Strange thing, though. There was no Internet, no email, text messages or phones. There weren't even computers. There was plenty of time for worldly things, the Investors said. Just not now.

Occasionally, Danny would hear a bell ring three times like a gong. Then he'd see boys heading for the Haystack and sometimes leaving it. Once, someone was carted away from it. An Investor was driving a utility vehicle and another old man was on the flatbed with the boy lying down. No one said much and the Investors stared straight ahead as they drove around the dormitory toward the Chimney.

In the first couple weeks, Danny saw the Chimney smoke three times.

Danny sat with his camp at lunch. He didn't know anyone else.

He half-listened to Sid layout their next game strategy and watched people move through the line. Another group returned from the Haystack, this one Hispanic. They hardly spoke.

One of them was a new poke. *The band-aid.*

Mr. Jones took Danny's band-aid off within the first week. He was a little more chill after the hand on the cheek incident. Danny decided if it happened again, he was swimming for it, screw the sharks. But Mr. Jones was cool. He just wanted to make sure Danny was getting everything he needed and followed his schedule. He had a knack of always finding Danny, but then he remembered the tracker in his neck. Mr. Jones could probably count the number of turds Danny dropped in the morning.

Danny peeled the band-aid off. Beneath it was a neat little hole. It wasn't red, wasn't sore. Just a hole. Mr. Jones wiped it with some alcohol, said the stent was healing just fine. He sensed Danny had a question – as anyone who woke up with a hole in the head would have – and said the hole was for healing. And not to worry.

Don't worry, my boy. He said that a lot.

"You listening?" Sid snapped his fingers in Danny's face. "Come on, man, you need to pay attention. This next battle is our last before we go to the Haystack. That's when it gets real, son. You're good with the gloves but things change when you get inside."

"Danny Boy isn't going to be any good the first round," Zin said, swallowing the last of his milk. "He shouldn't even be on the squad until he gets a few rounds inside the Haystack, you know that. You forget, he's a new poke."

"Yeah, just in case, Zinski."

"That's what we do in the Haystack?" Danny asked. "More games?"

Long silence.

Silence, every time the topic of the Haystack came up – and what the needle was. Danny knew what was likely to happen, it didn't take a genius. There was a needle and there was a hole in his head. It didn't take an engineer. Still, it was hard to imagine a needle going through his skull, so there had to be other explanations. He didn't want think about that.

When everyone was on another topic, Zin leaned over. "We're going inside the Haystack in two days. Everyone gets a little edgy, but don't let them worry you. It's all cool."

"So what happens, exactly?"

"It's a good time. You won't remember much, though."

"What are you going to be doing?"

"Uhhhh…" Zin looked around then smiled, mischievously. "Well, I don't know about the rest of these war mongers, but I'll be hooking up with my lady. If there's time, I might join them for some shoot 'em up, but that ain't my priority. I promise you."

"Girls?"

"Oh, yeah." Zin looked around again but no one was paying attention. He mouthed the word with a smile.

GIRLS.

They were going to see girls? There had never been one on the island – coming or going from the Haystack – unless they were dropped off on the back side of the island and snuck into the back of the building. Danny thought of the possibilities. Boys were in the Haystack alone for half a day or longer. If there were girls in there, too, then all kinds of things could be happening. So far, the island was a summer camp, but the way Zin was smiling made him wonder if it had some real-life sex education.

Just keeps getting better.

The last people in line were grabbing their trays off the dessert table. The last one was all alone, something Danny rarely saw. Everyone travelled in packs. There were no loners on the island, except for the guy at the end of the line – the long-haired kid Danny saw his first day. He moved slowly, carefully. Occasionally, he turned his head listening to something, looking around the cafeteria. Then he slid his tray along the service line.

"We're going to be down three men," Sid was saying. "Parker's going in with us but he ain't going to last long. He'll be smoked, after this. Am I right, Parker?"

Parker breathed through his mouth, holding an empty spoon over his tray. His food was untouched. He shrugged his shoulders when Sid snapped his fingers.

"Easy money," Sid said. "Anyway, Zin's right about Danny Boy clumping up like a vegetable, so we'll be short-handed. We'll have to play some defense."

"Who's the third person?" Zin asked.

"Oh." Sid twitched his chin at the loner in line. "Forgot to tell you, we got the freak."

There was a collective moan and some pissing to go along with it.

"Who is he?" Danny asked.

"That's Reed," Zin said. "Guy's been through, like, 100 rounds or something like that without taking the needle." Zin shook his head. "One tough dude, man. Someone said his head got all scrambled when he first got here. Ask me, I think he's just some badass that wants to piss in the Director's cereal."

"Where's he been?"

"He goes to the beach on the north end, stands there looking at the water all by himself. No one goes out to the beach, man. The bugs and the wind and no one's going swimming. There are a thousand better things to do, trust me."

"That makes him crazy?"

"You wait and see, no sane person would do what he's done. He just doesn't have any friends and no one wants to get near him, afraid his crazy will rub off. Can't say I disagree."

Reed stopped at the dessert table and held still like someone hit pause on him.

"See what I mean?" Zin said. "He's an odd dude named Reed, the kid that bends but don't break."

"What's that mean?"

"You'll see."

Reed nodded. He was either agreeing with himself or with the voices Zin said he was hearing. Reed left his tray on the dessert table and grabbed an apple. He left the cafeteria.

"I rest my case," Zin said. "Whack-a-do."

Reed didn't walk like he was crazy. Danny didn't exactly know what a crazy man would walk like, but it didn't seem like it would be confident, slow and steady. Just because someone doesn't fly with all the birds doesn't mean he's nuts.

The flock could be going in the wrong direction.

7

Danny woke up two hours before the sun rose. His eyes opened and refused to shut. He stared at the ceiling. The unknown was terrifying. Everyone else seemed excited. Danny rubbed his forehead, making a tiny circle around the hole. *No way they stick a needle in there.*

There was a soft knock.

Danny pulled the sheet up to his chin. Mr. Jones opened the door. Danny realized he looked pathetic, but he couldn't will himself to get up anymore than he could make himself sleep. Besides, he was in his underwear and even though Mr. Jones wasn't so creepy, there was no need to roll the dice.

"Good morning," Mr. Jones said.

Danny didn't answer.

Mr. Jones, usually cheery that time of the day – usually throwing open the curtains and welcoming the morning and telling Danny it was a great day to be alive – this time he went directly to the chest of drawers and began to fold Danny's clothes. When his shirts were organized, Mr. Jones put his hand on the desk. His cheeks moved like he was chewing on his tongue.

He sat on the bed, sinking into the mattress and rolling Danny closer. Thankfully, he placed his hands on his own lap.

"Danny Boy," he started and let out a sigh. "Today is a big day. It's a big day, my boy. You can't imagine what it means to me. The journey you're about to take will be revolutionary. You should know that, so that in your darkest hour you have something to hold onto. The Haystack is critical to what we do here on the island, you understand? We wouldn't do anything to hurt you, but sometimes you have to go to the dentist to stay well, am I right?"

Danny pulled the sheet just under his eyes. He wanted to pull it over his head but that wouldn't make the bogeyman go away.

"Here." Mr. Jones held a pill between his finger and thumb. "Put this under your tongue, it'll boost your immunity. I don't want you catching cold while you're in there, it just makes things harder."

Danny didn't move.

Mr. Jones had to pull the sheet down and put it on his lips. His fingers smelled like old leather. Danny let the pill fall into his mouth just so he'd get his hand away. It dissolved like candy.

Mr. Jones sighed again, looked at the ceiling. His eyes looked a little wet. It was times like this Danny thought he might be regretting something. He squeezed Danny's knee. "You're a hero, son. A real hero."

And then he got up, after two attempts, and went to the door looking more hunched over than usual. He put his hand on the knob and, without turning, said, "You go on and get dressed now, you hear? I'll be back up in an hour to escort you over to the building. No one goes into the Haystack alone, my boy."

The door clicked behind him. Danny stayed in bed with the sheet pulled up. He remained there for a while and only got dressed because he didn't want Mr. Jones in the room when he did.

All modesty was about to disappear from Danny's life.

Danny walked the Yard with Mr. Jones. This time he had no problem with his slow and steady gait. The others were walking with their Investors, too. They were all spread out, heading in the same direction: the multi-eyed round roof peeking above the distant trees. Their paths converged the closer they got.

They got in line as they entered a narrow path. There was little talking. But the silence was more than that; it was the sort of intense concentration that spontaneously happened before a big game, before surgery or some other life-altering event. Even Sid, walking a few bodies ahead of Danny, was quiet.

Suddenly, the path ended in an opening. The Haystack was at the far side. Its concrete wall was painted dark brown, stained with algae and sucker-cups that remained from vines stripped away. A man stood at the entrance with a clipboard in his folded arms. He was old, but kind of young among the old men. He had gentle gray eyes inside folds of skin. He began checking off items on his clipboard as they entered.

A bell rang three times.

Danny didn't look around but once. Zin was to his left. He lifted his eyebrows in mild celebration. Just past Zin was Parker as glassy-eyed and slack as ever. He wasn't looking around. He didn't even look like he knew anyone else was there.

"Welcome, young men," the man at the door suddenly said. "My name is Mr. Clark. I'll be supervising this round. Most of you know the drill. I know some of you are nervous, as would be expected, but I assure you that your experience will be just as exciting as the previous ones have been. For the newcomers, you will follow your Investor inside and he will orient you on what to do. But there's nothing to worry about, things are very simple inside."

Mr. Clark looked at his clipboard.

"Before we enter, are there any questions?" He looked around with the same welcoming smile. "Very well, then. Let's begin, shall we?"

He pushed the door open and stood to the side. Mr. Jones's hand fell on Danny's shoulder and squeezed reassuringly. Danny immediately tensed, but noticed every Investor was doing the same move with the hand on the shoulder, guiding their kid into the Haystack in some sort of ritual. Danny got in line. When they stepped inside, it was cold and dim.

It was the last time he would see the sun for quite some time.

Danny clenched up, a full-body seizure.

His knees locked and he pushed his weight against Mr. Jones's hand. It wasn't the dim light coming through the skylights or the giant steel fan that waited to chop them up or the smell of urine or the dank-dungeon cells that lined both sides of the aisle that made Danny step back. It was a sense of panic, of fear, that saturated the atmosphere like an electrical current, tingling in his bowels. The boys ahead of him didn't seize up, but they stutter-stepped. Like the end of a ship's plank was dead ahead.

Danny felt this type of fear spreading through his groin like cold fingers once before. A memory emerged in the soupy sea of memories inside his head. He remembered getting pulled out of the back seat of a car with his hands cuffed behind his back by someone. But then like everything he tried to remember, there were gaps.

There were FBI shirts, and big doors—

"It's all right, Danny Boy." Mr. Jones gently urged him forward.

Danny's knees refused to unbuckle. The cages were open and waiting. The boys ahead of him each walked inside one without resistance and their Investor closed the door.

"Come on!" someone shouted from outside. "We're waiting, Danny Boy!"

"Come along, my boy." Mr. Jones pressed forward, pushing Danny ahead. "It's all right. It's all right."

Danny walked with his weight leaning into Mr. Jones's hand. The old man showed surprising strength. His hand was like a talon. It guided him past the open cells. No cot or toilet or window on the walls. The boys were stripping off their shirts. That's when Danny realized the cold wasn't just fear eating away his innards but the humid cold air dimpling his skin.

They stopped about halfway down the aisle. Mr. Jones turned Danny to the left. He tried to squirm away but the old man's claw shoved him inside the open cell. The door latched closed before he could turn around.

Mr. Jones grabbed the bars.

"Why are you doing this?" Danny suddenly wanted to be back in his bed. He didn't mind if Mr. Jones sat on the bed and patted his knee. He would let him touch his face, if that's what he wanted.

"Danny Boy, trust me. Everything will be all right. It'll be better than okay, you just trust me now, son. These boys have been through this already and they're doing better, I promise."

No one else needed to be pushed inside a cell. They knew the deal and didn't seem to mind. They didn't look happy, but they weren't freaking out.

"We're about healing the world," Mr. Jones said, quietly. "This is the work that we ask you to do. As with any work, it is not always easy. But it will be rewarding, my boy. Richly."

The Haystack was silent except for the somber mutterings of a few Investors. The rest of the boys were taking off their clothes. First their shirts. Then shoes, socks and pants. And finally underwear.

Completely naked!

Mr. Jones held out his hands. "You need to hand me your clothes, Danny Boy. We enter the work like we enter life, completely exposed to the world. We are reborn into our flesh, revealing our humility for everyone to witness."

Danny backed up. The others were folding their clothes and passing them between the bars, neatly stacked. They stood unabashed with various amounts of pubic hair. The cold had shriveled most of them to embarrassing sizes, but no one seemed to care all that much. None of them were looking around like Danny.

"No one can touch you, Danny Boy."

Mr. Jones was right. There was a gap between the cells on each side. Even if he reached all the way through, he wouldn't be able to touch the person imprisoned next to him. He noticed the walls were set inside slots that could slide but it only looked like the cell could get smaller.

"You're safe inside the cell. No one will bother you."

"But… but why? Why do we have to do this?" Danny's voice cracked with an embarrassing whine.

"You'll understand. You'll just have to trust me."

Danny hugged himself. “I just don’t want to. You can’t just expect me to… I’m not just going to get naked because everyone else is. I’m not doing it.”

“Stop pissing around, Danny Boy!” Sid shouted from across the aisle. His penis had shrunk into the bush of pubic hair that crawled up and around his belly button. “The longer you go on like that, the longer it takes… NOW GET NAKED, BOY!”

Investors were already leaving. Mr. Jones stood with his hands around the bars. His expression was silent and sympathetic. Sid was growling and pacing inside his cell. But Danny couldn’t break the grip the cold hand of fear had on him. He just wasn’t going to do it. He just wanted to close his eyes and disappear. He wished this would all go away, that he could somehow escape his body and go somewhere nice and warm and safe.

“Hey.” Zin was pulling his shirt over his head in the cell next to him. “Listen, you got to do this. I know it’s all weird, but it’s no big deal. It’s like showering in the gym. I can tell you, nothing happens.”

“Then why do we have to do it?”

Zin shrugged while he stepped out of his shorts. “To make the first part more uncomfortable, I guess. To humiliate us, to make us want the needle. I don’t give two craps either way. All I know is that we got to get this thing going or it’s going to suck being here even longer.”

Zin folded his shorts and shirt into a stack and placed his flip-flops on top. His Investor gave him a nod and left.

“Danny Boy,” Mr. Jones said. “You should understand that in life, there is joy and there is suffering. Your work includes everything. The Haystack is designed to allow you to experience suffering safely, to learn to let go of your physical body so that you may experience another level of your existence. But I can’t make you, Danny Boy. I can’t make you do it. You’ll have to do it on your own.” Mr. Jones held out his hands. “You’ll have to walk naked alone.”

Others had joined Sid in the taunting. Danny could see there was no way to escape. And the others had been through it and they didn't seem to mind. Zin, too.

Danny's shirt came off, first. The cold air pulled his skin tight and his nipples were like BBs. He was shaking when he took off his shorts. Despite Sid screaming to go faster, he took his time getting his shoes off.

His underwear was last.

He took a long shaky breath before pulling them down. Unlike Sid and Zin, he didn't have much hair downstairs. What little he did have was bright red and barely covered his boyhood that looked more like a mushroom cap.

He threw the clothes at Mr. Jones's feet and cupped his hands over his genitalia.

"I'll need you to fold the clothes, Danny Boy." Mr. Jones didn't stoop to pick them up. "It's our attention to every moment of our life that matters. To make room for this very moment, to allow it to unfold. To care for life. Now, please, hand me your clothes properly."

Danny squatted down and did his best to put his clothes in order like Zin had done. Mr. Jones didn't seem completely pleased with the quality of his stack, but he nodded and stepped back. He nodded again and without another word, exited the Haystack.

The wrath of the others didn't stop. Danny backed up until he pressed against the bars, wishing it was dark enough to hide him. He kept his hands over his privates. The room had become loud with anger, vibrating inside Danny's head. Even Zin had his hands on the bars, shouting obscenities until finally one Investor was followed by another until they were all gone.

Sid tried to shake the solid bars on his cage, shouting, "Come on! Come on, already! LET'S GO!"

It seemed to go on forever. Danny's shoulder blades had numbed on the cold steel when a loud clank erupted from the ceiling. Everyone cheered as the dim light began to fade. Shutters inside the skylights were turning. What little light was available disappeared.

Danny shivered in the dark.

“Danny Boy?” Zin called.

“Yeah?”

“Welcome to the Haystack.”

8

Danny moved to the center of the cell. It was so dark that it didn't matter where he stood, no one would see him. The worst part was the concrete, slick and cold. Danny began to pace to keep warm.

"Save your strength."

There was a lump in the darkness to Danny's right. Slowly, the details of the room began to return with grainy, gray detail and fuzzy edges. The lump was Zin, sitting in the center of his cell with his knees pulled against his chest and his arms wrapped around his shins.

"You want to protect your core, Danny Boy," Zin said. "Do whatever you can to conserve your body heat. Walking around is only going to waste it. It might feel good now but you'll pay for it later."

"Why are they doing this, Zin?"

"Sit down and do what I told you," he snapped. "And use your legs to keep your balls from touching the floor. You don't want those getting cold."

He didn't have to worry about his scrotum touching anything. It had shriveled up like a mummified prune. The floor felt like a glacier. He stopped rocking back and forth before Zin snapped at him again, but he couldn't control the shivering.

"You good?" Zin asked. "Now, get into a breathing rhythm. Slowly, take in a breath and let it exhale on its own. In." Zin sucked air through his nostrils, loudly. "Out," he said, letting it leak out. He did it again, and again.

Danny followed his example. The chattering continued, but he felt less scattered. A little more settled. The fear that was strangling his insides had subsided to mild warmth. The muscles that were bunched around his shoulders released.

In.

Out.

He continued.

The room was mostly silent. Some of the others were talking. There was subtle laughter. Someone was whimpering.

"Here's the deal," Zin finally said. "We come here every two weeks, get naked and wait for the needle."

"What's that?"

"You'll find out. After this round, we'll screw around for two weeks like we've been doing until the next one. You get the picture."

"How long do we do this?"

"Don't ask that question. Just count your breath, that's all you need to know."

Laughter crackled through the room. Someone said to shut the hell up, then added, "God, I hate this freaking part."

Danny went back to breathing like Zin. It wasn't helping, he was getting colder. But there wasn't much choice. Danny could make out more details, could see that Zin was sitting with his back straight and legs folded beneath him, his hands in his lap. His chest rose and fell.

Danny didn't know who was in the cell on the other side, but he was standing and shrouded in darkness. He hadn't uttered a word.

Across the aisle, Parker had not moved. He stood in his cell hunched over. He looked disconnected already. He didn't seem to care whether it was hot or cold, whether he suffered or not. Like some spirit from another world.

The seconds stitched together and became minutes. Zin told him when to get up and walk around, when to rub some feeling back into his buttocks, and when to sit still and breathe. Danny was still shivering. There were moments when he swallowed the knot in his throat that threatened to break out sobs.

Danny lost count of how many times he and Zin walked, how many times he rubbed the feeling back into his buns, and how many breaths he'd counted. But he would remember for the rest of his life the sound the fan made when it engaged.

It started with a buzz. The long blades began to crawl in a circle. After one rotation, they picked up speed and the breeze came down with a slow helicopter sound.

Wop-wop-wop-wop-wop.

Then came the hiss of the sprinklers. A fine mist swirled in the current and settled on the floor and everything else.

"I won't talk after this, Danny Boy, no offense," Zin said. "This is where the real work begins. Just remember when the needle drops, push your tongue against the roof of your mouth."

"Why?"

Zin began to pace. "Or else you'll bite it off."

And that's when the lump in Danny's throat broke. He tried to smother the sobs but failed. No one said anything.

No one laughed.

The fan would stop. So would the mist.

Then start again.

Danny stopped the breathing exercise. He hadn't done it since the fan began. He was curled up on his side with his legs drawn up to his chest. He had cried out all his tears. His stomach ached.

He found strength watching Zin. He sat so still. He was getting up more often and walking back and forth with a steady, measured pace; his hands folded over his stomach. His head was slightly bowed.

And on and on, it went.

On and on, it went.

There were large patches of forgetting.

Danny wasn't sure if he'd fallen asleep or just blanked out. The floor had begun to grind into his hip and his neck hurt from lying down. He started to walk like Zin but didn't talk to him. It was just back and forth, back and forth.

The guy in the other cell turned out to be Reed. Danny only guessed from the long hair. He faced the other direction. He didn't fidget. Didn't much move. He just remained steady.

The fan finished another cycle of turning and they were in for a short reprieve. The following silence was interrupted by shuffling and a cough or a moan. Droplets of water condensed on the bars until they fell with a heavy drip.

But there was a new sound.

Above Danny's cell, a tiny mechanized motor turned.

The atmosphere changed. A heavy pause, like a collective breath.

Everyone stared up.

Danny saw a black box fastened in the center of the barred ceiling of his cell. Something was moving inside it. He didn't see the tiny door open, but heard the wire and straps fall out.

A jubilant roar shook the room.

The others were on their feet, calling to each other. There was laughter. They all reached up.

Zin stopped pacing. He paused for one final breath before reaching for the black box and pulling down a gaggle of straps and wire. He sat down and pulled the line from the box until there was plenty of slack on the floor. Then he took the straps and fastened them over his head like some sort of wrestling gear, but instead of ear protection there was a single knob that centered over the middle of his forehead. He didn't look at Danny, only took a deep breath and lay on his back.

His body convulsed once, his back arching off the floor for a long moment.

Then it went limp.

Everyone was in the same position. It was suddenly silent. No labored breathing. No groans or whimpers. Just complete silence.

He reached for the mess dangling from his cell. His joints ached. The straps were cold leather; the wire a thick cable. The knob was hard. He was reluctant, despite the agony. There was a needle inside the knob, he knew it had to be. It would plunge into the hole.

The thought was as cold as the floor.

He sat down, unable to put it on. But when the fan began to whir, Danny was in motion. His body moved on its own. He couldn't stand the cold, wet air anymore. Not when everyone around him was so peaceful. He just wanted out.

Away from this body.

The strap fit snugly around his head. He pulled extra cable from above until it pooled at his side. He shifted the knob over his forehead. If there were any tears left, Danny might have squeezed out a few. Instead, he just squeezed his eyes shut.

The knob began to squirm like flagellating lips, like the bottom of a snail. It numbed the skin beneath the knob. A cold fire spread into his forehead, like a river of icy water gushing inside his brain. His bladder released; a warm puddle grew between his legs. It was embarrassing, but he didn't care.

He just wanted out.

The cell walls shifted. The one next to him got smaller. Reed had turned around, staring down at him.

Then came the needle.

9

Danny tasted steel.

The needle plunged into the frontal lobe. The pain was minimal, but his body thrashed on the concrete, scraping his elbows and cutting the back of his head.

All Danny felt was the dull blunt force of metal and the crunching sound of the hole reopening. He no longer felt the cold floor or the frigid mist blowing over his naked body or the warm blood seeping from the back of his head. He was in another type of darkness.

Bodiless. Sightless.

Somewhere else.

Once he'd ridden a three-story water slide. He flung himself into the dark tube and plunged into the unknown where turns tossed him left and right and the water surged over his head. His stomach twisted with fear and excitement until he was shot out the bottom of the ride.

He remembered that. The whole thing.

The memory seeped into his mind from somewhere in the dark.

Danny was on another sort of ride that caused his stomach – if he still had a stomach – to buck and he was thrown through a series of twisting turns. But this ride swirled up and down and side to side, and it kept going and going. Until, finally, he fell through the bottom into a soft pit that was still black. Still nowhere.

There was a sense of floating. It was amniotic, thick and fluid. He tried to shout but had no lips, no throat. He was just somewhere, and that somewhere was better than his flesh.

He was seven years old. He slept in tee-pees and ran through icy streams and shot arrows and threw knives. He didn't change his underwear once. It was the best week of his life.

That was summer camp. He remembered! The memory was whole again. It was him.

A small man with a badge on his belt put his hand on Danny's shoulder and walked him up wide concrete steps that led to big wooden doors.

He had done something seriously wrong. He and some friends got caught writing computer code and hacking into websites. They did it as a goof, didn't think they'd get caught. And if they did, they were only seven or eight years old at the time. What were they going to do, put them in prison? They were kids. But the men and women waiting for Danny inside the wooden doors wore FBI t-shirts.

The needle was bringing back his memories. He felt more like himself.

There were sounds. It was distant, as if coming through a long pipe stuffed with towels. At first, it didn't sound like much, but then it took form. It sounded more like… laughter. The kind that comes from a playground.

He tried to swim towards it, but he was just floating, just listening. But it got louder. Words were popping up, now and then. They seemed to be running past him.

"Danny Boy!" It was right in front of him, just on the other side of the darkness. On the other side… of… his eyelids?

"I knew it," the voice said. "He ain't worth crap and in the middle of the field. Someone get him out of the way!"

There were footsteps. More voices. Some very far away, others going past him. Someone was nearby, out of breath from running.

"This is Danny Boy."

Zin! He's right there, just out of reach.

"That's him?" There was a girl with him. A *girl.* Colors swirled in the dark when Danny had the thought. "I thought you said he was some big deal," she said. "He's barely old enough to be here."

"Yeah, well you never saw him in the game room. The kid's some kind of prodigy with the computer sticks in his hands. I mean, there are kids on the island that have been here longer than me that aren't half as good as Danny Boy."

"Video games?" She sighed. "Seriously, who cares, Zin?"

"You want to help me move him, Sandy?"

The darkness shifted. Danny had a sense of the ground below him, the open sky above. Zin hooked his arms under Danny's armpits and Sandy took his feet. He felt the jostling of their footsteps. The breeze whistled past him and the grass was soft on his cheek when they put him down.

"Zin!" Sid called. "Don't get lost, I want you at the sundial when it hits noon, you got it?"

"Aye—aye, Capitan!"

"You're not really going to play that game again, are you?" the girl said.

"Naaaaaw."

"Seriously, Zin. We don't know how many rounds we have together and you're going to waste time gaming?"

And they went back and forth. Danny imagined the wry smile on Zin's face, what he usually looked like when he lied right in your face but still made you laugh. The image looked so clear and vivid, like he was looking right at it. Then he heard someone laugh.

Zin and Sandy were quiet. There was laughter again, and this time he felt it.

It was him.

"Danny Boy! Holy crap, did I tell you this kid was a winner, Sandy?"

Zin was very close, his voice soft but loud.

"Open your eyes, kid. Get here, man. Get all the way inside?"

Danny didn't know how to open his eyes. It was like telling a quadriplegic to move his legs when he didn't even know where they were. But then he felt pressure from the outside and recognized his face. There were hands on him. Once he knew where his cheeks were, he followed the pattern to his eyes.

They opened with a crunch, like years of sleep were crusted on his eyelids. There were blurs of color. A few blinks and smudges merged into a face. Zin was inches away, a big smile warping his lips.

"Danny Boy, you did it, man. You went fully lucid on your first round. How about that?" Zin looked back at Sandy. "Did I tell you? Who goes lucid on the first round? No one does, that's who. No one except Danny Boy. Freaking all the way inside on his first round."

Danny felt a smile on the inside, but he was still completely numb. His eyelids were already too heavy to keep open. Zin lightly slapped him.

"Not yet, don't go to sleep yet."

"Let him go down, Zinny," Sandy said. "He's not going to be able to move and I want to spend some time with you. The clock is ticking."

"I know, baby. I know. I just want to keep him lucid as long as possible. That will make the next round a lot easier."

Zin reached under Danny and propped him against a wall so that he was looking across a green field. He blinked and thought he was dreaming. He was sitting against the dormitory looking at the Yard and it didn't look a whole lot different.

"You see that, Danny Boy? We're inside the needle, somewhere between your mind and the Haystack's network. The needle is sunk inside your brain right now, boy. It's realigning your synapses so the computers can link directly with your frontal lobe. You're about as useful as a bowl of pudding, but you can see, Danny Boy. You can see, and the next time you'll be moving around. Next time, you'll be able to do this."

Zin lifted a boulder above his head. He tossed it over the distant trees.

"Peter Pan went to Neverland, but this is Foreverland, Danny Boy! We can do anything here. ANYTHING! There are no rules, no laws. Where gravity doesn't exist if we don't want it to. Where magic is limited only by our imagination."

Zin opened his hand and a long-stemmed rose grew from his palm. He took a knee in front of Sandy and kissed her hand. She rolled her eyes. She pointed over her shoulder and a truck squeezed out of her finger like a cartoon, but bounced on the ground like a ton of steel.

"It's not magic if everyone can do it," she said.

"Magic is not defined by the number of people that can perform it, but by the manner in which it is done."

"Okay, Socrates." She wrapped her arm around his neck and whispered. "Can we go?"

She whispered something else. Zin smiled wide.

He twirled his arm in front of his stomach and half-bowed. "I must bid you adieu, Danny Boy. There's only so much time and we work so hard to get here." He began to backpedal while Sandy pulled at him. "But don't give up hope. The first round sucks because you suffer without a payoff, but you'll see, Danny Boy. The next one will be better, you'll see!"

And they were off, running across the field, gleefully trotting like long lost lovers.

Danny didn't stay awake long. He managed to keep his eyes open to see the magic Zin was talking about. What seemed so ordinary when he first opened his eyes quickly turned into Foreverland. People were shapeshifting into lions and tigers and eagles. A mastodon thundered past with a horde of spear-chucking warriors that jumped off and floated away with their arms spread out.

It was everything that made dreams. But it was so real.

A long blink and the sun was lower. The field was nearly empty. There was half a spaceship buried a hundred yards away, its back half was on fire. It looked like the Millennium Falcon. There were distant explosions and gunfire. Someone shouted orders nearby. Another person went flying past on the back of a dinosaur.

Another long blink and it was night.

The ship was gone, replaced by an empty crater. Two moons were high, one full and the other half-crescent. There were several campfires in the field. Some people were singing, others laughed loudly while chasing each other. Girls squealed. It looked a lot like summer camp. Except for the people flying past the moon.

Dawn arrived.

The Yard was empty, except for the crater and dead campfires.

The sun was rising somewhere behind him. The shadows were long and dusky and the sunlight turned the trees a weird shimmery magenta. The quiet was disturbed by an occasional frog. Danny closed his eyes again. He was going to sleep when he felt someone very close. It was a girl.

She was inches from his face. Her eyes were green and her hair red, like candy. Her nostrils flared and her eyes searched his face. There was desperation in them, the eyes wide enough to expose the whites around her irises. She leaned in and pressed her cheek to his. She smelled like a beautiful flower.

“Find him,” she said. “Tell him we found you.”

And then she was off.

Danny hadn’t even blinked. She moved so fast, it was like she hadn’t been there. Maybe he would’ve believed he imagined it if not for the lingering scent.

He went to sleep for the last time. The next time he would wake, it would be in his bed, back in his body. But he would wake with her smell upon him and her words.

Tell him we found you.

ROUND
2

One-Car Accident; One Dead, One Missing

HOBART, Oklahoma. – A blue Ford F-150 hit a tree off route 55 and caught fire. Both occupants were ejected from the vehicle. One was a female in her late teens and pronounced dead on arrival. The other occupant is a male, also in his late teens, and severely injured. Neither person had identification on their body.

The female was Caucasian, 5' 7", 130 pounds, long red hair and green eyes. The male is Caucasian, 5' 10", 180 pounds, shoulder-length black hair, and brown eyes. He was taken to Elkview Hospital but was mysteriously missing shortly after being admitted. He was last seen wearing denim jeans, work boots and a brown t-shirt.

If you have any information regarding their identification and the male's whereabouts, please contact local police.

10

Danny stared at the popcorn texture of the ceiling. His face was fat; his lips rubbery. Every joint in his body ached.

The curtains were closed. A sliver of light etched the dusty air, falling on a plastic cup on a tray next to his bed. Danny reached for it, winced when the scabs on his elbows cracked and his entire head throbbed, front to back. The crown of his head was crusty and bruised. He leaned on one elbow and took the cup, drinking the water in three swift gulps, noticing the medical equipment on the tray, the blood pressure cuff, thermometer, and bandages.

Mr. Jones's smell was all over the place. Danny threw the covers off and sat up, the floor cold on his bare feet. *Nothing but underwear.*

He didn't want to think about Mr. Jones putting him in bed. Problem was, he couldn't remember anything. A cloud filled his head. He dropped his face into his hands to think a moment but it was hopeless. There was a strange taste in the back of his throat and all he could think about was more water.

He took the cup to the sink. There, in the mirror staring back, was a circular bandage in the middle of his forehead. He touched it, gently.

The fog cleared.

The Haystack and the fan and the mist. *The needle.*

Vertigo smacked him. He held onto the sink. It got worse. He sank to his knees and crawled to the bed while the memories settled. It was strange how his mind was like water and the memories swirled like grains of sand. There was something he was supposed to remember but it was so hard. Summer camp? FBI? Damn, he couldn't remember it now.

He had journeyed through the needle to some… dream. *Foreverland.*

It was torture to get there.

The taste still lingered, but it wasn't just in his mouth. It was in his head, too. *Metallic. The taste of the needle.*

The price to pay for reality limited only by the imagination. Danny looked at his hands, turned them over and studied the creases in his palms. *Is this Foreverland, still?*

He decided it wasn't. But it was hard to tell.

When the doorknob slowly turned, Danny threw the covers over his lap. The door cracked open. An eyeball slid into the opening and the door closed again. Before he could decide if it was Mr. Jones's eyeball, the door flew open and banged on the wall, followed by a mob.

"Danny Boy!"

Zin was the first one in the room. The others were right behind him. Danny curled up under the covers just before they piled onto him. They were slapping his back, his legs, his butt, shouting his name and whooping loudly.

"What a player!" Zin threw open the curtains, stabbing Danny's eyes with light. "The kid went lucid on his first round! ON HIS FIRST ROUND!"

There were high-fives and another dog pile on top of Danny. Zin mercifully pulled them off. The celebration continued in the center of the room.

"You all right, Danny Boy?" Zin asked

"A few aches."

"Yeah, but you did it," Zin said. "You did the impossible, you opened your eyes. No one does that."

The room got quiet. They stood like they were posing for a group photo, waiting for Danny's words of wisdom. He had none. They looked at him, expectantly. Everyone was there, except Parker.

"Poof."

That was Sid's explanation for Parker. He snapped his fingers, said, "Ole Parker is a puff of smoke, Danny Boy. He's gone on to bigger and better, my friend. Bigger and better."

No one explained it much beyond that, other than Parker graduated and was likely on his way back home, all healed up.

Bigger and better.

The slam dance of celebration began again. "And now you need to get out of bed, son! You've been sleeping for two damn days while we've been back in the real world. We need you, Danny Boy. We've been holding your slot open in the game room and we're about to drop in the standings. We can't wait any longer."

"Relax, Sid." Zin stood between them. "The kid hasn't eaten in two days, either."

"Then let's eat," Sid said. "Get dressed, we'll eat. We'll game. Daylight's burning, son."

Danny put his hand up to pause the ceaseless slam dance. It was hurting his head.

"Give him some privacy," Zin said. "Kid's in his underwear."

"He was butt naked two days ago. Underwear is a step up," Sid countered.

"All right, well, give him a second. We'll meet down in the cafeteria, right, Danny Boy? When you're ready, you come down. What do you say?"

Danny nodded with his eyes closed. He listened to Zin push them out. The chaos faded down the hallway. Danny dropped his head on the pillow. He needed some silence, just enough space to let the sand settle in his head. The last grains were falling into place.

We found you.

Mr. Jones was the happiest Danny had ever seen him.

No more hunching over. He walked upright and smiled all the time. He was proud of Danny, he said so every day. Looked like he was about to cry once or twice. Even the other Investors took notice. They shook Mr. Jones's hand and congratulated him, like he'd done something himself. Mr. Jones stood up and shook their hands back vigorously. Once, when he was walking with Danny to the cafeteria, another Investor stopped to congratulate him. The old man didn't pay much attention to Danny when he shook

Mr. Jones's hand and said, "You got a good one there, Jonsy. Lucky you."

"Maybe he'll graduate in five rounds," Mr. Jones said.

"Wouldn't that be something."

They parted ways and the old man didn't look back. Danny kept thinking. *Got a good one there... lucky you.*

Like the pick of the litter.

Danny didn't feel special. All he did was follow everyone else into the Haystack, put the needle on his head and wake up two days later. It wasn't like he did anything.

Evidently, others thought different.

He got high-fives in the game room, and those that didn't raise their hand were staring. Zin was out front, making room for them to walk to the central game dock where Sid and the others were waiting. Danny strapped on the gear and felt the pressure of half the game room gathering around to watch.

"Word gets around," Zin said, pulling on his gloves. "Don't disappoint."

And he didn't.

Danny took control of the game and Sid let him. Like before, he didn't feel like he was doing anything special, it just happened. He thought faster and clearer. He knew where his enemy was going, like he knew their thoughts. He'd operated with the efficiency of a computer, and when he snuck into the enemy camp and put a bullet through the last one's throat, the entire game room erupted.

He forgot they were even there.

Danny had discussed the first round with Mr. Jones, how he opened his eyes and what he saw. Mr. Jones listened, jotting down the details on a clipboard. When Danny was finished, he asked him to start from the top and go through it one more time, just in case there was something he was missing. "It's sort of like dreams, Danny Boy," he said. "The more you think about them, the more you remember. So one more time, my boy."

The more he remembered. That was the strange thing. Danny had the sense he got a bunch of his memories back when he was inside the needle, but now he couldn't remember them. Just something about summer camp and the FBI.

Danny got the feeling Mr. Jones just wanted to hear about it again. He added a few more details about people flying and the weird creatures that spawned from the ground (*Oh, yeah, and the Millennium Falcon had crashed; weird, huh?*).

"That's good. Good." When Danny stared at the floor, twisting his fingers, Mr. Jones said, "Anything else?"

"No," Danny said. "No, that's it."

But there was something else. He left out the girl. That felt secret and a gut-feeling decided to keep that part to himself. He waited another week before he did what the girl asked him to do.

Danny went to the beach.

11

Danny found the narrow path somewhere near the Haystack.

It meandered without apparent direction. Clearly one less traveled.

Palm fronds hung across it like soft arms blocking the way. He was wet from the dew and eventually found a stick to push them out of the way while knocking down spider webs.

The path eventually turned sandy and ended on a wide dune. He climbed over the soft mound of sand to the hard-packed beach. The wind was strong on this side of the island. The surf drove towards the shore in ten-foot waves, crashing hard only thirty yards out and leaving foamy residue on the beach. Danny could see the jagged edges of coral just under the surface, too dangerous to surf.

A lone figure was far down to Danny's left. He sat in the loose sand of the dunes. Danny started in that direction. His stomach tightened with nerves. And even though the sun was biting his white skin, he felt shivers the closer he got to him.

Reed didn't look up, not even when Danny was a few feet away. He sat with his arms resting on his knees, staring at the ocean. His bare chest was red. The edges of his shoulders poked out like his skin was hanging on him like an old shirt. The tracker bulged on his neck.

Danny started to say something but the sound of the surf blotted out his hesitant words and then he just didn't know what to say, so he swallowed the lump and looked at the water, too.

"What do you think's out there?" Reed finally asked.

Danny squinted, shading his eyes to search the horizon but nothing disrupted the flat line. No ship or island or rock, just water.

"Home," Danny said.

Reed didn't tell him if he was wrong or right. He got the feeling he was wrong.

Danny continued to search the horizon. Just because he couldn't see it didn't mean it wasn't there. He came from someplace and it wasn't the island. Out there, somewhere, were his parents and a place he called home. And when he graduated, he would see them again.

"Tell me what home looks like," Reed said, without looking up. "Better yet, tell me about your favorite Christmas. Think about the best Christmas you ever had, when you got everything you asked for and the world was the greatest place to be. Tell me what it was like."

Easy.

It was the time he got a skateboard half-pipe. He came down the stairs rubbing his eyes and his little brother was opening these big boxes from Santa and all Danny had was a green envelope. It was a message to look out the kitchen window. Danny pressed his hands on the cold glass. There, standing six feet tall and filling the back yard was the thing he wanted most in the world.

The half-pipe was covered in all his favorite stickers – Fallen and Zero and the fiery red head of Spitfire. His mother, wearing her pink robe with dyed blond hair hanging in her eyes, went onto the back deck with him.

But when Danny went through the back door, he stepped in three feet of snow. His mother was wearing a coat and her hair was black and short and she was smoking a cigarette. And his dad was there, too. He was fat and unshaven with a cigarette stuck in his lips. He handed Danny an air rifle and said Merry Christmas and aim for the cans he set up in the back yard. The yard was empty except for a dozen Budweisers.

Danny looked back to his mom because he had a half-pipe, not a rifle, but now she was shorter and wearing a tank top and the snow was gone and there were palm trees next to the house.

"They didn't erase our memories, Danny Boy." Reed still hadn't looked up. "They filled us with random ones, layered them one on top the other until we don't know which ones belong to us, which ones are false."

He was right. They didn't feel like his memories. And they were never the same parents. But Foreverland, that was different. "In the Haystack… I remembered…"

"They put your memories inside the needle. Every time you go inside, you get more of them back but you come back to the flesh, they get mixed with an ocean of random ones that aren't yours."

"Why?"

"The more you go inside the needle, the more you feel like yourself. The more you like it."

Danny tried to remember Christmas again. He knew who he was, he remembered getting what he wanted. He remembered the half-pipe covered with stickers and the sound of the skateboard clapping on the metal coping. But then he couldn't actually remember skating.

Then he realized he didn't know how to skate.

"She sent you," Reed said. "She told you to come find me, didn't she?"

There wasn't a hole in Reed's forehead, only a scar where it used to be. He went into the Haystack and endured the suffering without taking the needle. After Danny went to sleep, Reed stayed in that dreadful room. He'd done it before, Danny had been told. Reed was a sick puppy, he was told.

"How do you know that?" Danny asked.

Reed remained still and quiet. "You can trust her," he finally said.

"Do you know her?"

"I did, once upon a time." Again, quiet. A slight shrug. "Or maybe I just think I do. It's an ocean of thoughts, Danny Boy."

Danny wanted to ask him a hundred questions. Everyone on the island was buying everything the Investors were selling, gobbling it up like a bunch of hungry fish, and here was a kid that seemed to know something. Danny wanted to know why they were on the island and why Reed didn't take the needle and who the girl was…

But then a cart came over the dune and began driving down the hard-packed beach, the water skimming beneath it. Reed never looked at it, just continued staring. The cart stopped in front of them. Mr. Jones rested his hands on the steering wheel and stared at Reed. It was the first time since Danny had come out of the Haystack that the old man didn't look happy. He patted the empty seat next to him.

"Come along, Danny Boy. Your camp is looking for you, they've been waiting at the game room. You don't want to disappoint, now do you?"

Mr. Jones's eyes flickered at Reed when he said that. Reed didn't notice. Or seem to care. He just stared at the ocean, not looking for anything, almost like he was waiting for a ship to arrive. The girl said to tell Reed that they found him. He did that.

Now what?

Danny got on the cart. They left Reed behind. He'd stay there the remainder of the day. Maybe longer.

The next time Danny would see him was through the bars of his cell.

12

Reed had spent time on every section of the island. Most were sandy beaches; a few sections were cliffs. At first, he explored these areas in search of an escape while all the other boys wasted time in the game room. It didn't take long to see the futility of the choppy surf and rocky coral. Of course, he hadn't seen the south end where the old men lived where hope may still exist.

But hope was no longer in Reed's vocabulary. He extinguished it. Twenty-five trips – now, twenty-six – through the Haystack will scrub that out of any person. Boy or man.

Reed spent his time on the north end because no one else did. He would remain on the beach for days while the sun spread warmth deep into his bones where the cold torture felt unreachable.

He rarely saw anyone on the north end. Not even Mr. Smith, especially since he wasn't talking to Reed anymore. Mr. Smith didn't show up when the last round ended. Reed walked back to his room and curled up under the covers, chattering in and out of fitful sleep where he dreamed of turning blades and endless rain.

Reed came to the beach just before the sun rose, when the sky was glowing orange and purple. He sat, watching the waves come in. There was a time when he decided escape was impossible but still looked for a sign that he was wrong.

Not anymore.

Now he just watched the waves crash, reminding him of the one sustaining lesson: *hopelessness.*

Reed had given up hope that he would one day find a way off the island, to discover home somewhere out there, to be rid of the ceaseless random thoughts churning in his head. Because to hope was to reject the present moment, the only thing that was real, regardless of its misery. Reed clung to the present moment like a buoy. Reality had frayed. He didn't know who he was.

He hadn't given up, only the hope that things would be different. He found his suffering was bearable when he did so, that he accepted the totality of life, regardless how he felt about it, whether he liked it or not.

And like it, he did not.

Reed couldn't look at Danny. If he did, he would risk clinging to hope again.

He wasn't surprised he'd come. He had an intuition that he would seek him out. Reed's intuition didn't come in words or thoughts, it came in dreams. The only consistent thing about them was the image that followed them: red hair.

He didn't know who she was. He sensed her presence the day he woke up in a lab staring at Mr. Smith's hopeful grin. Her essence warmed him. At first, he thought he'd imagined it like all the other random thoughts, but the essence that accompanied her was different than all the others.

It was fragrant.

He didn't know her name. Didn't know if she meant anything to him or if she was real. He may have given up hope for escape, but he wasn't able to expel hope concerning her, hope that she was real, hope that he meant something to her. When things were darkest it was hope that he would see her one day that warmed him.

But that was as far as he hoped. That was it.

He couldn't look at Danny because he'd see the hope in his eyes. Danny needed to accept and understand where he was. This was the island. It was the end of the world. Home didn't exist, not anymore. If he hoped to find something better, he would eventually look inside the needle. But the answer wasn't in there.

But he would go inside. They all did.

Reed wasn't disappointed when he did. Danny confirmed what he suspected. *She's in there, too.*

It was harder to know that she was in there than suffering through the Haystack, knowing that if he took the needle he would find her. But he would have to stay strong. In his dreams, she told him to resist. She told him that someone would come for him and show him the way.

And then Danny appeared at the beach and he knew it. He just knew it. Maybe he was the one that would put an end to all the suffering. Maybe he would give them hope.

That was why he couldn't look at him.

13

Class was in session.

About thirty of them in small desks arranged in tidy rows and the teacher discussing the world economy. He was propped on the corner of the desk. He was mostly bald and his bottom lip glistened when he took a moment to gather his thoughts.

Some of the guys in the back row were asleep, carefully hiding their faces behind the people in front of them. Danny was up front and had taken to doodling on a piece of lined notebook paper. It started out as a tapestry of curly lines, but then a face took shape in the middle of it all. First the eyes, then the petit nose. He began to darken the hair—

"Danny Boy?" The teacher had crossed his arms, scowling over his glasses. "Art class is not today. I'll advise you to join the discussion or I'll be forced to report you to your Investor for tutoring."

Danny folded the paper.

After a long, uncomfortable pause, the teacher continued in the same droning tone about the recent flash crash of the New York Stock Exchange. Millions of dollars were lost in a matter of moments. The market closed early that day and all trading suspended. A week later, the culprit was found: some dopey day trader that lived in his parents' basement that hacked his way into the market and over reached.

"You don't mess with money, boys," the teacher intoned with a gurgle. He cleared his throat. "Money is power and it will find you."

The teacher asked for questions. He was answered by the sound of soft snoring somewhere in the back but didn't hear it. He had no idea why everyone started laughing.

"Okay, I understand this is not a stimulating topic," he said, finally standing up with a grunt, "that's why I got special permission to do an exercise today."

Their interest piqued.

"We're going to use tablets for our class discussion today."

There was no buzz, no excitement. There was a fully-loaded game room in the next building, why would anyone care about a tablet?

The teacher unlocked a cabinet in the corner of the room. He pulled a box off the bottom shelf and slid it across the floor. The guys sleeping in the back continued sleeping. The others looked bored. Danny listened.

They were going to begin a business in a simulated program. It could be anything: services, goods, investing, whatever. All they had to do was show they could create a fake business that made fake money in the fake world inside the tablet and that would prove they had some understanding of economics.

A few of the guys started taking them out of the box. The teacher stopped them by holding up a knobby finger. "And remember, these tablets are not allowed out of this room. The repercussions of such an infraction will be severe."

Ass = grass.

When he dropped his hand, Danny was the first one to the box. He found a seat next to one of the Sleeping Beauties. The tablet felt warm in his hand. It fit nicely.

The teacher got stern with the rest of the boys barely making an effort.

"We'll be here all day," he said. "Until you finish, I swear to God."

Every second in the class was a second away from the game room. They began breaking down into small groups. Even woke up the sleepers. The teacher advised them on how to begin. Danny, though, stroked the smooth glass as instincts bubbled inside him. He ignored the instructions and, with all the excited chaos, called up a virtual keyboard on the touchscreen.

His fingers raced over the keys with the tablet snuggly cradled in his left hand. He swiftly hit a combination of keys to override the operating system. The screen went black. A cursor blinked in the upper left corner. He began typing again.

The commands came from somewhere deep in his subconscious. He didn't stop to think about the letters or the meaning of what he was writing, he just let it flow through his fingertips until line after line of code began scrolling rapidly from top to bottom. He was looking for a combination of words that would give him an encrypted password. He didn't know what it was, just trusted he'd know it when he saw it.

AW34uT!69fEW&8990.

There it is.

He tapped the glass and stopped the word flow, then dragged his fingertip over the password and dropped it into the upper right corner. The screen went black again. One second. Two. Three.

And then color swirled into focus.

A light blinked in the upper right. He had hacked into the network. That blinking light meant he had access to the Internet. To the world outside.

Danny began to download a browser from an FTP site that popped into memory—

"Aw, what?"

Every single tablet went blank.

Danny looked up. The class was moaning, some of them trying to shake their tablet back to life. "What happened?" someone whined.

"Class! Class!" The teacher held up his hands. "I need you to hand the tablets back to me in an orderly fashion…"

Danny quickly slipped into the middle of the room and exchanged his tablet with one of many abandoned on a desk. Then he switched with another one, careful no one was watching.

"Class, please!" The old man cleared his throat. "Please! It's important you give me your tablet so we don't lose your data. Line up, keep orderly, please. Keep orderly."

Danny did what everyone else did and began moaning. He told the guy next to him about the idea he had for a lemonade stand. When he was checked off and dismissed, he left the classroom smiling.

We're not alone. There is an outside world.

14

They had a match in the game room in an hour.

It had only been a week since Danny woke from his first round and he'd put them firmly in first place. In fact, they were so far ahead they would still be in first after the second round. Sid didn't even pretend to be running the crew anymore. When they talked about strategy, he got everyone quiet and then looked at Danny.

They were in the cafeteria, talking about the second round only days away. Most had met new girls in the first round and Sid was having a hard time getting them to agree on another match once they were inside the needle.

Danny pushed his tray away and checked out of the conversation. He looked around for Reed. He had to come back to eat but maybe he did it at night when everyone was sleeping.

Danny pulled a sheet of paper from his back pocket. He had continued the doodling he started in economics class and fleshed out the details of the girl's hair, added plump lips and eyebrows. He hoped to see her again once he was inside. Danny didn't know what he was supposed to do and craved some direction. Craved some answers.

"What's that?" Zin plucked the paper out of his hand. "Ooo, you're a Michelangelo *and* a war hero, huh? Who would've guessed?"

Danny snatched it back. Zin didn't seem alarmed by the overreaction.

"That your girlfriend?" Zin asked.

"Yeah," Danny said. "I meet her every night in my dreams."

Zin opened a box of juice and sipped, absently. When no one seemed interested in what they were doing, Danny unfolded the paper and smoothed out the wrinkles.

"You ever see her, Zin?"

He glanced. "No. Why, you?"

"No, no. I was just wondering, you know, for the next time we're..." Danny stumbled over his directionless conversation. Again, Zin took no notice.

"Where do they come from?" Danny asked.

"The girls?"

"Yeah. I mean, are they real or just part of Foreverland?"

"No, they're real all right."

"How do you know?"

He shrugged. "Sandy describes a camp kind of like ours. They do the same things we do, only they don't call it the Haystack. I think they call it the Vase, or something girly."

"How do you know it's real?"

He shrugged, again. "I don't, but it makes sense. We're a boys' camp and they're a girls' camp. Why not?"

Danny looked at the face in the doodle. She was different than the rest. Maybe she wasn't real.

"But how do you know?" he said. "Who says that this, right here, isn't real? Maybe this is the dream."

Zin shook his head, took another sip and grimaced.

"I mean, what proof do I have that any of this is real? Maybe this is just another Foreverland that we think we woke up in and we're really still in a dark room somewhere freezing our asses off while we wander around another Foreverland—"

"Look! This is real!" Zin slammed his juice down. "It just is, so get that through your little punctured skull, all right? This is real, Foreverland is real, it's all real." He grabbed the paper and held it up to Danny's face. "She's real, too, Danny Boy. You know why?"

Danny backed off.

"Because we got nothing else. It's just this, and that's all. My girl is real, you got it? Stop pissing all over my party, why don't you?"

He finished the drink in one long sip and crushed the carton on the table. His leg was shaking. Then he got up and left.

Sid didn't see any of it, just figured Zin was making an early exit for the game room. In seconds, all of them followed Zin out. Everyone on the island had a nerve, Zin once told him.

Danny just stepped on Zin's.

15

Danny woke early for the second round.

Mr. Jones walked him to the Haystack. They walked inside without introductions from another clipboard carrier as the last bell faded.

Danny wasn't nervous until the air inside hit him and the steel fan loomed overhead and the smell of dank misery crawled up his nose. By the time he reached his cell, his insides had turned to jelly. Mr. Jones had sensed his hesitancy and placed a firm comforting hand on his shoulder. Danny turned quickly into his cell to get away. He waited until everyone was inside their cells before getting undressed, doing it quickly and folding everything neatly so that Mr. Jones would leave.

"Hey, Danny Boy," Sid shouted. "I want you fully lucid this time and get to the sundial, my man. You hear? Once you're inside the needle, none of this exploring crap like a new poke, you stay in the Yard and meet us at the sundial. We need to clock some real kills in the game, son. We only need to stay in first place another week!"

Someone whooped and shouted, "FIRST PLACE!"

And then everyone joined the seemingly random celebration.

"Zin, you, too!" Sid shouted above the melee. "You be at the sundial, boy, or I'll dot both your eyes. You're screwing with my time if you get lost inside the needle."

And the chant continued. *FIRST PLACE! FIRST PLACE!*

"What's the obsession with the game?" Danny said.

Zin was already sitting on the floor with his back straight. "There's a reward for any team that captures first place for three straight weeks. They drop the needle as soon as we get here. No getting naked and no suffering."

"Why didn't anyone tell me?" Danny grabbed the bars. He wanted to pull them apart and throttle Zin sitting so composed and unmoved. *No suffering? I'd be in that game room every waking second!*

"Bad luck to tell you," Zin said. "It's a jinx."

Danny wanted to argue, but he was right. They were in first.

"Don't fight it, Danny Boy." Zin took a deep breath. "Suffering is part of life. Either way, we go inside the needle."

"You mean you like this?"

"Hell, no. But it doesn't matter how I feel." Another deep breath. "Be here, no matter what."

"Fine." Danny crossed his arms and began pacing. "If you want to freeze your ass off, be my guest. I want out."

Reed was standing in his cell with his back to Danny. He was as motionless as Zin was sitting. The skylights began to turn, followed by another round of cheers. Light faded. Darkness settled like thick soup. Forms disappeared. Voices became bodiless chatter.

The second round had begun.

"Danny Boy?"

Zin's voice was soft, blending in with the docile conversations that were beginning to trail off into the silence of impending pain.

"The game, it's a waste of time," he said. "We're going to explore once we're inside the needle. I'm going to give you the tour, show you Foreverland."

Danny resumed breathing like Zin had taught him. He finished his count to ten. "Sid's going to be pissed."

"Good thing he's not running the show."

"Then who is?"

"You are, Danny Boy."

"Me?" He cringed, hoping Sid didn't hear him. "Dude, I'm a poke, I'm not running anything."

"Don't be a clown, you're the whole reason this place was cheering about a half hour ago. They're all watching you, Danny Boy. Not Sid. He's just a cheerleader."

"You're cracked, man," Danny hissed. "Sid will put a black mark under my eyes after he's done with you."

"You think the old men are going to let him do anything to you or me or any kid in this place? Nothing's going to happen, Danny Boy. This place is locked down tight."

Danny imagined a mob of old men charging through the Yard wielding stun guns. It wouldn't matter if they were carrying nuclear weapons, they'd throw a hip before they got anything under control.

"What about when they threw you in a trash can?"

"It was a trash can, who cares. It was funny. Even I laughed."

"So how's a bunch of crypt keepers going to keep us from getting pummeled?"

"Right here." Zin's dim figure tapped the tracker on the back of his neck. "They got some sort of remote in their pocket. They put their hand in there and they can kick a volt or two into your spine and you're sleeping, my friend. And Sid knows it. The geezers load you on a cart and it's over."

"What're you saying over there?" Sid's voice carried from across the dark aisle. "You got something to say about me?"

"Nothing, Cap-i-tan," Zin said. "Just girl talk over here, that's all."

Sid grunted. His teeth ground together. He said, "You just make sure—"

Click. Hmmmmmmmm.

The fan engaged. The blades began to crawl.

Conversation died.

"Let's get on with the suffering," Zin said.

Danny was already counting his breath. He glanced at Reed, still standing, still facing the other direction. It would be long and hard for him. Maybe if they held first place, he'd get a reprieve.

But he wouldn't take the needle, so then what?

Danny thought about doing the same. He could talk to Reed when everyone was out. He could tell Danny more about the underlying secrets of the island, the red-headed girl, and why he resisted. Maybe they could talk long enough to sort through each other's memories, figure out which ones were their own without having to go inside the needle.

But then the sprinklers began to hiss.

Moments later, Danny looked at the top of his cage. He knew he'd reach for the needle as soon as it dropped. Just like everyone else.

16

Reed settled into the rhythm of breathing.

The wet cold had reached his bones, but he found peace with it. Even the shivers seemed to fall into rhythm. He was at peace with misery.

He didn't like the suffering, didn't prefer it. If the gates opened, he'd gladly leave. But he didn't resist it.

He found space for it.

Mr. Smith's familiar walk-shuffle came down the aisle. Reed could smell him.

In-out, he breathed. *In-out*.

"Reed, look at me."

Reed saw a haggard face that was losing the battle with time and gravity, the cheeks sagging like an old dog that needed putting down. The eyes were hidden in the shadows.

"You've put me in a very difficult position, my boy. In an effort to convince you what's best, the Director and I have decided to alter your experience. We hope you'll make the best of your opportunity."

Reed drew a long breath through his nostrils.

"You understand we put you under duress to facilitate your progress. It's not meant to harm you, you see. Only to propel you forward. But you refuse our guidance, Reed; therefore, we'll need to push harder."

The back of the cell began closing. It did not stop until the bars were pressed against his chest and back. Reed was sandwiched tightly in place, barely able to move. The lucid gear dropped from the top of his cage and brushed the top of his head. He would only need to lift himself onto his toes to let it slide into place.

Mr. Smith clamped something on the bars, turning the wingnuts with his arthritic fingers. It was a metal frame, box-like. An empty bracket was centered twelve inches from Reed's face.

Mr. Smith remained a few seconds longer, then headed for the exit.

Reed closed his eyes. He squirmed against the bars and panic threatened to overwhelm him. He just wanted to move.

The lucid gear touched his head. They were making escape easy.

Each breath was forced to be shallow and quick as his chest was constricted by the bars. He wasn't able to turn his head. Thoughts of being buried alive piled up. Trapped, he focused his efforts on breathing, again.

Mr. Smith returned. He was dragging something long and snake-like.

Reed wouldn't look. He barely controlled his breathing.

Mr. Smith fastened it onto the metal bracket, turning wingnuts to hold it into place. He left the Haystack, the heavy door clicked shut. Locking the darkness inside.

Reed was tempted to lift up and take the needle. *What if it's a box of rats?*

Water hit his face.

He choked. Struggled to breathe. Unable to turn his head, he was forced to swallow too much of it, choking on the rest. He managed to hold his breath until it stopped. He coughed up excess liquid.

Drowning.

A hose was locked into the metal frame.

When he had regained his breath, when the burning subsided in his chest, when the bars weren't pressing as hard, the water came again.

And again.

17

Floating in darkness.

Not exactly floating, that implied motion.

Danny was just nowhere. There was no sound, smell or flesh. No nothing.

When the needle had dropped, Danny couldn't pull it down fast enough. He didn't bother looking at Reed. He was shivering too much to care about anything but escape. The suffering was worse than the first time. Felt longer, colder. He welcomed the needle like a savior.

The strap numbed his forehead. The needle hit the stent with a dull thump. His back arched. And then he went to the dark place.

And it was better than the Haystack.

Boundaries formed.

What felt like an endless void shaped into arms and legs and a body. He had no sense of up or down, just a feeling of being curled up in a fetal position.

Slowly, there was something hard beneath him. Gravity pulled the weight of his body against it. A rhythmic beating throbbed distantly, got louder. *Heartbeat.* Blood rushed past his ears.

The ground thundered beneath him.

The world spun and pain struck his arms—

"Don't challenge me, son." The voice was modulated and robotic. "Wake up."

Danny's head bobbled and neck popped. His eyes began to open. First, light. Then color. Then the details of a mechanical face. Danny was twenty feet off the ground, in the clutches of giant mechanical hands.

Danny's world shook violently, again. A word vibrated in his throat but didn't make it out.

"You ever have any delusions about who runs our camp, let this be a reminder," the thing said.

Danny's arms filled with sparking pain. The monster squeezed until they were painfully numb.

"You might be a hero in the game room, but you're a little thirteen year old bitch. You got that? Life on the island is short, and I've been here way longer than you, so get in line, son. I don't care what Zin told you about the tracker volts, I'll stuff your head up your cornhole before they konk me out. You'll be tasting last night's dinner for weeks."

The lower jaw jutted out. Flames ignited on the incisors like pilot lights.

"Try me again and I'll set your head on fire. You hear?"

When Danny didn't respond, his world shook. The popping in his neck was louder.

"You hear—"

"Whoa, whoa there, Sid. You're going to turn him into a jellyfish if you're not—"

Danny crumpled on the ground. The mechanical beast's enormous hand clamped around Zin and lifted him up. The fingers squeezed so hard that Zin bulged like a water balloon. Then he melted, dripped to the ground like mercury, coagulating and reforming. Zin was whole again.

"I'm not kidding, Zinski! You start putting ideas in Danny Boy's head and I'll cook you both."

"Sid, you got to remember that he just got here. He's still a poke, man. He needs a little introduction to the needle before you start throwing him in the Foreverland game room. Just give him a second to get used to it, will you? You remember what it was like on your second round?"

Zin was engulfed in a cloud of fire. He was unfazed when the fire died, pinching off a small flame dancing on his sleeve.

"Both of you." Sid pointed back and forth. "Don't jerk off all day, you hear? If we lose and you're MIA, then it's cornhole time. Got it?"

Danny nodded. Zin gave him a thumbs up.

The ground shuddered as the monster trotted across the Yard. Danny bounced with each step.

How'd you do that? Those words were stuck inside Danny.

Zin grabbed his arm and lifted him to his feet. "Lean against the sundial and stand there a minute."

It vibrated beneath his hand, penetrating into his chest until he was filled with warmth. The aches from Sid's punishment faded. He noticed other sensations, too. The breeze brushed his cheeks. The grass tickled between his toes. He noticed the shouting and laughter from across the Yard. People running. People flying.

"Welcome to Foreverland, Danny Boy." Zin let go of his arm. "You're all the way inside this time, my friend."

A body began to appear in the empty space only a few feet away. It first appeared translucent and ghostly, slowly solidified into one of the new pokes that came to the island shortly after Danny. He was sucking his thumb, eyes closed.

"That's what most people look like on the second round," Zin said. "Don't tell Sid, but I heard he sucked his thumb for five rounds." He looked around, suspiciously, whispered too loudly, "Even sucked his thumb inside the Haystack."

Danny laughed.

"How'd you do all that?" Danny asked, weakly.

"What? Turn to water? Old trick, man. Sid was just trying to scare you. He knew you'd be lucid enough to feel it but not enough to control the pain. After this round, Danny Boy, you'll be able to do anything. You can feel as much pleasure or as little pain as you want."

Zin splayed his hand on the sundial. He pulled a meat cleaver from his pocket and rammed it through the back of his hand. No blood. He didn't even flinch.

"See?" Zin held up his hand, the tip sticking through his palm. "If I wanted to feel that, I could. But I don't."

Danny felt dizzy. The blade sticking through the flesh and people flying like birds and the ground swaying and—

"Whoa, hold on there." Zin placed Danny's hands on the sundial before he fell over. "Hang on a bit longer, Danny Boy."

Feelings of seasickness subsided. The ground held still. The alternate reality felt normal again and the urge to vomit disappeared.

"You good?" Zin asked.

Danny nodded.

"All right, give it another minute. The sundial is the center of Foreverland, where we feel most solid when we get inside. It helps to touch it when you first get here. After while, you'll just hit the ground running."

"Where are we?"

"You mean you don't know?"

Danny shook his head.

Zin laughed. "We're inside a computer, Danny Boy! This is a program, a digital environment. Our identity has been sucked out of our heads, and the needle is doing the sucking. Hell of lot better than freezing your ass off on that concrete floor, right?"

Danny smiled. *Yeah, it is.*

"Once you're fully here, fully present, you'll figure out how to control this body. You can dial up pleasure, push out pain, turn yourself into a baboon or swim to the bottom of the ocean… whatever you want to do. The sky's the limit, Danny Boy. And the sky has none."

Zin pulled Danny from the sundial. They walked around the poke curled on the ground. Danny felt shaky the further they got from the sundial, but he was still solid. He had a new body, one he could control with a thought.

"So what do you want to do, Danny Boy? What'll it be?"

Danny stepped away from Zin. The Yard was exactly like it was on the island. The same buildings, same trees. Even the Haystack. But it was different. It all felt interconnected. Danny could feel the grass shifting in the wind. He could feel it crush when a footstep landed. He sensed the birds singing and the crackle of heat as a fire erupted in the trees. He was one with everything.

Not separate. But one. And the sky was the limit.

"That," Danny said. "I want to do that."

Zin looked up. "All right."

The island was lushly shaped like the state of South Carolina, dominated by trees with a bald spot of turf in the middle.

Tears streamed down Danny's cheeks in the cold wind. He kept his arms out for balance, like walking a tightrope for the first time, 3000 miles above the ground. Zin flew next to him on his back with his hands laced behind his head. For him, it was as thrilling as riding a bike for the thousandth time. For Danny, it was everything he imagined.

The ocean was choppy, but the distant horizon disappeared in a gray haze. Even the sky above them looked more gray than blue, like they were inside a fuzzy dome.

"What's all that?" Danny shouted above the wind.

"The Nowhere." Zin made hardly any effort to speak, but his words resounded clearly across the whistling wind. "You can't go out there, it's the edge of the program. Where your memories are."

"Wait. What?"

"Your memories." Zin put a finger on Danny's forehead. Inside Foreverland, there was no hole. "Haven't you noticed?"

Danny concentrated on flying straight, but he was remembering the time he stepped on a nail when he was six and had to get a tetanus shot; the time he got caught smoking his mom's cigarette and had to finish the pack in front of her as punishment. The time he kissed a girl behind the garage on a dare—

He began to wobble. Zin grabbed his arm to straighten him out.

"I don't get it," Danny shouted.

"It's part of the reprogramming, Danny Boy. The healing. They sucked our memories out so our bad habits get fixed. You know, like addiction and stealing and whatever else the bunch of us lowlifes did wrong before we got here. Inside the needle, we get them back until we're whole again."

"Reed said we'll get sucked inside the needle."

"Yeah, well, he's not exactly the voice of reason." Zin resumed his relaxed posture. "But he might not be all that crazy."

"Why?"

"You might not want to remember everything, Danny Boy. There's a reason we're here."

He didn't have a chance to ask for more. Zin floated farther away, eyes closed. Not so happy. If they were a bunch of screw-ups before they got to the island, it wouldn't be so rosy to remember.

They soared over the beach. The waves were just as angry as the day he went to visit Reed but the beach was empty. Reed was still back in the Haystack, forced to stand in the blowing cold. *How would he know what was going on if he'd never been inside the needle?*

Danny liked the way it felt, remembering his life. He wasn't sure it made sense, how it was fixing him, but if he was broken then maybe he shouldn't know how it worked. Just because he was regaining memories, though, didn't make him more of who he was.

Is that what I am, memories? Or am I something else?

It was too confusing to think about. He was perfectly fine with the thrilling sensation of flying, of being so far off the ground without the fear of falling. If they just did circles all day, it would be a good one.

There were no girls on the ground. Zin was flying with his eyes closed. Danny wanted to ask about them, even about the redheaded one, but then a squad of boys blasted between them in v-shaped formation and tossed Danny head over heel. He went tumbling.

I'm going to crash, I'm going to die!

Zin studied him. "You got to watch it. If you let your thoughts get a hold of you, you'll divebomb out, man. You crash, it's going to hurt. You're not ready to control your pain so if you split a bone, you're going to feel it. Remember, they're just thoughts. *You* are not your thoughts. Stay focused. Sometimes it helps to imagine a dot in the middle of your brain. Breathe in and out of it until there's nothing left but the dot. You'll get the hang of it."

He did that. First, with his eyes closed. Next, eyes open.

They did a complete circle around the island. The second time around, he felt a little more in control. In fact, he put his arms down and did a Superman pose. Zin was pretending to swim.

They were over the south end of the island where the Investors' Mansion divided the trees from the coast. They soared around it and cut across the middle of the island. Zin turned on the jets and did loops around the Chimney.

The Chimney, where everyone woke up and everyone disappeared. Graduated. *Smoked.* But no one knew what really happened. Would Foreverland really show them what was inside?

"Get to the ground, Danny Boy," he said. "I don't want you crashing and burning, my man."

"Where you going?"

Zin pointed down. Danny could see the girls popping into existence near the sundial. "Girl plus boy… you do the math."

They landed safely. Danny didn't see Zin after that.

The two moons had fallen below the tree line. There was a castle in the Yard with smolder holes in it. The moat was on fire. Danny watched Vikings carry out chests of gold. They celebrated around a fire with pre-historic turkey legs and vats of beer, wine or whatever was slurring their speech. Apparently, they won.

Danny had gone to the beach. It was empty. No sign of the redhead. He explored the island, messed around inside the castle and went swimming. He even went to the game room and helped the team win.

(They were getting slaughtered before he showed up.)

DA-NNY! DA-NNY! DA-NNY!

Sid was all happy.

Danny looked for the redhead some more. He ended up where he first met her on the Yard. The castle had crumbled into dust by then. The moat continued to burn with eerie red flames.

Campfires were all around it. When the moons began to fade, they were hugging and saying goodbye. Some of them were crying. Danny watched from the edge of the trees, alone.

Someone walked toward him.

"You Danny Boy?" It was one of the girls. "Someone found this by the fire."

She handed him a gift. It was wrapped in red paper that sparkled in the dimming light. He opened the card taped to the top.

Merry Christmas, Danny Boy.

He could hardly see his hands as he ripped the paper from the box. The fires were nearly gone when he pulled the top open. He put his hand inside.

Sand.

ROUND 3

Fire Takes Life of Mother and Son

GILBERT, Arizona. – The Gilbert Fire Department responded to a call at 4:22 AM where a two-story house belonging to Allison Forrester was engulfed in flames. Fire fighters were able to keep the blaze from jumping to neighboring houses but unable to rescue the occupants. Once the fire was extinguished, two unidentified bodies were discovered inside. One is believed to be Allison Forrester, 47, and her son, Daniel Forrester, 13.

The cause of the fire is unknown.

18

She neared the edge of the gray boundary, dared not go any closer.

But she could see… all of Foreverland.

Danny flew by with the other boy. He was quite… good.

Quite.

She… she was right. He was who she needed. She needed someone to watch Reed. Needed someone to help her… to put an end…

She watched, she watched.

He would need the practice. He would need to learn the ways of Foreverland. He would need to be stronger. She couldn't wait long, but she… she needed to wait for now. To give him time to get stronger.

She left him a present. A gift. A clue.

He would use it.

To find her next time.

In the…

Nowhere.

19

Light softly flooded the Haystack. Danny shivered.

The boys were slowly coming to life. Zin was still on his back. Reed's cell was empty. Danny didn't bother wondering where he was or if he was alive, he just needed to get out. The others were already ahead of him, scurrying for the exit. No one spoke.

Danny's clothes were near the opening of his cell, the door slung open. He quickly got dressed and hurried for the outdoors, to get heat into his bones. They exited into the shade of the trees, but the air was so much warmer than inside the Haystack. They trotted down the path to the end. *Sun.*

Danny stopped as he entered the Yard, savoring the warmth on his face, the smell of green grass and the sound of birds.

Something flashed.

He shaded his eyes and picked up a small twinkle in the top floor of the Chimney behind the black windows. He gave it little thought. Instead, he started for the dorms to get some rest. He hadn't moved all day, but all that healing was exhausting. He couldn't exactly remember what had happened.

Danny crossed the Yard.

Zin was still inside the Haystack, shivering on the floor.

20

The Director scrubbed his hair with a towel.

It had been days since he'd showered. Work was demanding. Sometimes he forgot what he smelled like. But when a man stays locked away on the top floor of a luxury penthouse-style apartment, it didn't matter what he smelled like. But a shower was in order. He needed to get outside and stretch a bit, see his island. Reconnect with the reason he came to it in the first place.

Things have evolved so quickly.

He saw the line of boys emerging from the trees.

The Director threw the towel over the back of a chair and aimed one of his telescopes. He dialed the knob until the faces came into focus. They were exhausted and shivering. Eight hours of bone-chilling cold would make a polar bear chatter. Those boys had no idea what their bodies were enduring while they were away.

Foreverland, they called it.

The Director couldn't have come up with a better name. Then again, he never could have envisioned what his island had become. Not in a million years.

These kids had no idea what a gift they'd received. If they knew what their lives had been like before he brought them to this paradise, they'd break down like rag dolls. Then again, if they knew the price they were paying for such freedom, for the unadulterated alternate reality, they might not exactly drop to their knees in thanks.

Evolution works that way. The weak feed the strong.

The boys continued to exit the trees, crossing the Yard toward their warm beds. They'd stop for some food but then they'd sleep the night away. The Director kept his telescope focused on the trees until he came out. The kid stopped, shaded his eyes and glanced in the direction of the Director.

Danny Boy.

He was filled with the urge to mix a drink.

The Director questioned that acquisition, the young little redheaded hacker. He wasn't the typical candidate for his program. He was too smart. Too skilled. He needed kids that were physically fit. Not necessarily retarded, but he didn't need a genius, either. Just an ordinary kid that would follow the pack.

But that Mr. Jones persuaded him it was the right choice. Said the kid had enhanced brain activity that would open new avenues in the program. The Director knew Jones was only in it for himself, but he made sense.

The Director was reluctant because the program was delicate. There were so many unknown factors that a risk was dangerous. But if he didn't push into the unknown, the program would stagnate. In fact, if the problem – *the problem* – hadn't already started, he would've told Jones to go slam his head in the sand. But he needed some solutions, and, damnit, Jones made sense.

Reed created the problem. The Director needed to keep him around to solve it. So far, that wasn't working. He couldn't make Reed take the needle. It just wouldn't work if he didn't want it, if he wasn't open to it. If the Director punched it through his skull against his will, it would do more harm than good.

Danny Boy, though, could be the key. He'd already reached out to Reed on the beach. The Director knew it had something to do with the girl that confronted him in the first round.

She is the problem.

She was still hiding in the Nowhere. She was careful, sent the kid a clue. The Director didn't know what she had in mind, but he would keep following. And like all his enemies, she would be destroyed in the end. He rubbed the small hole in his forehead. After all, she couldn't escape. He knew where she was, he just couldn't reach her.

"Director?" the intercom squawked.

"Yes," he answered.

"We're ready."

The Director watched Danny cross the Yard. He was too sleepy, too damn cold, to do anything else. He'd go to his room and sleep off the experience for the next day. That would give the Director some time to figure out something for the next round.

He decided he'd mix that drink after all. Tomato juice and vodka mixed over three ice cubes. The Director stirred it with a stalk of celery. He took a swig, hit it with a dash of pepper. He crossed to the other side and stood over another telescope, this one pointed over Geezer Mansion. He munched the celery and looked at the water beyond.

He focused on the horizon. There was nothing but the sharp edge where water met the sky. He often imagined he could see land beyond it. But that was too far for a telescope. He hadn't seen it in many years.

"Director?" The voice was impatient. "We would like to begin—"

"Don't interrupt, Mr. Jackson."

The intercom remained silent.

The Director finished his drink. When he was good and ready, he went to the elevator to assume his position as Director of a revolutionary program.

The world would remember him long after they forgot Jesus.

21

Parker lay on a bed. Mouth open. His lips were dry and cracked; his hair springing out in all directions.

A needle in his forehead.

A bald old man pulled aside a curtain that divided the room in half. "We're clear, Director."

"Thank you, Mr. Jackson."

The Director stood at the foot of the bed. The room was hospitable with soothing blue walls and the white curtain. There was a large glass window with half a dozen old men staring at them. At one time, the Investors stood in the room with the Director. Now, they were sequestered in the sound-proof booth. The Director needed peace and quiet when he worked his magic.

The Director would've banished them altogether, but these old men funded the project. The Director had proven to be a smart man in science and politics, so he let them watch. They didn't like it, but they were smart men, as well. They eventually stopped complaining and the Director eventually forgot they were there. Besides, he wanted them to see him perform the miracle. The Director was not a magician.

He was a savior.

Parker's eyes began rapid eye movement. The Director moved next to the bed. The eyes danced beneath the lids.

"Come on, now," the Director said, gently. "Come on."

Sometimes he lost them in the final leg of the journey; they just needed to connect the mind with the body. The sound of his voice gave them guidance. Previous patients said it was like a beacon bringing them home. It was very dark and directionless where they were; the mind drifting in unknown territory.

He cradled Parker's head, careful not to bump the wire protruding from the end of the needle that connected to a bedside computer. He brushed the wild hair back and stroked his cheeks, anything to stimulate the nervous system, give the mind direction.

"You're almost there." The eyes bounced faster. "Almost. Come on, now."

The eyes stopped.

Opened.

Parker stared at the Director without seeing him. Slowly, they came into focus. The Director pulled the needle from his forehead and stood back, gave him space. Parker sat up like a spring. He jerked his head around, surveying the room, eyes wide with wonder. He looked at his hands, turning them over, palm to back to palm.

"You did it," he said. "I've never felt… this good."

The men in the booth were waiting for a sign. Parker lifted his hand and waved. He saw them silently clap. The Director stopped Parker from standing.

"The password."

Parker jittered like a kid hopped up on energy drinks. He watched the men in the booth, mouthing out the words, *He did it, he did it!*

The Director squeezed his arms. "Password."

Parker focused on him. His lips moved but the word wouldn't come. He searched the Director's face for the answer. Mr. Jackson appeared from around the curtain, hiding a syringe behind his back. The Director glanced at him.

The old men settled.

"Last time," he said. "Password, please."

Panic jittered in Parker's stomach. The Director gave him a password before the journey to ensure he had made it. Without it, he couldn't be sure.

He knew the moment was about to pass by and he was about to lose everything he worked for. The Director let go of him and sat back. Parker sat still, thinking. A word was coming. He felt Mr. Jackson take a step and held up a finger to give him more time. He knew there was a needle behind his back. He knew if he didn't give the Director the word they would put him out and try it again. Next time, he might not return from that dark, drifting place.

He looked up.

Eyes bright.

"Foreverland."

The Director nodded. Smiled. "Foreverland, indeed."

He grabbed Parker's arm and held it up. They turned to the booth and the expectant faces inside.

"We've saved another one, gentlemen!" the Director shouted.

The old men entered the lab with cheers, shaking Parker's hand vigorously and patting him on the back. The Director stood back and watched. It was his favorite moment. The fruit of his labor. They brought Parker a glass of water and – in between sips – listened to him describe the details of his journey. They listened with bright eyes.

Mr. Jackson sheathed the syringe and stepped next to the Director.

"Check his vitals," the Director said. "And run him through cognition testing. If everything checks out, put him on the standard quarantine for six weeks. His body's in good shape, but we don't want him slipping away after all this hard work."

Parker touched his forehead, tenderly.

"Wait to remove the stent until the quarantine is complete," the Director added. "Just in case we need to go inside again. Otherwise, he won't need that anymore." He smiled at Mr. Jackson. "At least not for quite some time."

"And the garbage?"

"Hold it in the freezer for a few days, then the oven."

Mr. Jackson went behind the curtain.

The Director put his arm around Parker's shoulders and shook hands with all the men.

"We're saving the world one life at a time, gentlemen." He smiled through the scraggly beard. "One life at a time."

22

"Boom!" Sid slammed down the Jack of Spades. "That's game, you hole-headed freaks!"

The others threw their cards down. Sid swept them up. They were two days out of the Haystack and the damp cold was still inside them. Lying in bed just wasn't the same as letting the sun heat them up. They sat around the table killing time while they slow-roasted their bodies in the mid-afternoon heat.

Danny had been to the beach. He was expecting Reed to be warming up on the dune, but it was empty. He wanted to tell him.

Merry Christmas, Danny Boy.

It was from her. The red wrapping, the same bright red of her hair. The sand, he figured, maybe that meant the beach. *Meet her at the beach inside the needle? Was that it? Or meet Reed at the beach when he got back? And Merry Christmas?*

"Zinski!" Sid slapped Zin. "Wake up, boy. It's your deal."

Zin had his elbows on the table, staring at the mess of cards. He was yawning. Danny caught him shivering, earlier. Zin slowly unraveled the cards, stacking them all in one direction. He attempted to shuffle but they sprayed over the table.

"I think Zinski's heading for the Chimney, boys," Sid announced. "You feeling a little foggy, son? A little muddled in the noodle?"

Zin batted his arm away. "I'm waking up, fool."

"Oooooo…" Sid poked the cards out of his hands. "This dog's got some bite."

Zin carefully picked them up and began putting them back together. He was sluggish. Maybe he was tired, but he was breathing through his mouth. Vacancy lingered in his eyes now and then. How long before the Chimney took him?

Danny didn't want to think about it. He just got here and now Zin was looking more like Parker. Danny got up and stretched.

"Where you going?" Sid scooped up the cards as Zin dealt them.

"A walk, I guess."

"Maybe you're going to the beach with Reed."

"Why would I do that?" Danny snapped.

"I don't know. You been there a couple times, I thought maybe you two were dating."

"Give him a break," Danny said. "Who on this island is normal?"

"That's my point, you lunatic. He's standout crazy on an island of crazies. Right, Zinski?"

Zin blocked Sid's attempt to rustle his hair.

"Reed's in his room," Zin said. "I heard him in there before I came down."

"Well, good," Sid said. "Maybe they finally broke through his granite skull and he'll pop the needle like the rest of us." Sid played a card. "He thinks he's too good, that's his problem. He's special or something, all high and mighty that he can't damage his royal head. Friggin idiot, is what he is."

"You hit it right on the money." Danny stepped closer. "He's so stuck up that he would rather suffer than go inside the needle. All this time I thought he was trying to work something out or maybe he was just afraid we're all doing the wrong thing, but now you've made so much sense, Sid. He's an asshole! Why didn't I think of that?"

The game stopped. Sid tapped his cards on the table. "What's your problem, kid? You got a crush on Looney Tunes?"

"You ever stop to think why we're here, Sid?"

"We're here because we're sick." Sid nodded at the others. "This is a revolutionary method of healing, or did you miss orientation?"

"You buying that?" Danny looked around. "We've all had our memories sucked out and scrambled and we're marched into a prison cell and forced to get naked before they torture us until we stick a needle in our brains… that's what you're buying, no questions asked?"

"It's revolutionary, dummy."

"Or something else," Danny said.

Silence settled.

Sid tapped his cards into a neat stack and placed them face down. He was thinking. They all were. It was the line of questions that was always ignored. No one wanted to think about it. Even Danny.

But it was out there like the Ace of Spades.

"Okay, hotshot." Sid was expressionless. "Why don't you do something about it?"

Danny clenched his fists so no one would see him shaking. He didn't have any more balls to do something about it than any of the rest of them. He was reaching for the needle just like they were; swimming towards a bone-crushing waterfall.

Danny opened his hands. His fingers trembled.

"That's what I thought." Sid picked up his cards. "So why don't you shut your little cake hole and play some cards."

Sid shouted for the next play. Zin was staring, mouth open.

23

Danny went to the beach a couple of times that week. Always empty.

He avoided Sid and company and they didn't seem to care. They had locked up first place so they didn't need Danny anymore. They went to the game room without him while he was lying in the middle of the Yard with an unobstructed view of the Chimney. The smoke stack was leaking fumes. It was hardly noticeable, just a thin discolored wisp.

Danny dozed off. It felt good to be so warm and alone. Sometimes when he felt that good, he forgot about the island. He thought about a time when he was sitting in the kitchen at home when a warm breeze made brightly colored curtains dance in the windowpane. It smelled like cut grass. And his mom was there with macaroni and cheese in a plastic bowl.

It didn't bother him that it probably wasn't his memory. He enjoyed it, nonetheless.

"Danny Boy?" A shadow passed over. "You all right, my boy?"

Danny refused to open his eyes. He was sick of being Mr. Jones's *boy.* "Yes, sir. Just enjoying the weather, that's all."

"Okay." Mr. Jones's laugh was grating. "Well, your camp is going to the cafeteria. I thought maybe you'd be with them."

"I'm not hungry."

"You're not sick, are you?" Mr. Jones's took a knee and his old-smelling hand landed on his forehead. It was soft, untouched by manual labor. "Perhaps you should get some rest in your room so you don't get sunburned."

"Maybe I'll do that." It was best not to argue. "I'm waiting for Zin, though."

"Isn't he in his room?"

"He's coming." Danny lied.

"Are you boys going to the game room?"

"No, sir. I think we'll do some exploring. Maybe hike over to the beach or something."

"That's a fine idea, Danny Boy. A little exercise is good for you. Maybe you could grab an apple before you head off. You know what they say, an apple a day…"

"Keeps the doctor away," Danny finished.

And Mr. Jones laughed. He grunted as he stood up but kept on laughing. "At a boy," he said. "You're a good boy, Danny Boy. A good one."

Mr. Jones smacked the grass off his hands. There was an awkward silence. Danny hadn't opened his eyes. Mr. Jones finally said, "Well, I'm going to turn in for a nap and sleep for the both of us, my boy." That was punctuated by a short laugh and Danny cringed. "If you need anything, ask one of the Investors and they'll be in touch with me."

"Yes, sir."

And the shadow was gone.

Mr. Jones was halfway across the Yard before a cart picked him up. It looked like Zin's Investor (Danny was getting accustomed to the subtle differences in gray hair). A few minutes later, another cart pulled up to the dormitory and the Investor (he didn't recognize this one) went inside.

Zin's curtains were closed. Only one other room had the curtains drawn: two to the left of Zin's. *Reed.* He was sleeping, too. Or hiding.

Danny could get at least one of them to go on a hike.

Or a ride.

"What are you doing?" Zin stopped short of the golf cart.

Danny shoved him onto the seat. The Yard was mostly empty. He swung around to the driver's seat and stomped on the accelerator. The cart jerked forward and Zin nearly fell off. He went around the dorm at full speed. Zin grabbed onto the roof.

"Hold on!" Danny shouted. "We're out of control, Zin! We're out of control!"

Zin's eyes were wide open for the first time since they'd finished the last round. A smile had returned, too. Danny saw it. They made the next turn even faster and Zin held on to keep from sliding off. No one saw them hit a narrow path and disappear into the trees.

Danny was breaking the rules. He was doing something bad. It felt *gooood.*

The wooded turns were hard to manage at full speed. They sideswiped a couple branches, gouging the side of the cart. But the laughter never stopped. They drove past the Chimney where, luckily, no one was around and they got to the path on the other side without being seen. Several minutes later and a close call with a tree, Danny slammed the brakes. Zin nearly went over the dashboard.

"There it is." Danny huffed.

The path ended a hundred yards away at steps leading to gigantic palms that framed doors at the top.

"Geezer Mansion?" Zin said.

Danny smiled wide. "Let's storm it."

"Reed's rubbing off on you."

"What are they going to do? Ground us? Stick a needle in our head?"

Zin thought about it, then was overcome with laughter. "Let's ditch the cart and ambush these old bastards."

Danny started up the cart again. They each hung a foot over the edge as they approached the end of the path. Just before they hit the opening, he gunned it and they leaped out, rolling into the scrubby palms. The boys crawled out in time to see the cart come to a stop at the bottom step.

Perfect landing.

"What are we doing?" Zin asked.

They were crouched just inside the tree line, watching the front doors. "We're going to see what the old men got inside there."

"No, I mean why are we hiding? It's not against the rules to be here."

"We hijacked a cart. There's a really pissed-off Investor back at the dorm."

They waited another five minutes.

When nothing happened, they stepped into the opening. The Mansion was more intimidating in the real than it was flying overhead when it was Foreverland. It was only one story tall. The walls were white and smooth with a wide soffit that would keep anyone from climbing on top. The trees were kept twenty feet away, preventing anyone from climbing up one and leaping to the roof. The infrequent windows were a hundred feet apart, interspersed with single garage doors for the golf carts.

But it was long.

In both directions, the building was a solid barrier that extended all the way to each coast, cutting off the southern tip from the rest of the island. That much he had seen in Foreverland, and it was dead-on.

"You believe this?" Danny said. "It looks like a prison wall to keep us out."

"Or keep them in. You got any ideas besides bum-rushing the front door?"

They stared at the doors. There was nothing but the sounds of the jungle all around.

"If we time it right—"

"I'm kidding. That idea sucks," Zin said. "They'll jolt our trackers before we're two steps inside."

"How do you know?"

"You want to try it?" Zin stepped to the side and gestured.

Danny hadn't given it much thought. He wasn't serious about getting inside, but now that they were on the doorstep, it didn't sound so bad. Danny looked in both directions. He started to his left.

"Where you going?" Zin asked.

"Looking for a mouse hole. What else?"

"You scared of getting smoked?" Danny asked.

They'd been walking for twenty minutes. Zin faded in and out, not like he was deep in thought but more like he was just absent, staring at the ground while his body was on autopilot. Then he'd come back and they'd be talking again. Danny wasn't all that sure Zin even knew it was happening.

He didn't snap his fingers or clap. That was something Sid would do. Danny just gave him space because Zin always came back and then they'd pick up where they left off. Most of the time, they just walked. The Mansion was nothing but a long wall with an occasional window and not one of them accidentally left open.

Danny was about to ask the question again when Zin answered.

"No," he said. "I'm not. I just want it to be over."

Danny gave that answer a good twenty steps. "You giving up hope?"

"Since when was there hope? Like it or not, Danny Boy, we all get sucked into the needle. You want to swim against the current, you're just going to get tired. Just sit back and enjoy the ride, that's all you can do, son. And hope you come out the other side."

"Where's that?"

"The Chimney, where else?"

They reached the end of the building. It dropped off a sheer cliff about thirty feet. The Mansion was built flush against it. And just in case someone figured out a way to get down, tangles of barbed wire extended down to the water.

"Figured as much," Zin said.

"Man, they don't want us in there. Think there's any reason to go to the other side?"

"Not unless you want to see a mirror image of this."

The breeze was nice. They stayed there until the sweat evaporated from their cheeks. Five minutes back down the trail, they were wiping sweat off their brows. Zin seemed present, although he wasn't talking.

"What'd you think they're doing in there?" Danny asked.

"Healing, I guess."

"How, though?"

"Who knows?"

"That's what I mean," Danny said. "They tell us they're healing, but we don't see anyone after they've graduated."

"Maybe we're all infected with something, it's a quarantine."

"You believe that?"

"Hell, I don't know, Danny Boy. You think salmon wonder why they're swimming up stream?"

"They should. Bears eat them."

Zin shrugged. A few seconds later, he glazed over. He'd been on the island much longer than Danny and asked all the same questions, made all the same arguments when he first woke up in the Chimney. But you bang your head with a hammer long enough, you come to realize it only hurts when you swing. He'd put the hammer down long before Danny arrived. Explanations only made his head hurt.

"What's it like?" Danny asked.

Zin still seemed absent, but then coughed. "What?"

"Fading out like that, what's it feel like? Where do you go?"

He thought about it. "It's like… becoming hollow."

"You mean like a log?"

"Kind of," Zin said. "I'm tired, but not the regular tired. It's more like I'm just not connected with my body like I'm supposed to be." He swung his hands around like his identity was a ghost floating around him. "I am out there and I'm attached to this body by these invisible filaments, like a puppet." He began to zone. "And they're breaking, Danny Boy."

"What happens when they all break?"

"I guess I go to Foreverland."

"Why do you say that?"

"Because that's where I want to be. I don't remember much of anything when I'm back here. When we go inside the needle, that's when I feel like myself. I get my life back and it feels good. You know what I mean."

"But that's a computer program, you said so yourself."

"So, what's the difference?"

"It's not real. And if you're not real, you're dead."

"Like I said, Danny Boy, why fight it."

Zin went into the zone and didn't come back out, almost like the argument exhausted him. Danny could see the cart still parked at the steps, exactly where they left it. He couldn't stand the look on Zin's face, remembered how the joy ride brought him back. Maybe joy rides would reattach those filaments and Zin wouldn't go away so much. Maybe he just needed to live life in the real world and make some new memories. He could reverse the tide.

He was about to ask Zin if he wanted to drive the cart this time when the front doors opened.

Danny yanked Zin into the trees.

Just as the garage door to the left of the steps began to open, someone came down the steps. He didn't take them one at a time and he wasn't hunched over a cane. The kid went three at a time, hit the ground with both feet and sprang into a somersault!

Danny didn't recognize him because he'd never seen him with that much energy. He'd been a zombie from the day Danny woke up.

But Zin knew him.

"Parker?"

The kid was climbing onto the driver's seat.

"Parker, dude." Zin said. "Is that you?"

Parker stood, slowly. The boundless energy dissipated. He looked from Zin to Danny and back again. The knot in his throat bobbed up and down.

"Danny Boy, look. It's Parker! He's right here. Oh, man." Zin grabbed Parker's hand and shook. "Me and Danny Boy here were just talking about never seeing anyone that graduated and here you are… man, it's good to see you!"

The handshake shook Parker's whole body. The zombie look that Danny associated with Parker was gone. He was confused but completely focused. He looked exactly the same, except for the hair. The wild shag was gone, replaced by a proper haircut above the ears and combed to the side. The part was so sharp and neat that it looked like a white line on the side of his head.

"I almost didn't recognize you, man." Zin tried to muss up the hair but Parker jerked away. Zin didn't notice the rage that flashed across his face. "Are you living inside the Mansion? Is that where the graduates go?" Zin turned to Danny. "Holy crap, you know what that means? They're not lying, Danny Boy. They're really healing us, I mean look at Parker. I never seen this kid so… alive."

One thing Danny couldn't argue with, he looked good. Half an hour ago, Danny thought there was a chance they might be chucking the graduates into an oven that smoked out the top of the Chimney. Now, there was proof they weren't.

"Can you get us inside?" Danny looked inside the open garage. "We'll hide in the garage until night, what do you say?"

"Oh, hell yeah," Zin said. "How about it, Parker? Maybe you can give us a sneak preview?"

Parker's eyes widened. The knob was bobbing non-stop. He started backing up the steps and tripped backwards.

"I don't know, Zin." Danny watched Parker crab-walk his way up the steps. "Something isn't right."

Zin was catching on. "You remember us, Parker?"

When Zin took a step towards him, he crawled faster.

"That's enough."

The deep authoritative voice sent shivers through Danny's guts. A round old man was at the front doors. He stepped aside and two old men came out to help Parker inside. The round old man kept Danny and Zin frozen in place with a baggy-eyed stare.

"Danny Boy?" Mr. Jones came out. "What are you doing here, son?"

The gentle, grandfatherly look that distinguished Mr. Jones from all the other old men quickly darkened. Danny experienced another familiar feeling.

Getting caught.

24

Danny lifted the desk onto his bed and sat on top of it. It was mid-day and most people were in the game room or the cafeteria. Only three guys were in the Yard playing catch with a long-distance disc.

Danny hadn't been outside in three days.

Mr. Jones put him on room-restriction for two days and threatened to send him to the Director if he got to misbehaving like that again. None of that bothered Danny. To prove it, he volunteered to stay in his room a third day. Who knows, maybe he'd stay there until they dragged him to the Haystack for the third round.

He spent the day staring at a spot on the ceiling and counting his breath, practicing his focus like Zin taught him. *You'll need it to control yourself when you're inside the needle. Find your point of existence and breathe into it.*

There were a dozen old men that were eventually lured out of the Mansion when they got caught. When Mr. Jones got the full story – how they hijacked the golf cart and conspired to break inside – his face turned dark red. A jagged vein throbbed on his right temple. Danny thought it might wriggle out and explode.

Zin's Investor, Mr. Stevens, didn't change color. He arrived ten minutes later and calmly took Zin aside while Mr. Jones ushered Danny down the steps with a stranglehold on his arm. Anger transformed his feeble task-master into a thundering disciplinarian. They went to the dormitory on the very same cart that Danny swiped.

"You love trouble, Danny Boy," he said. "You have to have self-control. Chaos leads to anarchy, my boy. It'll lead you down the wrong path. It led you here."

Thought I was here for healing.

Mr. Jones strangled the steering wheel. "There are much worse places than here, I promise. You go back to trouble and you'll find out."

Mr. Jones was telling Danny more than he should've and Danny knew it. Most thirteen year old boys would've been reduced to a trembling mess under the glare of those father figures, but not Danny. It was thrilling. And the more Mr. Jones frowned – the more he shook his finger – the more fun Danny was having. He was forced to look away before he began laughing. Mr. Jones thought it was because he felt shame and, out of compassion, left the boy alone. He was hopeful Danny was punishing himself and that maybe, just maybe, he was mentoring this boy to a better life.

But authority doesn't scare me, Mr. Jones.

And neither did Sid.

Self-preservation should've instilled some fear in him since all the above could cause a great deal of pain. Maybe worse. Danny knew he was good with computers, that perhaps he'd been arrested for hacking a federal agency, and that he loved trouble. It was a start.

He also knew something else: Parker was alive and healthy. Maybe a little confused but, besides the creepy haircut, he looked good. That ended speculation that the old men were using them for firewood. But Parker didn't look excited to help them out.

Something had changed.

Danny had a future date with the Director, he was sure of it. And it might be sooner than later if he didn't curb his behavior and he had no plans to do that. He was just starting to flex his muscles and he liked it.

The boys had stopped throwing the disc and headed inside. Someone else was crossing the Yard.

Reed finally left his room.

Danny's self-imposed restriction came to an end.

25

Reed felt smaller, frailer. Vulnerable.

I'm breaking.

Reed stayed in the room because he didn't trust himself. He craved the sun's warmth but the ocean would be so near. If he went to the beach, all he'd have to do was step into the water and let the undertow sweep him out. It was moments like this – moments that revealed cracks in his will – that made him ask the question.

Why?

Why keep going?

Sleep came in short bursts. His body continuously ached. Dreams were fitful. He had delusions of falling, of shattering, of dying. He dreamed of drowning, over and over and over. Sometimes waking up gulping air. He didn't find a restful night.

Until she came.

He was in a field of soybeans. The rows ran over the hills like a sea of green. He walked them and picked the heads off foxtail and stripped the seeds to chew on the bitter stalks. When the sun had peaked, someone appeared in the row ahead of him.

Her hair was below the shoulders, a halo of cherry red. She walked toward him in a fluttering white summer dress. She took his hand and led him to a lone elm tree in the middle of the field. Her smell was like a dewy morning. Her laughter, pure joy.

It was a dream. A long one. A safe one.

He lay back on the grassy knoll. The grass tickled his shoulders. "If I take the needle, we'll be together," he said. "I won't have to dream anymore."

"If you take the needle, you'll never see me again."

"Why?"

"I don't know." She looked off. The dappled shade mottled her complexion. "I just know that you must wait. You must resist."

"I don't think I can anymore."

"You must. Not for you and me, but for everyone on the island and everyone that will come. This is bigger than us."

"But this is just a dream. Maybe I'm imagining this. Imagining you. Maybe none of this is true."

She ran her finger over the bridge of his nose, touched his lips. "It's all a dream. We just need to wake up."

He took her hand and traced the blue veins on her wrist.

"If any of this matters," he whispered, "then why can't I remember you?"

"You will, Reed."

"But I don't even know your name."

She took his hand and pressed it to her chest. Her pulse beat steadily into his palm. He slid his hand into her hair. The sun was low and the shadows hid her face as he drew her closer. Her cheek was warm against his.

The sun set.

Reed didn't understand dreams. He might be delusional. All his bravado misguided. His suffering, useless.

But it was all he had.

When he woke, he returned to the beach.

The water lapped against his ankles.

He walked the length of the north shore until he reached the rocky outcroppings. He went no deeper into the water, just enough to keep his feet wet. He turned back, his footprints washed away.

His life was like his footprints: no trace of his past. Everything he could remember he disregarded as chatter. None of it was true, there was no reason to give it space. He just walked and walked, one foot in front of the other. The footprints dissolved behind him.

Up ahead, Danny was on the dune. He looked different. His chest was out, his gaze patiently set upon the horizon. He paid no attention to Reed's approach.

Reed plunked down and leaned back on his elbows. He was tempted to take his shirt off and let the sun warm him but didn't want Danny to see what had become of him. His appetite had waned and it was beginning to show.

Danny sat next to him. The wind scoured their shins with sand.

And the waves rolled.

"They're healing us, Reed. Just like they promised."

He told him about Parker, how he looked, how he acted. He wasn't dead, not a zombie. He was vibrant, happy to be alive.

"You believe that?" Reed spoke just loud enough to be heard.

Danny took a breath, started to answer. He picked up a shell, instead, rubbing the shiny backside with his thumb. He wanted to say yes, he believed it. They were doing exactly what they told us and there was the proof. Parker was alive. *He's alive! They're not killing us.*

But are they healing us?

It was what they all wanted to believe. And he saw it with his own eyes.

He started to say *yes* again, but stood up. He walked to the water and threw the shell sidearm, skipping it on the thin water racing over the hardpacked sand. He remembered throwing flat rocks on a pond and counting the number of skips when he was a little kid. He was fishing with his dad.

Someone's dad.

Someone's memory.

He'd come to the beach to bring good news: they were being saved.

Reed shattered it with three words. Cut right to the heart of Danny's doubt.

He picked up another shell, this one as big as his hand, and carried it back to the dune. He rubbed the inside of the shell, the pearly white inside. Half a clam.

Where was the other half?

Danny picked up sand, let it sift between his fingers. It scattered in a gust of wind.

"I remember hiking," he said, grabbing another handful. "Hunting and fishing and fighting. Once, I got stuck on a trail without water for a day and nearly dehydrated before I got back. My ankle was twisted, too. Lost ten pounds on that trip."

He smacked his empty hands, the grains of sand lost on the dune.

"The thing is, I know none of those memories are mine. I don't hike and I don't fish."

Reed nodded.

"What I'm trying to say is, maybe you don't know her. Maybe she's someone else's memory and you're just hanging onto it and you're wasting your time resisting."

"I *don't* remember her."

"Then what are you doing?"

Reed looked far away. "I dream about her."

Danny hadn't dreamed once since he woke up on the island. In fact, he always woke up with a buzzing noise, like static. And it had gotten louder since the second round. Was the needle killing their dreams?

"I didn't see her in the last round. But she gave me something. She left a gift just before it ended, or at least I think it was from her. It was wrapped in red paper, the same color of her hair. It said *Merry Christmas, Danny Boy.* And inside was sand."

Reed tensed.

Describing her made him cringe.

He didn't like to think of her inside Foreverland. Not when he was outside.

"What do you think it means?" Danny asked.

"It's a clue."

"A box of sand, but what does it mean?"

"You need to find her. It'll make sense the next time."

"Why don't you go with me and help find her?"

Reed didn't bother responding. He'd been through enough pain and suffering that a bit of guilt wasn't going to get him to take the needle.

"Why is she hiding?" Danny asked.

"I don't know," he said, quickly. "But you need to find her."

Danny played with another shell, sifted more sand. Reed didn't have anything else to tell him so he got up, whacking the sand off his legs. He started back over the dune without saying goodbye.

"Danny Boy!"

Danny turned around but Reed was sitting still, facing the ocean. Maybe Danny imagined him shouting his name. The waves were so loud. He left him on the dune, all alone. But even when he was sitting next to him, he seemed so alone. Hollowed out by the suffering, a shell of a boy.

And the waves rolled.

26

"Keep your clothes on, gentlemen," Mr. Clark said. "You've earned a reprieve for your masterful skills in the game room."

The boys gathered outside the Haystack and gave a rousing cheer. The Investors applauded. Sid lifted his arms and strutted around. He stood next to Mr. Clark, jutting like a rooster. Mr. Clark pushed him gently back toward the boys.

"Yes," he said. "Your appetite for killing in a virtual environment was unparalleled."

The Investors chuckled but the boys didn't catch the sarcasm. They were still slapping hands.

"As you know, you will be ineligible for another hiatus until the fifth round, so I encourage you to enjoy the reprieve. Please, take advantage of this gift bestowed upon you by the Director."

Again, only the Investors noticed the sarcasm.

"You may enter the Haystack and your prospective cells." He opened the door.

They lined up single file, as usual, but there was no need for the Investors to guide them with a hand on the shoulder. The damp cold was nothing to fear, only a temporary nuisance.

Danny found his cell and Mr. Jones closed it for him with a curt nod and a quick exit. Danny blew into his cupped hands watching the others find their place. He wasn't going to lie on the concrete until the skylights went out. Zin entered his cell with his head bowed. He dropped to the floor and crossed his legs, falling into his typical breathing pattern. Reed stepped into his cell alone. His Investor wasn't with him.

"Zin." Danny bent down. "Zin, hey!"

Zin took a long breath and turned to Danny. A slight smile curled on his lips. That was all Danny wanted to see.

The Haystack door closed and the room became a shade darker. Only one Investor remained inside. Mr. Smith paced the aisle and stopped in front of Reed's cell.

"Reed, you are ineligible for the reprieve, son. I'll need you to—"

"Wait a second," Danny said. "He's part of this camp, he gets the same treatment as the rest of us."

Mr. Smith waited for the interruption to end. "I'll need you to hand me your clothes."

"Listen to me, dammit!" Danny screamed. "You're being unfair!"

Mr. Smith was unperturbed. His gaze was trained on Reed like crosshairs.

"He deserves it, Danny Boy," Sid chimed from across the aisle. "What the hell has he done to get reprieve? I'll tell you what: *squat*. He's done nothing, Danny Boy. He's a waste of time. They should put a bullet through his skull instead of a needle."

"Mr. Smith, please." Danny hugged the bars. "Reed needs the reprieve, sir. You're going to break him. He's not going to take the needle, you know that. There's got to be another way. Have a heart, man."

Mr. Smith's stare did not waver.

Reed stripped off his shirt. His shoulder blades knifed from his back and every one of his vertebrae could be played like a xylophone.

"Mr. Smith…" Danny said.

"Ah-hah-hahaha!" Sid bellowed. "Look at the goon! It's Halloween in cell six, boys. Reed's got an eating disorder, the crazy mutt!"

Reed slipped off his pants. His pelvis poked from his hips.

Danny couldn't watch. He'd sat with him on the beach, but seeing him bared to the world told of every second he'd endured since he'd been on the island. Even his face looked like a barren skull in the shadows.

Danny took off his shirt.

"Hey, look at Danny Boy!" Sid laughed. "He's copying his boyfriend. I knew the two were gay for each other."

Mr. Smith finally looked Danny's way. He muttered something. By the time Danny had his pants off, the door to the Haystack swung open and a crowd of Investors rushed inside.

"Danny Boy." Mr. Jones grabbed the bars on his cell. "What are you doing, my boy? You don't need to do this, you have a reprieve. You can't worry what the others are doing, you need to keep yourself in line, son."

Danny removed his underwear and began folding his clothes.

"You're a good boy, Danny Boy. You're a good boy. This is so…" Mr. Jones looked at the other old men. "Danny! Look at me! LOOK AT ME, BOY!"

Danny turned his back.

"Stop this madness, son. This is just so unnecessary… I mean, you don't need to go through the suffering. You don't need…" He chuckled nervously, then reached through the bars but Danny was out of reach.

The other Investors murmured. "It'll be all right," they said. "He'll get right, Mr. Jones, don't worry. The kid will get right. Let things go at their own pace, you can't make him do it."

Reed placed his clothes at the foot of the cell door. Mr. Smith retrieved them and left. The Investors consoled Mr. Jones until he let go of the cage. He muttered on the way out, leaving Danny's clothes behind. When the door closed, the Haystack was quiet.

"You're as crazy as he is, Danny Boy," Sid said. "You're a pair of cracked pots, son. A pair of them."

Reed turned his back on Danny and started a breathing routine.

The skylights began to close and darkness settled.

Danny began pacing to combat the chill running up and down his body. The camp began talking in half-hushed tones. He didn't care.

It was impulse. He didn't plan on joining Reed, but he just didn't want to follow the rest of them into the needle. It was too much celebration, they were embracing it too happily. *Someone needs to resist.*

But the lights had gone down and he was already shivering.

The cages whirred. The needles began to lower. The excitement had been dampened by the weirdness of Danny's voluntary nudity, but it didn't slow any of them from reaching. The lines whined as they were stretched to the floor.

Zin was still sitting, unaware that the needle had dropped into the cage until it lowered to the top of his head. He reached up, mechanically, and began to fit it around his head.

"Zin," Danny said. "Come back, all right. Don't… just come back."

Reed still had his back to Danny. And Zin was reaching for the needle and Danny realized it might be for the last time. If he got smoked on this round, Danny would be completely alone.

"Zin!" Danny just wanted him to hear it, to make sure. "You hear me?"

"Isn't that lovely, boys?" Sid's voice echoed in the dark. "Danny Boy's afraid for Zinski. Hot damn, I'm tearing up over here. It's breaking my heart."

"Zin." Danny tried to keep it quiet, but it was impossible. "Just look at me, man. Just, don't smoke out. Not yet."

"He's a goner, Danny Boy," Sid said. "Say goodbye."

"Shut up!" Danny rushed the front of his cell and reached into the dark aisle. "SHUT THE HELL UP, SID!"

Silence fell as heavy as the cold air. Faint rustling told Danny that none of the boys had gone inside the needle, yet. They were listening. A drop of water fell from one of the sprinklers.

Sid laughed. "You think you're a man, now? You're Danny BOY, son. You better mind your manners."

"I quit, Sid. I ain't never stepping foot inside the game room again."

"I don't need you."

"You were nothing before I got here. You and the rest of these clowns were just running around in circles until I saved your asses again and again because you're an idiot. It's over, now. All you dumbasses, you're on your own. I'm done."

The silence grew heavy, again. It was undercut by growling.

"I hope you learned how to control the pain response, Danny Boy," he said. "Because when you get inside the needle, I'm going to pull you apart like a bug, son. I'm going to pour acid in your eyeballs and piss in the holes." Sid laughed, but no one joined him. It was as dark as the room around them. "You think it's torture in here, wait until I get a hold of you in Foreverland."

Danny was grateful for the cloak of darkness, but it couldn't hide the shivers in his voice. "I'm not going inside the needle."

"Of course not." And Sid laughed again. It carried down to the floor and faded off. Soon, the entire room no longer moved except for the heavy mouth-breathing. They were all inside the needle.

It was just Danny and Reed.

"Danny Boy?" Zin's voice was scratchy, just above a whisper. "I'm coming back."

Danny leaned his head against the bars.

The big fan clicked.

And the breeze came down.

"What are you doing?" Reed had turned around. Danny couldn't make out his expression in the dark but he could see him latched onto the bars facing him. "This is my fight, not yours."

"I'm not letting you do this alone."

"It doesn't prove anything."

"Then follow your own advice!" Danny shouted. "You're not doing anything by staying here."

Reed remained at the side of his cell. He dropped his hands and went back to the center. Danny could hear his breath fall back into rhythm. He was not going to waste words.

Danny began pacing again. The cold crept into his ankles. The fan was on but not the sprinklers. With the rest of the camp wearing clothes, maybe they didn't want to keep them soaked. Still, it was plenty uncomfortable, especially since Sid promised something much worse on the inside. Danny wasn't sure he could control the pain response. He hadn't even tried.

Zin will protect me.

But would he even remember Danny? Parker didn't seem to know anything near the end. Perhaps his memory completely evaporated.

An hour elapsed.

Danny was cold but without the mist it was easier to stay in rhythm. If it remained this way, he could tolerate the suffering like Reed. Maybe the hole would even heal. Maybe the others would see the wisdom in fighting the system and they could form a revolt. If everyone refused the needle, they could make a difference.

That's when the door opened.

He knew it wasn't Mr. Jones, unless he hurt his knee in the last hour. An old man appeared in the darkened aisle dragging a bum leg. Mr. Smith passed Danny's cell. He was carrying tubes attached by a cord that dangled and swayed between his hands.

"Reed." The old man stopped at his cell. "I need to see your hands, son."

Reed took a deep breath and turned.

"What're you doing?" Danny said. He was ignored.

Mr. Smith held up the tubes. "Put your hands through the bars."

"Don't do it, Reed," Danny said. "They can't make you."

But Reed voluntarily went to the front of his cell and offered his hands. Mr. Smith slipped the tubes over his thumbs and adjusted clips on the sides. He stepped back and watched the cell begin to collapse.

"The pressure will increase over time, Reed. Please don't be stubborn. You're not accomplishing anything by the needless suffering."

The cell continued to shrink until it sandwiched Reed, pressing deeply into his chest and back. Mr. Smith stared at Reed. They were unflinching in their hatred. Until the pressure clamped down on his knuckles and pinched the webbing between his thumb and finger, pressing on a nerve that buckled his knees. He would've fallen had the bars not held him tightly.

The lucid gear dropped just inches from the top of his head.

"Stop this," Danny said. "This isn't fair, he doesn't want the needle. You can't do this. YOU CAN'T DO THIS!"

But they could. They did.

Mr. Smith began to take his leave.

"Come back here, you old bastard!" Danny reached through the bars, losing sight of the limping man. "YOU HEARTLESS BASTARD!"

Light cut through the Haystack as the door at the end of the aisle opened. Danny turned away as it hit him in the face, but for a moment he saw Reed's quivering hands and the shackles squeezing his thumbs. He didn't see the expression of agony. But he heard it.

Danny paced back and forth. Reed's pained breathing was worse than anything inside the Haystack. He'd rather they come put the thumb shackles on him.

There was nothing he could do.

He had to find the girl.

Danny pulled the lucid gear from the top. It whined as the cord unreeled to the floor. He dropped hard on the concrete and pulled it quickly over his head. The needle numbed his forehead, searching for the stent.

Before it jolted inside his brain, before he arched off the pavement, he muttered something to Reed. He doubted he would hear it.

"I'm sorry."

And then the needle took him.

27

Danny visualized a spot.

He imagined it was a glowing dot floating in the darkness where he was drifting. He put his breath into it. *One. Two. Three.*

It abolished thoughts.

It brought focus. Presence.

And when he felt his body forming near the sundial, he willed it to become numb. There would be no pain when Sid pulled out his intestines. He would melt like water and blow like wind. Nothing would hurt him.

The grass was beneath him. Sunlight and wind. And the screaming of engines.

Danny opened his eyes.

An asphalt racetrack circled the Yard and rocket-shaped cars roared around it, disappearing into the trees. The engines called from the jungle and soon wound around him before reentering the Yard behind him and making another lap.

He was alone. Sid was nowhere to be seen. Maybe he got bored. Or perhaps he was setting a trap. Didn't matter. Danny needed to get to the business of finding a Christmas present. And it would be much easier if he was invisible when he did it.

He put both hands on the sundial and felt the power vibrate through his arms. He pictured the focal dot and willed transparency to enter his body. What was his body other than data, really? Danny knew how to handle data. It helped to think of it that way, that he was computer code that needed to be manipulated. He breathed in and out, in and out.

Opened his eyes.

He was still there, but he could see the sundial through his hands.

"Translucency. Okay, close enough."

He wasn't invisible, but he'd faded enough that no one would notice unless they were looking right at him. He crotched down and – as the rocket cars came around – leaped into the sky.

Danny hovered just inside a cloud.

The gray haze on the horizon seemed closer than it did the last time. No one would see him, especially being half-faded. As long as no one flew into him, he could stay there all day. Since it seemed everyone was part of the race, he took his time.

The track serpentined around the entire island – through the trees and over the cliffs. The rocket cars even made a loop into the water. Occasionally, one would fire a weapon and there would be an explosion and parts flying.

The only other oddity about the island was tiny lights twinkling on top of random trees. He floated around the cloud and willed his vision to zoom on one of the trees. It appeared to be a star set on top, along with smaller lights strung from the branches.

Christmas trees. They're all Christmas trees.

It would've been an easy clue to follow, but there was easily a hundred of them scattered over the island. Even one that appeared to be floating out at sea. He cloud-hopped around the sky, zooming in on several trees but couldn't make out any substantial differences.

"I'm going to have to go down," he muttered to no one. Then said like he was the one answering, "Yep, going to have to go down."

The sun was already falling toward the horizon. Time in Foreverland went faster than it did in the flesh. He had wasted half of Foreverland's day in the Haystack. Maybe he already blew it.

He dropped from the sky and hit the ground like a stone. He was able to quell the pain from the impact. He was getting the hang of it. He dusted off the dirt and stared at the twenty foot tall Christmas tree that shaded a dozen red-wrapped gifts. Nothing else was around. There was no time to waste.

Danny began ripping open presents.

He had been to nearly fifty trees. Each one had a pile of gifts that he tore open to find more sand. By the time he got to the tree in front of the Mansion, the sun had dropped below the trees and the sky had turned orange and was quickly dimming. He wasn't going to get to all the trees, but he couldn't sit around and think about it.

This tree was near the entrance. A golf cart had been abandoned exactly where Danny and Zin had left one a week earlier. Seemed odd, but Danny was focused on the tree and the dozen gifts beneath it. He tore through them, sifting sand from each one, finding nothing new. He crouched down to bounce back into the sky to find the next one when lights inside the Mansion caught his eye.

One of the double doors was open. An enormous tree glittered inside the dark entrance.

Danny climbed the steps. The doors had been vandalized with spray-painted graffiti and skateboard stickers. The hinges creaked as he pushed the door open. The tree stood beyond the foyer against the far back window with a view to the ocean where lights twinkled. More trees.

He sighed. He'd never get to all of them. She was killing him. And yet he couldn't forget what Reed must be going through. He opened the dozen presents to find more sand. Danny threw the last one across the room. He grabbed the tree and launched it through the window. Shards of glass exploded.

His curses echoed down the empty halls.

But he was wasting time. Every second that was wasted was a second that Reed endured needless suffering.

He went back to the front doors. There was a narrow closet door on both sides of the foyer, both closed. But the one on the right had a sticker. Danny stopped.

It was a Spitfire sticker; the flaming head smiling at him.

One sticker. The rest of the room was in order, just the one sticker.

Merry Christmas.

Sand.

Christmas on the beach.

Tell me your favorite Christmas.

Reed asked Danny on the beach and Danny remembered the thing he wanted most in the world: the half-pipe covered in stickers. But no one would have known that, he didn't tell anyone about it. He wasn't even sure it was his memory. But there it was, a Spitfire sticker in an otherwise pristine Mansion without a half-pipe in sight.

Danny put his hand on the door knob. He turned it slowly and cracked the door open. An odd grainy light spilled out. It crept out in misty tendrils. Danny tried to slam it closed but the foggy light wrapped around him. Liquefied him.

And sucked him inside.

28

The mist had texture.

Grainy particles, scratching.

Momma?

A boy. He sounded sad, crying for—

First! I'm first!

On the right. Someone excited, someone—

You go first!

Where am I?

How long until we eat? I'm hungry.

The voices bunched together, above and below. They were everywhere, but nothing came out of the gray mist. The bodiless words whizzing by like passing trains.

The mist thickened.

The grains pelted his face like sand. He looked at his hands, saw his feet and realized he was standing on something solid. The wind began pulling away, revealing a white floor.

A spot of color developed ahead of him. It was soft and faded, like a beacon appearing in a blizzard. It was pink.

Then red.

Bright red.

The mist swirled out like an ever-widening hurricane. And then it was gone. He was in a round room, walls white. And she was sitting in the center, hands on her lap. The bright red hair cut below the shoulders.

"I'm sorry for the inconvenience," she said, softly. "But you couldn't know where you were going. He would've known, he would've followed… he was watching."

"Who?"

"Whoever runs… Foreverland."

"The Director?"

She shrugged.

Her eyes were large, the pupils engorged and the irises brilliant green. She was almost cartoonish, the colors saturated.

The room was barren, except for the chair she was sitting on, legs crossed, hands on lap. She stood up, her bare feet touched the floor silently; toenails the same color as her hair.

Olly-olly-oxen-free! The voices soared through the wall.

"Where are we?" Danny asked.

"The boys call this the Nowhere," she said. "It's outside… the eyes of Foreverland. Outside the reach of he who… is Foreverland."

"Those are memories?"

"In a way…" Her cheeks suddenly matched the color of her hair and toenails. "I know you have questions and I'll answer them the best I can, but the truth is… I don't know much and we don't have much time…" She wrapped her arms around her chest like she was hugging herself. "I'm sorry. It's just… he hurts so much… and you're our only chance… and I never…"

She trailed off. She had difficulty finding words, like she had to search for them.

"You mean Reed?" Danny asked.

She nodded, hugging herself again.

"Who are you?" Danny shook his head. *That sounded rude.* "I'm sorry, I just don't know much about Reed. Or you."

She thought, staring blankly. "I don't really know, Danny Boy. I just woke up here..."

Danny remembered the confusion of waking up on the paper-covered table and Mr. Jones staring at him with his white lab coat. He didn't know anything before that moment. She had the same experience, only she woke up in Foreverland.

Is she real? Definitely rude. *But is she a memory? Reed's memory? But she's here, alive. She had to be something other than a memory, right?*

"If you're in here, how do you know about Reed?" Danny asked.

"I see the boys' thoughts. I see what they bring in from the island… I know the suffering they go through… before the needle."

That's how she knew about the half-pipe at Christmas. She saw it in my thoughts.

"Then you know Reed is—"

She began shaking her head and rocking in her self-hug.

Damn.

She was still muttering about Reed. Danny stopped her. "How can I help?"

Her oversized eyes were glassy. Her brow furrowed when she pointed at the chair.

"Sit."

Danny went to the chair. When he sat down, a desk appeared from the floor and circled all the way around him. Several keyboards appeared.

"You don't really need the keyboards or the monitors… but you're familiar with that medium… so that's what you'll start with."

She glared at him.

"You need to understand… I'm as much a prisoner in here as you are out there."

"But Foreverland is a computer program."

"I don't know what this is, Danny Boy. You need to help us find out… what it is."

"How?"

She lifted her arms and the walls flickered like the entire room was a monitor. The walls were blue with white puffy clouds, like the wallpaper of a computer desktop. Danny brushed his fingers over the keyboard and felt something for the first time since arriving.

A familiar thrill.

A bead of sweat trickled down his cheek. Strange, this was an illusion but his body believed it.

It took several minutes to get familiar with the 360-degree monitor and multiple keyboards, but the keystrokes were the same as any computer. He accessed the mainframe and was soon sneaking around the security firewalls. The system was like one he'd never encountered. The code seemed to evolve like a living organism. Maybe it was a program that believed it was alive, just like he was sweating.

He synchronized several programs and let them run like digital wrecking balls smashing holes in databases and security code. He spun on his chair to unravel the next layer of the firewall. The security system operated like a virtual vault that continued to change the combination. Danny learned its tendencies and began to solve the complex code. His fingers blurred across the keyboards but it wasn't fast enough.

I'm inside my head. I don't need the keyboards.

He began to call out commands instead of typing and they were executed just as if he'd pecked them on the keyboard. He swiveled around to watch geometric shapes of computer code connect, shift and reconnect like organic chemistry. He stopped seeing the numbers and letters and began to see the computer language in three-dimensional objects that began to float off the walls. He shouted at them, made them change direction, change form, merge or divide. He was looking for the arrangement that would open the door to the system that was driving Foreverland.

Still, he was behind the evolving firewall that was always half a step ahead.

In the mind.

He focused inwardly, forming his next command into a sharpened thought instead of a spoken word. Then he created another one. And another. The shapes began to move again. Silently, Danny looked around the room and sent the thought-commands out. The room was in continuous movement, washed in morphing shapes and colors. Danny stopped looking at what they were doing so that he wasn't limited by his eyes. He connected with his mind; he began to construct the code, predicting outcomes, glancing only to verify what they were becoming. He was in the center of another universe that operated on numbers and formulas and colors, looking for the right combination—

The room went black. Something clicked.

A spot of light hung over his head.

"What is it?" the girl said.

He'd forgotten she was there. "The firewall cracked."

"What's that mean?"

More clicking, like blocks were stacking and pieces latching and uncoupling. The spot of light shrunk to a pinpoint and began to dim. The clicking ended. Something fell into place like a key sliding into a lock. And turning.

The point exploded in blinding light.

And then they were flying above planet Earth.

"We're through," Danny said.

"Where?"

Danny stood up. "It's the outside world."

It exists.

There was an outside world. The desks and keyboard had disappeared. Danny walked on clouds, looking at the blue ocean thousands of feet below.

"We're seeing the world through satellites," he said.

"Where's the island?"

Danny put together a few thought-commands, requesting the location of the portal he'd just hacked. The view spun like the planet rotated below. They were in the middle of the South Atlantic Ocean, halfway between South America and Africa.

Nothing but water.

[Enhance,] he thought.

The view zoomed toward the water and two tiny islands came into view. The southern one was very small and narrow. There appeared to be an airstrip the length of it. The larger island to the north was shaped like South Carolina.

"That's it," Danny muttered. "That's where we are."

"It's in the middle of nowhere."

"Exactly."

He began pacing around, observing the two islands. The details were sharper than what he'd seen in his flying sessions in Foreverland. There was the Yard in the center of the larger island

and the horseshoe-shaped dormitory and the top of the Haystack nestled in the trees.

That's where I am. Right now.

He scrolled the view to the south end, over the Mansion. He enhanced the view until he was walking right over the roof. The area behind the Mansion was a resort with swimming pools and lounging areas. There was a large pier attached to the shore with a yacht.

He looked at the smaller island, now off in the distance about five miles.

"They must fly into that island." Danny took a few steps and the view scrolled beneath him until the airstrip was just below their feet. There was a hangar at one end and an empty pier on shore. "And then bring people over on the yacht."

The girl stood next to him. "What do you think they're doing?"

The view returned to the Mansion. Someone was swimming. One of the Investors was taking long, smooth strokes to the end of the pool before turning to backstroke in the other direction.

"Looks like they're on vacation," he said.

After scrolling over the rest of the Mansion yard and finding nothing unusual, he began to look at the rest of the island. The view – directly overhead – looked like a privately owned tropical island. If someone flew over it, there would be nothing out of the ordinary.

"There's not much time." The girl had been walking along Danny's side, looking where he was looking but watching for his reaction. "Is there anything here that helps?"

He grunted. "Not really."

Danny continued walking, looking for anything that would be of interest. The Yard had a few people in it. The Chimney was highest in the sky, the stovepipe quiet. The waves were crashing violently on the north shore. The beach was empty, of course, because Reed was still in the Haystack with those vicious looking things on his hands.

Danny turned.

The girl was standing in the middle of the room, her hands clutched in front of her. She saw his thought and her eyes were big but not glassy this time.

"How do you know Reed?" he asked.

"It's hard to know… my memories…"

"They're mixed up?"

She shrugged.

"But you're stuck in here?" Danny asked. "You can't get out of Foreverland?"

"I don't know… I just remember suddenly being here… something was after me when I woke up…"

Danny waited, but she seemed more confused than before. "So you escaped into the Nowhere?"

Quick nod, again. "No one can come out here. Not even him."

The Director.

"You know that Reed dreams about you. He thinks you're telling him not to come, that he has to—"

"I know… I just… want him to be okay."

She turned away so Danny couldn't see her face. Her shoulders tensed. He thought she might be weeping, but when she turned back around, Danny thought it was anger fading from her expression.

Her fists were clenched. "What are we going to do… to make all this end?"

An old man was getting out of the pool. He wrapped a towel over his shoulders and waved to someone back at the Mansion. A young man ran down the wide, curving steps off the balcony. *Parker.*

"I'll figure something out before the next round," Danny said. "Can you bring me back here?"

"Yes, but it'll have to be like the last time… just look for a fight and I'll get you back."

Danny looked across the island at the Haystack where Sid's body was twenty feet away from his. "That shouldn't be too hard."

The random voices began penetrating the walls and the grainy mist twisted across the floor, obscuring the view below.

"There isn't much… time. You need to figure something out… fast."

"I know," he said. "I know."

The light began to fade.

"Goodbye, Danny Boy."

The fog swirled around him. Her red hair faded to pink. "Wait! What's your name?"

The voices were louder, one after another. The gray fog thickened, wrapping him in a cocoon of silky darkness. The voices got farther away. Danny slid back to the space between Foreverland and the Haystack.

Just before he felt his flesh and the hard concrete on his back, he heard one last word from far away.

Lucinda.

ROUND
4

Real Estate Tycoon Missing at Sea

LAS VEGAS, Nevada. – Local real estate and business billionaire, Franklin Constantino, 82, was reported missing after taking his yacht for a solo excursion out of San Francisco into the Pacific Ocean.

Constantino had been diagnosed with lung cancer two months before his disappearance. According to one of his staff, he rarely boarded his 70' yacht without a captain and crew, but insisted on a lone journey for some "soul searching".

The Coast Guard received distress calls about fifty miles off the coast but were unable to locate the ship. Evidence suggests the ship may have sunk but nothing has been confirmed.

29

The top floor of the Chimney hummed as the electric motors began winding up the shades. Evening light – diffused by the window's tint – filled the room.

The Director was stretched out on a comfortable recliner. His lips began twitching before his eyes fluttered open. He stared vacantly at the black ceiling for a few moments before reaching up. He slid the needle out of the stent. He quivered. The sensation of the lubricated needle was a queer one that tickled the inside of his brain.

He rubbed salve over the hole and sighed while the Foreverland world faded. It would take a few minutes before he felt all the way back in his body. He drummed his fingers on the cushiony armrests while the chair's internal rolling pins massaged his back, legs and buttocks. Circulation was important after lying still for so long. When the tingling faded, he put his feet on the ground and slowly stood.

He hadn't eaten since he'd gone "inside the needle" (another term the boys invented) but he wasn't thinking of food. He was thinking of what he just saw.

He found her.

The Director mixed a drink.

He stooped over a telescope aimed across the empty Yard. The boys would exit the Haystack in a half hour or so. It always took them a bit longer to return to the flesh when a round had ended. After all, the Director had been doing it for years, one of the few people to master the ability to go inside the needle. They were still rookies.

Only Danny Boy's third round and he'd already managed to get control of his body. Maybe she was helping him, but he somehow doubted that was it. The kid was brilliant. The Director secretly wished he could somehow cryogenically freeze him for about twenty years; he could save the kid for his own personal use. But he didn't have that technology. Not yet.

The drink warmed him.

She was clever, of course. He continued to underestimate her. She left that Christmas present as a clue and then sent the kid on a wild chase throughout the island. The Director already had a lot of responsibility keeping Foreverland stable, so keeping track of Danny Boy racing around was difficult. Somehow, she managed to construct a trapdoor in the Mansion and the kid found it without knowing it. By the time the Director realized what had happened, she'd collapsed the tunnel that led to the outer perimeter of the Nowhere. Out of his reach.

She's learning, that's what's happening.

And learning was a problem.

Before she infected Foreverland, it was an expanding universe that started at the sundial and extended hundreds of miles past the shoreline. The Director envisioned it encompassing the planet, the solar system, and eventually the universe. The growth was exponential and the system operated flawlessly. He had great plans for humanity's next evolutionary step. Foreverland wasn't just an imaginary place where the kids went to play.

Everything was right on schedule. Until they inoculated Reed.

He appeared to be a healthy, normal subject. As he lay in a medically induced coma – after his body healed from the car accident – they strapped him with the initial needle-piercing for false memory infusion, but when they drew his memories out, this girl had slipped out of his subconscious. Memories always ended up floating around the Nowhere like bits of chicken in a bowl of soup.

But the girl was conscious!

Initially, she was merely a nuisance, a cockroach that would eventually run into the bottom of the Director's heel. But she found cover in the Nowhere where the Director was blind. And ever since then, Foreverland had been collapsing.

The misty Nowhere was less than five miles off the shore, shrinking every day. He predicted that it would take a month to collapse all the way back to the sundial. If there was no

Foreverland, the program would come to a screeching halt. The Investors would not be pleased. Not with the sums of money they were putting up.

But Danny Boy found her and that wasn't necessarily a bad thing.

It was the first time she'd stuck her neck out of the Nowhere. The Director missed it, this time. He wouldn't the next. She wanted Danny Boy and that meant she would do it again. If he caught her – no, not if… *when* he caught her, he would put a stop to the collapse. And then he could continue with the original plan: get Reed inside. He knew that once Reed was inside Foreverland, he would absorb her like a memory. Because that's what she was. She would go back inside his mind and leave Foreverland.

And Foreverland would grow, once again.

Why Reed had resisted all this time he still couldn't understand. Somehow, the kid seemed to know he was the antidote to the Director's problem. That's why he needed Danny Boy. He needed him to tell Reed about what she was doing, what she looked like, how much she needed him. Danny Boy would apply the pressure the Director needed, he would help bring him to Foreverland.

He swallowed the drink and mixed another.

Someone was crossing the Yard. Reed was the first one out, clutching his hands to his stomach. There were Soldiers of Fortune that didn't have balls half the size as his. The Director would have to get medieval, very soon. Reed would discover that every human had a breaking point.

"Director?" the intercom called.

"Yes?"

"At your convenience, could you come down to the network floor? I think you'll find this interesting."

He finished the drink. He was tired and already a little buzzed. But there was data to observe from Foreverland.

30

Lucinda watched Foreverland recede.

She knew everything about the Nowhere. She knew all the thoughts of the boys that had been there. Knew all the… suffering, too. But it was Danny Boy that cracked the system open. He showed her how to work with the code, how to see into the network that helped operate… Foreverland.

The Nowhere fog circled the sundial as the boys went back to their bodies. And Foreverland went to sleep. Until the next round.

31

Danny woke on the floor, shivering. His clothes were still piled up where he left them. The door of his cell was open. A sharp pain gouged his ribs as he sat up. He couldn't remember falling before taking the needle. He got dressed and wiped something off his cheek, like snails raced across his face.

The Haystack was empty, except for Zin.

He was awake and sitting with his arms propped on his knees. His throat bobbed up and down like he was trying to swallow something that just wouldn't go down.

"Zin." Danny squatted in front of him. "You all right?"

A string of saliva dangled from his lip.

Danny pulled him onto his feet. At least he didn't have to dress him. He threw Zin's arm over his shoulders and guided him out of the Haystack and through the woods. Zin continued to swallow at nothing until they emerged into the Yard. When daylight hit their faces, Zin looked up. Focus returned.

"Thanks, Danny Boy."

They went straight to their rooms. Danny helped him crawl in bed and then went to his own. He was asleep as soon as his head hit the pillow.

There were no medical trays when Danny woke up. As far as he could tell, Mr. Jones hadn't been to his room. At least, he couldn't smell him.

He did come to his room a couple days later. He was apologetic, at first. He stood in the middle of the room with his hands behind his back like he was addressing the press.

"I'm sorry I lost control in the Haystack, Danny Boy. I understand you're under a lot of stress and it can be confusing about what to do. It's easy to become irrational, I know. We're all under a lot of stress."

Danny wondered what kind of stress Mr. Jones could be enduring. Did he have to swim three laps in the luxury pool instead of two?

"But what Reed is doing is borderline insanity. No, it *is* insanity." That was about the time the apology ended and the finger-waving began. "The fact that he's been allowed to remain in the program this long is unconscionable, Danny Boy."

And that was another first. *Program. He called this a program.*

"He's a terrible example," Mr. Jones said, pointing at Danny. "Refusing the lucid gear is an insult and a travesty and sabotages everything we strive to…" His tone softened. "Everything we strive to give you boys. It makes no sense, and I don't want to see you contaminated by his actions. You understand, Danny Boy?"

"I'm sorry, too," Danny said with his most convincing doe-eyes. "I just lost it in there, Mr. Jones. It didn't take long to realize my mistake, trust me. It won't happen again."

Mr. Jones smiled. He sat on the bed, permeating the sheets with his Mr. Jones smell.

"You know, I can't forbid you from talking to him. I just want you to understand how damaged he is. I don't want that to happen to you. You're a good kid, Danny Boy. You know what they say about spoiled apples."

"You don't have to worry about me, Mr. Jones."

Danny stopped from adding, *Golly gee. I love this place.* Mr. Jones would've bought it even if he did. He scrubbed Danny's head.

"A good kid, you are."

The camp was at the table, again, soaking up the sun and tossing cards. Danny mostly stayed in his room for a couple days and only snuck down to the cafeteria when they weren't there. Sid didn't seem to be looking for him but Danny wasn't taking any chances. He just needed some peace to sort through his thoughts.

Lucinda.

She woke up in Foreverland, but what was she? Part of the program? Something real?

It didn't matter. They all had the same goal: get off the island. He just needed to come up with a solution. He'd established contact with the outside world and no one that ran the place seemed to notice. But that didn't mean he wasn't being watched. He'd slipped through the firewall and he was sure he could do it again, at least once. And if he only had one chance, it needed to work.

He couldn't send for help, it would just look like a hoax. *We're a bunch of kids held on a tropical island given everything we could ever want and we go into a barn and get a needle shot into our heads so we can experience an alternate reality. Please help.*

The island was a slick operation. Surely they'd have a plan for visitors. Danny needed something that would get the world's attention, something that would piss off some important people and make them come looking for them. The next round wasn't for another week and a half. He had time to think and no distractions. He had to go into the fourth round with something ready to go.

And look for a fight.

The card table was empty. Sid and his band of merry men had gone to lunch. Zin hadn't left his room. His Investor was bringing up food and closing the door quietly on his way out. Danny had been checking up on him, too. He was tired, but at least he was alive. Maybe when this was all over, he'd find the old Zin in the Mansion. Or maybe a new and improved Zin.

Danny opened his door. The hallway was empty and Zin's door was closed. He lightly tapped on it. He was going to try the door knob and peek inside the room when someone said, "Zin's looking for you."

It was James. He was a fourteen year old kid that never gave Danny any crap.

"Where is he?"

James opened the door to his room and said, "I saw him going out back, said something about a joyride."

Danny went to his room and threw on clothes and started for the stairs. *A joyride?* Maybe the old Zin was putting up a fight after all.

He never bothered opening Zin's door.

32

"Preposterous." Mr. Jones threw his arms up. "You'll have a real problem on your hands if he's hurt, I promise you, Director. Something happens to my Danny Boy…"

Mr. Smith stood next to him. They were looking out the tinted windows of the Chimney's top floor. Mr. Smith calmly kept his hands latched behind his back, while Mr. Jones folded and unfolded his arms making a small sound each time he did, like he was choking on words until he had to spit them out.

"There will be hell to pay. I've invested too much time and money to take such a risk, you should've consulted me." He looked over his shoulder. "This is absurd!"

The Director was throwing a floral red and white shirt over his head. "Mr. Jones," he said, his flip-flops slapping his feet, "I don't consult my clients. You pay me to do the thinking."

The Director stood next to Mr. Smith. They were looking at the back of the dormitory.

"Besides," he said, "you don't exist, so don't make idle threats."

Mr. Jones's face went red. "You're punishing him for what? For going in the Nowhere? I'm a fair man, Director, and this has nothing to do with fairness."

The Director looked at Mr. Jones. His beard did not conceal the smile. *Fair man? His delusion knows no bounds.*

The program thrived from the self-centeredness of these old men, the infection of false entitlements that comes from money and power. Their universe revolved around their petty concerns and anything that affected them. They couldn't see the bigger picture, they couldn't see opportunity when they looked in only one direction. *Stay open to life, gentlemen. Let it unfold and the universe will provide you with endless paths on your journey.*

Fact is, they got lucky.

The Director expected Danny to be risky, but he never would've guessed the kid would *hack through the security firewall and spread across the world!* He did it through a vast web of communications. He didn't attempt any communication because he was smart. Any other frightened kid would've shouted out to the world, *Help! Help!* The Director had answers for that, but that wasn't what Danny Boy did. He was patient, scoping out his potential. He would do something the next time, something the Director might not be able to stop.

But, more importantly, he showed the Director how the world's vast communication network had become a living body that just needed a soul to breathe. Danny Boy merged his identity with the network. He became the network.

Danny showed him just how short-sighted he had been all this time.

"We're making him stronger," the Director said. "He needs this to push through his psychological barriers."

"On what basis do you make these assessments?" Mr. Jones said. "Those barriers were put in place by us! He's not supposed to remember his past in the flesh, Director. Like every boy on this island, he only recovers them inside the needle, and now you want to remove the barriers that prevent him from remembering in the flesh? Director, I must question your motivations—"

"Question nothing, Mr. Jones," he snapped. "Every boy on this island is different, each needs the program tailored to his individual needs. May I remind you that you were the one that argued to recruit this young man against my better judgment, that he would bring problems that would be dealt with in an unorthodox manner. Do you recall that conversation?"

Mr. Jones folded his arms, once again. "You are introducing anarchy. I hardly see how that will benefit those involved."

"Sometimes death provides life, Mr. Jones. I believe that is something we can all agree upon."

They watched the scene unfold behind the dormitory.

"I've had enough. I'm putting a stop to this now."

The Director didn't stop him from going to the elevator. The event was over.

Mr. Smith was nonplussed. It didn't involve his boy. In fact, it was for the benefit of Danny Boy *and* Reed. Therefore, Mr. Smith watched with great interest.

"Danny Boy is Reed's salvation," is what the Director told him before Mr. Jones had arrived. "He's our best chance to draw him inside the needle."

And the needle was what Mr. Smith needed him to take. Otherwise, he would have wasted his time and money. Money, he had. Time was what he was trying to buy.

So the Director's argument was very compelling. The pressure they had put on Reed still had not succeeded. The Director and Mr. Smith agreed that Reed was likely to die before succumbing to it. His health was already on the decline and his time was very short. It wasn't going to benefit Mr. Smith if he destroyed him. He was willing to try anything.

The Director twisted the curly whiskers on his upper lip. The event behind the dormitory was taking an unforeseen turn, but Mr. Smith didn't flinch. He watched as it unfolded. This made the Director smile. *He trusts me.*

"There's hope yet, Mr. Smith. The two are bonding. Keep them close, let them continue to develop a relationship."

"What about Mr. Jones? He will not be pleased with this approach."

"I'll handle Mr. Jones. Danny Boy made contact with Reed's 'problem' inside the needle. We can't let that opportunity go to waste."

The Director didn't lie. There was a problem. The extent of that problem, however, was not fully explained to any of the Investors. Reed's problem was a threat to all of them. Mr. Jones, included. If Danny Boy was part of the solution, there would be no discussion about how to handle it.

The boys behind the dormitory fell to the ground as Mr. Jones and other Investors arrived on the scene. Mr. Smith took his leave to attend to Reed.

"He's worth saving," the Director said, as Mr. Smith boarded the elevator. "They're all worth saving."

Not a lie. But not exactly the truth.

33

Danny ran towards the only door that opened to the back of the dormitory. Zin must have come out of it to swipe a golf cart. His Investor was going to flip. And Mr. Jones was going to drop a nuke. *That's right. Danny is not a good boy.*

Maybe they could scout the other end of the Mansion but this time take the cart, drop a brick on the accelerator and send it over the edge. It was a horrible idea, but he'd run it by Zin, see what he thought. If he was game, Danny wasn't going to stand in his way. May as well have some fun destroying personal property.

He threw open the door—

CRAAACK!

Danny tumbled with lights in his head and the side of his face numb, the tang of iron on his tongue.

"Booooom!" Sid shouted. "Where I come from, that's called a boom-shot, son!"

Danny touched his fat lips, pulled back bloody fingers. He spit a dark red pool into the dirt.

The camp was throwing high-fives at Sid. One of the guys was down at the corner on the lookout for Investors. James nearly tripped over Danny on his way out of the back door.

"Did I miss it?"

"Hell, yeah, you missed it." Sid shook his hand like it was hot. "I broke up his damn face. You should've seen the look he gave me right before I landed the boom-shot." He high-fived James. "That's what we call it where I come from."

Danny got on his hands and knees and spit red. "You don't know where you come from." He spit out a chunk of skin. "None of you morons do."

It got quiet. Sid squatted down. "I don't care where I'm from, that's what we call it."

He kicked Danny onto his back and got another round of hand-slapping.

"I'm king of this island, Danny Boy," Sid called. "And you're the trash. You and Reed, a couple of crazy bastards getting naked. What's wrong with your brains, son? Did the needle drive too deep? Did it suck the noodle out of your skull?"

"Maybe I've seen the truth."

"Yeah, the truth of your mental illness. What is there not to love about this place, idiot? We got everything we could want, we don't pay for a thing, and we got the best games in the world. I mean, sue me for not wanting to stay here forever."

"We get smoked, Sid," Danny said, spitting. "You forget?"

"Yeah, well we all got to die. That's a fact, brain surgeon. May as well do it happy."

The clowns around him agreed. A pack of lemmings.

"The Director is a genius," he said. "You should be kissing the man's feet."

"Excuse me for wanting to know what they're doing to us," Danny said.

"Who gives a flying fart?"

Danny was on his hands and knees, again.

"And another thing." Sid was back down at face level. "You're getting your ass back in that game room to put us back in first place. I got a taste of that freebee and I like. We want another pass, you hear?"

"Forget it."

"You might want to think about it because there's more where this came from." Sid kicked dirt in his face. "You got to sleep sometime."

"So do you."

They laughed. Sid led the way toward the corner of the building where they'd sit their fat asses on the card table and yuck it up. Danny just needed to sit it out until they were gone. He was going to need stitches, but what would he tell Mr. Jones? The truth would probably help the most, but that seemed boring. Besides, Danny sensed the thrill beneath the throbbing in his face. And that's what made him stand up.

"You forgot something!" He took a shuffle-step to catch his balance then threw up his middle finger. "Take this to the game room with you."

Sid thought about it. It would be easier to let this one go, but everyone was watching and Danny hadn't learned his lesson. And that was the whole point. How could Sid really be the king if a little punk gave him the finger and got away with it? If he walked off, Danny wins no matter how many stitches it takes.

Danny sealed the deal when he threw his hands out to the side. *Still standing, bitch.*

Sid got a running start.

Danny bent at the knees, balled his fists. He was going to start swinging before Sid got too close. He had no plan after that. But it didn't matter.

Sid launched himself – feet first.

Danny went flying like a limp doll. Before his wits returned, Sid was on top. He tasted gritty blood, now. Sid planted his knees on Danny's arms, grinding them into the dirt and sat on his chest. Danny's legs flailed behind Sid. He grabbed a handful of Danny's hair and held his head still. A bubbly glob of spit hung on Sid's lower lip, then fell.

"How's that, munchkin?" Sid said.

The others gathered around. Their shadows loomed.

"That loogey matches the one I dropped on you in the Haystack. That was from me and you're welcome."

The snail slime when I woke up.

The pain radiating from his arms had extinguished the thrill and replaced it with rage. But he was too small to do anything, helpless beneath 180 pounds of Sid. He tried to spit on him but it only landed on his own face.

"Listen, you crazy dwarf. What I say goes. You'll game and shut your bloody mouth or I'll spit in your eye every day you wake up. You'll be begging to get smoked when I'm done with you. You think you can out-crazy me? Well, I got news for you, I'm the real deal. I'm a psychopath. I'll climb inside you and eat your damn gizzard."

Danny started laughing. *Gizzard. What an idiot.*

This caught Sid off-guard. Danny's cheek lit up with a loud smack. But it only made him laugh harder. He didn't care about pain. Sid would have to break his teeth out to get him to shut up. And that's what he was about to do, pulling his fist behind his ear—

Sid went rolling across the ground.

Elbows flying.

Danny was back on his hands and knees, catching his breath, listening to grunts and the slap of skin-on-skin. Sid was on feet, dragging someone with him.

Reed.

His shirt was pulled over his head, revealing his bony chest. Sid pushed him into the group and two of them pinned his arms behind him. Reed's face was gaunt. Yellow-darkness hung beneath his eyes. He was out of breath.

"A hero, huh?" Sid paced closer. "Hold him still, let me show you what we do to heroes."

He pulled his fist behind his ear, again, lined up a shot that would break Reed's entire face—

They all dropped on the ground.

Sid, Reed, and all the rest. They fell like dead bodies.

"It's all right, Danny Boy." Mr. Jones was on one knee. "We got things under control."

Golf carts pulled up and old men unloaded, each one of them going to their camper. They rolled them over, cradled their heads. Their eyes were rolled back and the Investors talked to them. Slowly, they came out of the tracker-zapping stupor and their Investors – each with his own look of disapproval – guided them away.

"Come along." Mr. Jones helped Danny up. "Let's get you to the doctor to have a look. Don't worry about those boys, it's all right now."

Each of them was up and being cared for, tended to. All of them, except one.

Reed was alone and still unconscious.

34

It was Danny's second time inside the Chimney.

Mr. Jones took him to the big, silver elevator shaft in the center of the first floor. He held Mr. Jones's handkerchief to his mouth. It was white with major splotches of blood. They went to the second floor. Danny didn't see a stairwell. Either Mr. Jones was too tired to walk or this was ultra-security. The only way up was in the elevator.

Five floors in the Chimney. The third one was where I woke up. The second one is the doctor's office. The fifth one is the Director's penthouse. What's on the fourth?

The second floor was silent. Four hallways radiated from the center like spokes. They went down one of them and stopped outside an office door with a row of chairs against the wall.

"Would you have a seat, Danny Boy?" Mr. Jones asked. "I'd like to speak with the doctor."

Danny grunted through the handkerchief. Mr. Jones helped him into one of the chairs and went inside the office. Danny couldn't hear them talking. He flicked his tongue over his bottom lip, felt the hole carved out of it when Sid's fist crushed his face against his teeth. Mr. Jones assured him that would never happen again. If Sid got within fifty feet, an alarm would sound on his tracker. If he got closer than twenty, he'd get knocked out.

Danny wouldn't mind testing the system. Maybe sneak up on him while he was in the bathroom, watch him crumple up on the toilet. He'd be in trouble – major, big time – but it would be so worth it. So, so worth it.

He laid his head against the wall and closed his eyes. He was sinking in the chair, exhaustion weighing him down. He was breathing heavily when the elevator doors broke open. Two sets of footsteps came down the hallway. One was dragging a foot.

"Hello, Danny Boy," Mr. Smith said. "How's your mouth feeling?"

Danny shrugged. He could answer, but the bloody rag was a good excuse not to speak without being rude.

"Listen, son. You'll be all right. We've got a real sharp doctor on the island that will have you back to normal in a snap." Mr. Smith snapped his fingers to illustrate his point. "No one hurts for long around here."

Mr. Smith turned to Reed, mumbled something about sitting. "Let me go inside and talk with Mr. Jones and the doctor, all right?"

He winked at Danny, smiled, and went inside.

Reed hunched over, hiding his hands in his lap. The silence was enormous.

"You didn't have to do that back there."

Reed didn't respond. Danny took that as a sign to shut up. He said thanks. Move on. Danny pushed his tongue into the hole in his lip. The bleeding had stopped but he kept the handkerchief to his mouth.

"He's a psychopath, you know that," Reed mumbled.

"Yeah, he told me."

Reed sat back, holding his hands beneath his shirt. "Next time you'll get more than a bloody lip."

"There won't be a next time. Sid gets a warning if he's within fifty feet of me. Twenty feet and the tracker knocks his ass out. I might sneak up on him just to watch him twitch."

"You're playing with fire."

"We all are, Reed. May as well have some fun."

Zin would've liked that line; he'd tell him when he woke up.

"Why are you here?" Danny asked.

Reed hesitated. He unveiled his hands. The thumbs were purple and doubled in size. They stuck out like useless pegs. "To put Humpty Dumpty back together."

"So they can push you back off?"

"That seems to be the pattern."

Reed put his hands beneath his shirt, again. His breathing was a little shaky. It hurt just moving them. Danny couldn't imagine what it took to tackle Sid.

"Why don't you go inside the needle?" Danny asked.

Reed chuckled, smiled at the floor.

"What's so funny?" Danny asked. "It doesn't make sense, going through all this suffering when you know we're going to end up in Foreverland anyway. Come on, Reed, give yourself a break. You've suffered enough, you've proved your point. You can take a beating."

Reed was quiet. He drew a long breath and let it out, thoughtfully. Then threw his head back with laughter. It echoed up and down the hallway.

Danny watched him unravel. "You're losing it, Reed."

"What's so funny?" Reed said, wiping his eyes. "This is exactly what they want."

"Who?"

"Them." Reed gestured with a nod at the doctor's office. "They want us to be friends so that you'll talk me into taking the needle. And you're biting, Danny Boy. You're biting hard on the bait, son."

"I'm not biting on anything, I'm just making sense."

"You don't know what you're making."

"I saw her, Reed." The fits of laughter trailed off, quickly. "Want to know what she said?"

Reed hunched over, quietly.

"She sees you, Reed. She sees you in everyone's thoughts when they go inside the needle. She knows you're staying in the Haystack and suffering and refusing to come for her. She's alone and something is after her. You got to tell me why you're not going inside to help her."

Reed bowed his head lower like he barely had the strength to hold Danny's words.

"She's in your dreams," Danny added, "but that's a dream, man! Lucinda's alive, I'm telling you."

Reed jerked. He turned away. No sound came out of him. Just quiet convulsions.

"It's a trick, Danny Boy. The Director's got you fooled."

"It was no trick. She was—"

"YOU THINK I LIKE THIS?"

Reed shoved his hands in Danny's face. They weren't just swollen, they were misshapen and three different colors of purple, parts of them black. Thin red lines streaked down his wrists.

"You don't think I want to see her? That I just want to dream about her, that I don't want to touch her, smell her? That I don't want to be with her, Danny Boy, to know she's okay? To know she's alive? Is that what you think?"

Danny pulled his head back.

"It's hopeless, Danny Boy." Reed walked away. "It's all hopeless."

Lucinda.

Her name opened a memory.

Reed suddenly remembered, with fine clarity, a time he was driving a truck – a twenty year old pickup – with torn seat covers. He reached for the stick shift between her knees.

"We're doing it, Reed!" Lucinda said. "We're really doing it!"

The landscape rolled past them with long legs of corn and bushy fields of soybeans, dotted with silos and lonesome houses. The wind blew her red hair around. Lucinda grabbed Reed's face and planted a kiss. Her lips wet, warm and full.

Bip. It ended. Memory, over and out.

But it wasn't a dream, it was a memory. He remembered her.

He remembered that he loved her.

She's real.

Danny stepped next to him. They were at the end of the hall, standing at one of the glass walls that overlooked the dormitory and the Yard. And, beyond that, the Haystack.

"The world, it's out there, Reed." Danny told him about hacking the firewall, locating the island through the satellite system. "There's hope."

"Can you do it again?" Reed asked, staring out.

"I don't know, it was some wild code. It was evolving like an organism, never seen anything like it."

"You can't just send for help. They'll have that figured out."

"I know."

"It has to be something the whole world will see, Danny Boy. You got to give them a reason to search for us."

Reed hung his hands inside his shirt like a hammock. He couldn't fold his arms and it hurt too much to let them hang at his sides. Besides, hiding them kept Danny from staring. Reed just wanted to get to the beach where he could be in the sun alone with the memories. He wanted to drive down that country road, again. He wanted to kiss her.

Lucinda. You're in there and I'm out here. The Haystack is nothing compared to that.

"Danny Boy?" Mr. Jones called from the doctor's office. "Son, the doctor would like to see you now."

Danny waited a bit, turned and nodded at the old man. He started to say something to Reed then went on his way. Mr. Jones closed the door behind them. He'd get his lip fixed and be ready for the next round. Reed only hoped he could do it again. Yes, he hoped.

Because he wouldn't be able to resist much longer.

35

The cafeteria was full. But the table Danny was sitting at was empty.

He was in the corner, far away from the windows. The compartments on his lunch tray were filled with pudding, Jell-O and noodles. No chewing required. The doctor patched the gaping hole with a gel adhesive, but it didn't relieve the swelling. Pressure on his teeth hurt. His smile was lop-sided, but there wasn't much to smile about.

He slurped a spoonful of pudding and looked at the lined sheet of paper in front of him. He chose the corner of the room because it was the farthest spot from the rest of his camp eating at their regular table. They were in last place in the game room. Without Danny, they'd have to suffer every round they went inside the Haystack until they all got smoked. That gave him a little satisfaction. A few guys asked him to come back.

You've got to be kidding.

Danny glanced up and Sid flipped him the middle finger.

He also wanted privacy and the lighting was weak in the corner. He wrapped his arm around the paper to cast a shadow over his notes. It was stupid to write these things down, but he had to organize his thoughts. He was just writing bullet points but they were still clues:

- *Mutual Fund*
- *FBI*
- *Mt. Rushmore*

These were the three ideas he'd come up with to get the world's attention. The first one, mutual fund. Get control of the largest mutual fund in the world and sell all the assets. The stock market suffers a flash crash and people lose money.

Money is power and it will find you. If they found the rogue trader holed up in his parents' basement, they would find an island in the South Atlantic.

The second idea—

"Danny Boy." James flung a folded sheet of paper into his pudding. "Message."

Danny turned his notes over. James looked back. They were watching. And laughing. Danny wiped the chocolate smudge off and spread the note open.

Turdbrain. You die in the needle.

Sid was standing on the table with both birds flying. James nodded and smiled.

"Hey, you're a pal," Danny said. "Hang on a sec."

James waited for him to finish writing, watched him fold it back up.

"Don't peek now," Danny said. "I want it to be a surprise."

James opened it anyway. He carried it back to Sid still holding up middle fingers and still getting laughs. James handed it to him and Sid opened it. He sat down.

I'm running at you in five minutes.

Sid was sixty feet away. If Danny rushed him, he'd be less than twenty and pissing his pants. He could curse him all day long, but all it took was minus twenty feet and he'd be catatonic.

Second idea: destroy the FBI's database. Danny was drawing on previous memories. Crime-fighting agencies, like the FBI, were touchy when it came to their data. If he got inside their network, he could detonate everything digital. That was like kicking a hornet's nest. They wouldn't come to the Chimney asking questions, they'd kick the door down.

The third idea: blow something up. Destroying a national monument was surely going to set off a worldwide manhunt. If he dropped a building with a couple thousand people in it, they were as good as rescued, but Danny wasn't a killer. And there was the problem of getting explosives to detonate. It could be done; he could redirect a couple of military bases but that would get complicated.

It was down to the first two ideas. He was only going to get one chance. It had to work. But he wouldn't know until he was back inside the needle and tested the system. First, he had to find Lucinda.

Pick a fight.

Danny took his tray to the return window. Sid was in a conversation with someone across the table, but kept an eye on Danny as he filled a to-go box with food. Danny closed the lid and held up his hand for Sid to see, all four fingers and thumb.

He had Sid's full attention as he dropped one finger at a time. When he folded the last one into a fist, he started walking right at their table.

Sid was out the exit before twenty feet.

36

Danny tapped on the door. He didn't expect an answer. He turned the knob, poked his head inside, slowly. There was a lump on the bed. The curtains were closed. Danny didn't bother closing the door quietly. Zin had been asleep for two days.

"Zin, my man." Danny pulled one of the curtains open. "Let the sunshine in, brother."

The light fell on his face with no effect. His head was half-buried in the pillow, mouth open. His complexion was lighter, a grayishness mixed with mocha. But still dark beneath his eyes.

"Hey, man, wake up." Danny shook him. "You got to eat or you'll shrivel up like a leaf."

Zin moaned, smacking white slime between his lips. Danny sat him up. Zin's head lolled around. "What time is it?"

"Daytime," Danny said. "You need to join the living while you're still alive. I brought you some food, here." He doled out an apple, a turkey sandwich with spinach and tomato, a bag of chips and a container of pudding. "Get some of this in you before you fall asleep again."

Zin was beginning to collapse.

"Hey, come on." He shook his shoulders. "Throw some water on your face or something. Wake up."

Zin rubbed his eyes then shuffled to the sink. When he turned around, his eyes were at least open. So was his mouth.

"The mouth-breathing is starting to annoy me, you know," Danny said.

"Then look the other way."

"Can't you just breathe through your nose or something?"

"I'm too tired."

Zin started for the bed.

"Ah-ah-ah." Danny pulled the hard chair from the desk. "Have a seat, my friend. You're eating and then we're going to the Yard. If your skin gets any lighter, you'll officially be Caucasian."

"I didn't realize it was that easy."

"You see yourself lately? You're a ghost."

"Well, that's how I feel." He fell into the chair and limply unwrapped the sandwich. He leaned back and chewed with his mouth open. "This sucks, dude."

"Sorry. I would've taken your order but you were busy snoring."

"Not this." Zin held up the sandwich. "I feel like I'm barely here, like a puppet down to one string. I can barely remember anything. It's like everything that was me is still in Foreverland."

"Right now, get some of this highly nutritious food in you and stop complaining. We can get to the Yard and if we got time we can chase Sid around."

Zin was still awake but the distant gaze fogged over his eyes while he stuffed chips in his mouth. Danny had learned not to push. It was better to let him zone out from time to time. He was more responsive afterwards. As long as he was awake, he'd eventually come back. Danny pulled his notes out of his pocket. It wasn't much and he didn't need anything written down. It would be better to destroy it. He took a pen from the desk drawer and blacked out all the words.

"What's that?" Zin shot food out with the words.

"Nothing, just ideas."

Danny wadded up the paper and tossed it in the air, playing catch with himself. He couldn't decide which idea to go with. Maybe he could bounce them off Zin, he would know what to do, but it wasn't worth the chance. He was going to disappear after the next round and who knows if he talked in his sleep. He might blab the whole plan to his Investor and Danny would be screwed to the max.

Zin finished the sandwich and opened the pudding. "Maybe I can help."

He was behind on the conversation.

"You want to see these?"

Zin shrugged.

Danny went into a wind-up – an exaggerated kick – and threw a fastball right at him. It was a trick throw. When he brought his arm back, he flipped the paperball behind his back and threw an empty hand. Zin still didn't flinch.

Instead of a fastball hitting him square in the face, it gently lobbed from behind his back and bounced off Zin's chest.

Danny stared at it. Something happened. It was déjà-vu, he'd seen someone do that before. He learned it… from his father? He used to do that when he was a kid and it scared him the first time. The fake fastball, he called it. And when Danny's cousins came over, he'd do it to them and they'd laugh when they flinched. The fake fastball always tricked them. Always hit them right in the face. They never saw it coming.

It wasn't Danny's memory, but it didn't matter.

"That's what I'm going to do," Danny muttered. "Only I'm going to hit them right in the face with the fastball."

"What?"

"Nothing, nothing." Danny nodded at the empty desk. "You finished?"

"If you say so."

"Let's go, then. First, the Yard. After that, Sid-city."

Zin pushed himself out of the chair and took his time getting dressed in auto-pilot. Danny picked up the paperball. *Was it my father, really?*

Didn't matter. Danny was going to hit the island with something the United States military would notice.

37

The moon was just a sliver.

Danny didn't sleep that night. He lay in bed, working through the details of what he'd need to do when he got inside the needle. He'd have one chance. If he blew it, he'd be headed for the Chimney, and probably not to graduate.

No pressure.

He got dressed, stopped at Zin's room. It wasn't locked anymore, not unless Danny locked it on the way out. Danny didn't bother turning on the lights. He sat on the edge of the bed, felt a little like one of the Investors. Zin was on his back, mouth open, ripping wind through his throat.

"Zin." He shook him, over and over. "Zin, wake up."

Zin's eyes opened but remained unfocused. Danny gently slapped his cheek. He ended up dripping water on his face. "What the…" He looked around the room and couldn't see Danny right next to him. "What're you doing?"

"Two things." Danny held up two fingers. "First, I got to fight Sid when we get inside the needle so don't get in the way."

Zin nodded, sleepily.

"Repeat it," Danny said.

"You got to fight, got it. What's the other thing?"

"Let me in the Mansion when you get there."

Zin was thinking about it. Moments later, he got it. He nodded. *All right.*

Danny went to the door. Zin was still up on one elbow. It was the longest he'd stayed lucid in the last days. He watched Danny leave.

Danny stepped onto the dune. Black waves roared onto shore with white foam on top. The tide was high; the water skimming across the hardpacked sand.

He gripped the paper sack against the tug of the wind. It was too dark to see down the beach. Reed was usually on the left end.

A hundred yards proved him correct. His knees were pulled up to his chest, hair fluttering.

Danny had been on the island almost two months. In that time, Reed had become a withered camp survivor. Every bone was visible from the waist up. Danny sat next to him and pulled out two bananas and passed one to him. Reed took it. He held it for several moments before peeling it.

"You got to eat, Reed."

Reed chewed, slowly. "It only makes me feel better."

"Yeah, that's the idea."

"And that makes it harder."

When the bananas were gone, Danny handed him an apple. "You know what they say about apples."

"They don't say that here, Danny Boy. Besides, I don't think it's a good idea."

Reed pushed up his lip, revealed the black gap of a missing tooth. Danny hadn't noticed it when they were at the doctor's office. His teeth were falling out.

Danny bit a chunk and handed it to him. "Yeah, it's gross but there are worse things. You got to eat. I can't have you petering out before the next round ends."

Reed eyeballed the slice. Danny swore he could see him smile before taking it. Danny took another bite and held it out. He ate the entire apple that way.

"I'm going to drop a satellite, Reed."

Reed didn't respond.

"I'll hack the United States Air Force, direct one their Milstar satellites to make an emergency landing in the middle of the island. The government will be here before it lands."

"You think you can do that?"

Danny recalled the processing speed and the ease at which he maneuvered through the global communications network the last time. It had become more an effort of will than skill.

"I can."

Reed just nodded.

They listened to the ocean, to the rise and fall of the water.

Danny leaned back on his elbows. The sky was filled with a thousand points of light. He located the Big Dipper and Orion's Belt. He put his head down and closed his eyes. And the water lulled him to sleep.

A bird woke him. The waves glittered with morning light.

Reed was gone.

The fourth round was near.

Mr. Jones was waiting at the Haystack. The gongs had already passed.

He led Danny inside with a few encouraging words. The rest of the camp was in their cells, still dressed, waiting for Danny. They were glad he arrived but not happy to see him.

Reed was already nude with his back to Danny. He could count all the vertebrae.

Mr. Jones took Danny's clothes. Zin was the last to arrive. His Investor guided him inside with a hand on his shoulder. He was vacant, spastically swallowing. The Investor asked him three times for his clothes before he caught on. The boys grew impatient.

When the doors closed and the skylights darkened, Zin stood in the middle of his cell, shoulders slumped. Head down.

"Bye, Zin," Danny whispered.

He wasn't sure he heard him. But didn't expect him to.

38

The Director watched the sun set.

He awoke completely refreshed. He had not slept well until recently. He never slept well in the face of uncertainty. That was over now. He knew what needed to be done. And how to do it.

"Director," the intercom said. "We'll be dropping the lucid gear in thirty minutes."

"Thank you."

He changed into a clean shirt and settled into his reclining chair. The kneading rollers adjusted to his shifting weight, allowing him to settle into a comfortable position. The Director stared at the ceiling. Deep breath.

The network technician that monitored Foreverland showed him how Danny had somehow circumvented the security like some sort of science fiction mind meld. He became one with the environment and rode it into the Ethernet, around the world and all the way to the satellites.

He wouldn't do it again. They were ready for him.

In fact, he was hoping he would try.

He would watch closely this time. Even though he couldn't see into the Nowhere, there were ways to watch how Foreverland was being manipulated. It was a risk to let the kid's mind run free, but they were ready. But it was still a risk. *A risk worth taking*. The reward was far beyond his imagination.

Danny Boy was a jewel.

There was still the girl and there was Reed. They would be dealt with. For now, he needed to discover the potential Danny Boy had unveiled.

The Director reached for a tray next to the chair with two glass tubes. One contained a needle – two inches long – soaking in a solution with a thin cable extending from the end of it that went all the way to the third floor where rows of computers would help transform his mind into Foreverland. The boys – when they took the needle – would come to the Director's mind.

Foreverland wasn't a computer program, that was too artificial. It had to be organic. But the Director needed the assistance of his computer network to keep his mind stable, so that he could create the world of Foreverland, where the boys would find their thoughts. *Where he would eat their souls.*

Well, to say he ate their souls was a little dramatic. Their identities – whoever they are – were absorbed by the Director's mind. It made him bigger, stronger. It made him *more.*

And he liked that.

And his mind would continue to expand. Once the girl was gone.

The Director pulled the needle out and punctured the second glass tube that greased it with electrolytic salve. Careful not to touch it with his fingers, he lifted it to the hole in his forehead. The tip made contact with the stent just below the skin.

The Director took a deep breath. He pushed it through the stent and into his frontal lobe.

His vision quivered.

His body quaked.

He laid his arm at his side and closed his eyes.

Foreverland.

39

The grainy world was all that Lucinda knew.

There was no land to walk, no object… for her to lay her head. She existed in its endless vacuum. In the swirling gray of… voices.

The sound of static.

It was continuous in the Nowhere.

It was lonely.

Until a shockwave began.

It rippled outward, stimulating the grains of gray… excited atoms. The voices began to chatter, fleeing from an object that began to take shape. It was the color of sandstone, a pedestal with a triangular fin atop a circular disc. It was always the first to appear before Foreverland was reborn.

The gray scattered around it like insects. Colors bled from the base of the sundial. Lucinda hid deep in the Nowhere as… grass and trees and buildings and sky was born. She prepared to find her savior, hoping that he might bring her peace.

That he might bring them all peace.

40

Danny floated in the bodiless darkness. He escaped the suffering, forsaking his body for the needle. But he carried the image of Reed's naked body shivering in the cold.

The fan would blow on him. The sprinklers would mist.

But Mr. Smith would arrive with something much worse.

Danny couldn't fail.

Solid ground formed beneath him. He was next to the sundial. The entire camp had arrived, forming a half-circle around him.

"Welcome, dirtbag." Sid was a monster of fleshy muscle and blue, snaky veins. "I'm dedicating this round to your misery. I'm going to invent ways of torture, invent things even the Director wouldn't dream of doing to another human being, Danny Boy. There's going to burning, there's going to be cutting and ripping… just, all sorts of fun stuff."

He popped his knuckles like snapping timber.

"I'm going to do those things to you, Danny Boy. I'm going to do them all night long."

Foreverland was quiet. No one flying in the blue sky or miniature warriors racing across the Yard. They were all around the sundial to watch Sid perform surgery. Whether they wanted to watch or Sid told them to, they were there.

"Try to run, Danny Boy, and we'll catch you. Call for help, we'll shred whoever shows up."

Does he mean Zin?

"It's going to be the longest day of your life, my friend. You'll beg me to stop, but you missed that chance, son. You already sold your soul to the devil." Big toothy grin. "And I bought it."

He paced around the semi-circle, rolling his head like a mixed martial artist warming up for a big fight. He glared down at Danny. He was nearly twenty feet tall, and growing. Muscles writhed like snakes. He pulled a long breath through his nostrils. It came out like exhaust, blowing hotly in Danny's face.

Danny looked around.

"No one's coming, Danny Boy." Sid's voice dropped an octave, filled with gravel. "No one is here to save you, it's just us, punk. Just us."

Sid filled his chest with another deep breath. His shoulders bulged, his arms rippled. His skin turned a shade redder. Talons emerged from the tips of his fingers with razor edges.

"I'm really going to dig this," he blurted with a slight lisp as sharpened incisors bit into his lower lip. "I only wish Reed was here to make it double-dip ass whipping."

The others were growing, too. It would be like a pride of lions feeding on the lone antelope. Danny was not a lion. He closed his eyes, focused on a tiny point.

Stay numb. Until she comes.

Breathe, in and out.

"I love this place, Danny Boy," Sid stated, deeply. "I'm afraid you're really going to hate it."

Sid took one more long breath and let out a roar. He lifted his tree trunk arms, flexed the dagger-tipped claws, and slashed downward. He would dice Danny into cubes. He would put him back together and do it again. And again.

He was going to do it all night.

But then Lucinda arrived.

She emerged from the ground like a ghost.

She smacked the edge of the sundial with her fist. It rang like a gong struck with a hammer. The vibrations shook Foreverland.

Danny staggered. His vision doubled.

Only Lucinda remained in focus, unaffected by the tremors emanating from the sundial. She had let loose a never-ending earthquake.

"If you love this place," she said, "then you will never leave it."

Lucinda walked toward Sid as he lost his balance. She plunged her hand into his chest. He continued to convulse, but slowly – very slowly – he began to settle like a bell reaching the end of its ring until he was as unaffected as Lucinda.

His eyes were wide. His mouth was open.

He shrank back to normal-size. When she gently placed him on the ground, he had become Sid, the gangly kid back in the Haystack. His expression was not angry or scared.

It was vacant.

She took Danny's hand. Warmth penetrated his arm and filled him. And then they fell through a trapdoor that opened on the ground.

Into the grayness of the Nowhere.

Danny was on his knees when the circular room appeared.

His hands were splayed on the floor. Twenty fingers were jiggling out of focus, the sundial ringing between his ears. His stomach turned and twisted. He thought he might vomit, then thought it weird since he was a digital body and hadn't really eaten anything.

He closed his eyes, focused on the tiny dot. In and out, he breathed until things settled. When he opened his eyes, he had ten fingers again.

"He's a bad kid." Lucinda was sitting in the lone chair, center of the room. "I saw what he was doing… in the others' thoughts."

"I thought the fight was a clue. You just wanted Sid."

"He tortures Reed," she said. "He deserved what he got."

"What'd you do to him?"

"I gave him what he loves." She crossed her legs. "I gave him Foreverland."

It sounded like a bad thing.

Danny sat up, allowed a few moments to adjust before standing. The floor swayed a bit. He felt like he just stepped off a roller coaster. A chair appeared. He grabbed the back but didn't sit.

"What's that mean?" he asked. "How'd you give him Foreverland?"

"He'll never leave."

"You can do that?"

She glanced away. "You're all coming here, Danny Boy. You all join the voices in the Nowhere."

"I don't understand, Parker was better. He couldn't have stayed here."

She shrugged.

He'll join the voices? She couldn't have that right. Parker was there, he was back. It had to be some mirror image that remained in Foreverland, perhaps the ghosts of ideas and thoughts that weren't real to begin with. Perhaps that's what the program was about, cleansing our minds of impurity, erasing the habits of self-destruction and reprogramming us with desirable thoughts.

But then who would be deciding what to program? And who decided what was desirable?

Zin might already be scattered in the Nowhere.

"He is not," she said, sensing his thought. "But he's close."

"How do you know?"

"I just know… he's with his girlfriend. He's a good person, Danny Boy. I like Zin."

But none of that would matter if Danny couldn't do something because she was right. They were all heading for Foreverland. If they were really helping them become better people, then a satellite landing on the island wouldn't harm anything.

But if they weren't helping…

"Are you ready?" she asked.

Danny let go of the chair and nodded. She stood up and the chair disappeared. He took his place in the center.

Thought-commands lit up the room.

He was in the eye of a data storm.

The colors swirled around the room. Sometimes they appeared as shapes that connected with other shapes, sometimes merging, sometimes snapping together. Other colors were blurs or streaks or dots that interweaved and interlocked and became something larger.

Danny stood still, eyes closed.

He forgot he was in a room. Forgot he once inhabited a body. He had become the data, swimming through the ethereal universe of networks on the island, searching for the conduit that would let him leak out and spread across the outside world—

The colors stopped.

He opened his eyes. The room looked like the inside of a kaleidoscope.

"What's wrong?" Lucinda asked.

"It's too easy."

Danny walked the perimeter, thinking. He wanted to be sure. If he fell into a trap, everything ended. Game over. He made one loop around the room, started another. By the end of the second one, he was positive.

A bubble appeared in the middle of the room, hovering off the floor. Its surface swirled with colors reflecting from the walls.

"That's like the firewall that seals the island from the rest of the world," Danny said. "Last time, I exploited a line of communication."

He put his finger on a black dot floating on the surface.

"They only stay open for a millisecond because snoopers scour the entire firewall a thousand times a second looking for these inconsistencies and closing them. I was able to slip through one before they closed it."

"So? Do it again."

"But I shouldn't be able to. Snoopers are learning programs, they would fix the gap. It shouldn't be there."

The lights from the bubble scattered over her face, glimmering on her electric red hair.

"I think it's a trap," Danny said. "They might know what I'm doing."

"Then why set a trap?"

Good question. "I can't chance it. If I blow this, it's all over."

Lucinda gazed at the bubble. She gave him the space to think as the clock inside Foreverland ticked closer to the end of the day. Closer to his return to the Haystack.

"Is there another way to get out?" she asked.

A red dot began glowing in the center of the bubble. It took the form of a building with five floors and a smokestack. Danny reached inside and touched it.

"I'll go deeper."

Danny had become the colors, again. He had become the data streaming through the network pipelines like blood through the body's arteries. He swished through the Ethernet web, spreading out and observing the flow of data, reading its content, following multiple directions and destinations, searching for the center of activity. He experienced the sensation of shooting across space.

Lucinda watched quietly.

Many times, he disguised himself as quantifiable data as the security snoopers trolled the network for potential intruders. And then he'd be on the move again. But the closer he got to the center of activity – the mainframe processor – the slower his progress became. He spent long chunks of time idle. One slip and the security snoopers would trace his presence back to an identity known as Danny Boy. He had cloaked his identity, but they would eventually unravel it. And then everyone would know what he was up to. And on an island, it was hard to run and hide.

He began to doubt his intuition about the outer firewall, but he knew it was just wishful thinking. His new path was slow and tedious and dangerous, but he couldn't take forever. At some point, the needle would withdraw from his body and he'd return empty-handed.

His senses adjusted to the new reality of colorful data. He began to *see* it and feel it. The room reflected his experience. Lucinda watched as his experience reflected a recognizable reality in the room. They soared through slippery tunnels and past doorways and stopped inside empty rooms. They flew down hallways, beneath doors. Sometimes they went so fast it was just a blur. Something silver formed ahead of them. It was down a long hallway. It came into focus.

An elevator opened.

Danny moved for the first time in hours. He walked toward the elevator and then appeared to go inside it. The doors closed.

Lucinda wouldn't see him come back.

The Milstar communications system consisted of five satellites – each weighing approximately 10,000 pounds – positioned around the world to meet wartime requirements with a price tag just under $5 billion.

They'd notice one missing.

Danny went up to the fourth floor of the Chimney where the bulk of computer activity operated and streamed through a major conduit of data that was transferring updates to the outside world. He did a quick search of the Milstar program and found it linked to three locations: Los Angeles Air Force Base, Hanscom Air Force Base in Massachusetts, and Schriever Air Force Base in Colorado.

He was careful not to set off any alarms while snooping around each location. Since he resembled data, it only took seconds to cross the country for preliminary observations. Once he was certain, he penetrated Schriever Air Force Base.

There were very few gaps to exploit and the multi-layered security system was covered with alarms. But it wasn't evolving like the Chimney. Danny easily disguised himself as a top-secret document and streamed onto a secretary's computer in one of the outer offices. From there, he leaped into the network and passed through encrypted firewalls as a variety of updates and system maintenance. He avoided any sort of forced entry that might trigger a lockdown. He needed things to be open and fully operational.

Once he cleared security, he migrated to the central command processor and located the geosynchronized orbit of the satellites. He could take complete control of all five, if he wished, shoot all of them at the island like falling stars. But that was risky. Alarms would be triggered and there was a chance that a system override could override his actions. They would know the coordinates and likely investigate, but that wasn't as sure a thing as dropping 10,000 pounds of metal on the Mansion.

Danny tucked Trojan horses into the system that would lay dormant until one of the satellites was positioned over the island. Then they would send the satellite hurtling toward the South Atlantic. At that point, there would be nothing Milstar could do to restore power in time to alter the $1 billion belly flop.

Estimated impact: ten hours, twenty minutes.

Danny double-checked his work. When he was satisfied, he drifted back into the network. He took his time reentering the same portal inside the Chimney, trailing an email that was downloading onto the server. He ended up in the middle of the main database that contained phone calls, emails, and documents. He filtered through the information disguised as system maintenance, integrating with the content.

There were lists of clients, none of which Danny recognized; surveillance video showing "prospects" of teenage boys that were sometimes in hospitals, alone in poverty or abandoned in remote areas. Prospects had psychological evaluation documents attached to them, evaluating them as either viable candidates or not.

Nothing explained what they were doing with them.

Danny ventured out of the system, past highly secure compartments that controlled all the buildings, food storage, power and security features. He could shut down the island, if he needed to. But that wouldn't do any good without someone coming to the rescue.

He was about to return to the Nowhere when something stopped him. It was a large database called "Records".

Danny hesitated. Records would mean histories. The past.

Who I am.

Night had arrived in Foreverland.

Danny hurried inside the Records.

42

The atmosphere transformed into images. He was no longer amorphous data that streamed along the colorful conduit. The Records database took shape of something that resembled an enormous library with vaulted ceilings and hanging lights. The floor was hard and shiny and the walls covered with bookshelves. But there were no tables or chairs; there was no need to reach for the symbolic books that held the records of the island. Danny only needed to think and the information streamed into his consciousness. He could absorb and comprehend the data about everyone, but he was only interested in one person.

[Search for Danny...] he thought-commanded, suddenly realizing something he had been missing every since he woke up.

I don't know my last name.

It didn't seem important before. He was Danny and that was all he needed. It didn't even feel like he had a last name, like it had been erased.

The walls shifted. The bookshelves rotated and changed positions. Three books floated off the shelves and levitated in front of him, each with the name *Daniel* on the cover. He didn't recognize any of the last names, but two of them had two small words lettered in red just below the name.

Crossover Completed.

Danny sent them back to the shelves. The third one centered in front of him.

"Daniel Forrester," he said. "Let's see what you got."

He touched the cover. The book opened. There were no words on pages, only the colors of raw data. He put his hand on it and knew.

I'm Daniel Forrester.

Daniel Forrester was born in Gilbert, Arizona.

A healthy boy and an only child. His parents were John and Maggy Forrester. They were both only children, as well. The grandparents all deceased. The only extended family was a great aunt that lived in Rockford, Illinois. She was in her eighties and suffering from dementia.

Ideal candidate, it said.

That's what Danny was labeled, an ideal candidate for the program. He didn't know if that referred to his health or the dementia. Or maybe the lack of extended family.

His father was a finish carpenter.

Memories emerged of his father coming home when it was dark. Danny would be parked in front of the television when his truck pulled into the driveway. His father smelled of sweat and cedar. Sometimes he'd lug his double-saddle tool belt into the house loaded with every tool ever invented and work on a project at home, fixing a doorframe or building a new room. He knew where every tool was located in the tool belt, finding it without looking. And when he was done, he always slipped it back where it belonged, without looking.

He was very good.

Until he fell from a roof and severed his spinal cord.

Danny was nine when it happened. He was on the computer in the attic when his mother took him to the neighbor's house. She was crying and didn't tell Danny anything. She didn't come back to get him for three days. She didn't talk much then, either.

His father died on the operating table.

Danny held her hand at the funeral. It was cold. When he squeezed, she didn't squeeze back. Her eyes had become blank. No family attended, only neighbors and woodworkers. The house was very quiet that night.

His mother was not home much. She worked a lot. She had a prescription drug problem and washed it down with gin. She often never made it off the couch. This suited Danny's lifestyle just fine.

Danny learned how to hack computers when he was six. It started with online games. He and his friends hacked Xbox and PlayStation databases, rewriting the code for unlimited weapons.

They downloaded free music, movies, and games. Sometimes they had games before they were released.

By the time he was nine, it wasn't even a challenge. After his father died, he stepped up the stakes.

They hacked into the school and planted porn in the principal's inbox. They changed all the jocks' grades to Fs. They set off fire alarms ten times in a month.

They hacked their first bank when he was 10.

They set up a dummy account with false ATM deposits. They never let the balance go over five hundred dollars and they never withdrew the money as cash, simply used it to pay for things online. Because his mother was never home, they had clothes, shoes, computers and software shipped directly to his house.

It was a parole officer that busted him.

Danny skipped school, sitting up in the attic on the computer for days at a time. The cops came to the house and wanted to speak to his mother. It pissed Danny off, so he swiped the officer's identity, repossessed his car and foreclosed on his house. The man's credit was trashed. They couldn't prove he did anything.

He had all the money an 11 year old would want, but he wanted more. He began trolling Las Vegas casinos. At first, it was just jacking accounts and hacking online poker games. But the real money was in Vegas. His friends came over. It took a weekend and a case of Red Bull, but they managed to set up a dummy account with three million dollars and a penthouse timeshare waiting for them at the top of a resort. Their biggest problem was the fact that they were a bunch of eleven year olds.

But they ended up with bigger problems.

At first they thought they'd been discovered by Vegas security and they'd lose all the bones in their thumbs. They were relieved that it was just the FBI. They'd be in trouble, but at least they wouldn't be hung from a hook through the tongue.

The rest of them wanted to stop, but Danny wasn't going to lie down. He planted a data bomb inside the FBI network and wiped it out. Their evidence disappeared. But not all of it.

They came to the door disguised as the UPS man dropping off another package. Danny answered the door in his sweatpants. They put him in the back of a black Suburban. His friends sat next to him.

He was back home by the time he was thirteen.

Despite the federal shadow watching his every move, he went back to his Vegas accounts and set up two more. He could retire when he turned eighteen.

That's when the house burned down.

That's when Danny's life – as he knew it – ended.

Danny Forrester was acquired by Franklin Constantino.

The file said he'd been acquired by this man.

Acquired.

Franklin Constantino made his money in real estate and other businesses. He had lung cancer and had not been seen in public for quite some time. Some reports stated he had died in a boating accident.

But Danny knew he wasn't dead. Franklin Constantino stood in front of him as the record book projected his image before him.

Mr. Jones.

The house had burned down. The police found two bodies. One was a woman and the other was a boy. Each was beyond recognition but assumed to be the bodies of Danny and his mother. The fire started when she fell asleep on the couch and dropped a lit cigarette. Danny was asleep in the attic and couldn't escape.

None of it was true.

He didn't fall asleep in the attic. On the nights he did sleep, he went to his room. It was too cold upstairs and there was nowhere to lie down. But to the world, Danny was dead.

And there was no family left to care.

No family left to look.

Like the database at the Federal Bureau of Investigations, he had been erased from the world.

He had been *acquired.*

The record ended there.

No explanation how he got to the island. Only when he got there and who he belonged to.

Danny closed the book. It flew back to the shelf. So many books, each someone that had been acquired. And every one of them boys, each of them brought to the island, fed and cared for, each marched to the Haystack where they gladly stuck a needle in their head. Every one of them doing what they were told to do and the world would never know.

All of them following this trail to Foreverland. All of them but one.

[Reed...] Danny thought-commanded.

The room shifted. One book came out, front and center.

Reed Johnston, born in Wooster, Ohio.

He was an only child, too. Grew up on a farm. His mother had died when she delivered him.

He was raised by his father. He stopped going to school before he graduated so that he could help with the crops. Danny planted the fields and helped harvest at the end of the season. He also cleaned out the bottles of vodka that rolled from beneath the seat. When his father went on a real bender, he'd be the only one in the fields. He was the one that answered the door when the creditors came knocking and he was the one that called the bank when they needed money for seed.

Reed didn't socialize much. He wouldn't talk to anyone at school except for a girl that sat behind him in most of his classes. Her name was Lucinda Jones.

Lucinda lived with her aunt and uncle and their twelve kids. They weren't thrilled about it; they had enough mouths to feed. She was given custody to them when her father died serving in the military and her mother died of breast cancer two years later. Lucinda was only five.

She made plenty of trouble by the time she was ten.

Reed spent years watching her. He even went to church just to see her walk back from communion. He'd sit in the back row while his dad was sleeping off a long one and slip out before mass was over. But she knew he was watching.

She would meet him out in the field and they'd find the shade of a tree to sit and talk. She would sometimes sneak out after midnight and meet Reed waiting on the road in his father's old pick-up. They would drive the deserted country roads and look at the stars until she fell asleep in his arms. He would take her home and help her back through the window.

There was no mention of Reed being an ideal candidate.

When Reed was seventeen, he finished the morning rounds. The tractor needed parts. He ate lunch before heading into town. When he got back, his father was still asleep. At supper, he finally checked on him, found him dead in his bed.

Reed didn't bother calling an ambulance.

He buried his old man in the soybean field out behind the silo. No tombstone, no cross or words. He put him in the ground still wearing coveralls, his mouth slightly agape, and covered him with dirt. When he was done, he dropped the shovel and went inside and called Lucinda.

The next day, they were hundreds of miles away from home. Lucinda's suitcase was in the back. Reed's few belongings were in a paper sack. They were driving south. They didn't know where, they were just going to drive until they felt like stopping. They wanted to get married but they'd have to find someone that would wed seventeen year olds without parental consent. There was always Vegas.

Their truck went off the road somewhere in Oklahoma. The bumper wrapped around an oak tree.

Both of them went through the windshield.

Reed survived. He saw her body next to a tree. She wasn't moving. He tried to get to her, to help her, to breathe into her lungs, to touch her once more…

The record ended.

Reed Johnston was *acquired.*

And woke up on the island.

43

The Nowhere room was empty.

Lucinda wasn't there when Danny returned from the Records. He was relieved. He considered staying in the Records until the round ended but it was too risky. Lucinda would know his thoughts the moment he arrived. She would know that she was dead.

Lucinda is a memory.

When Reed arrived on the island, somehow she slipped out of his memories and came to life in Foreverland. She didn't know that she didn't exist outside in the real world.

She thinks she's alive. Does that make her real?

Did Reed know?

No, Reed was just as confused as she was. He dreamed of her, didn't know her name. Only Danny knew they had a real past. He knew they had parents, they were real people before they woke up on the island. But their parents were gone. There was nothing left of their lives.

No one would look for them.

Danny drifted back to his body, back to the Haystack and cold reality. He sat up, groggily. The cells were open and empty. Reed was gone. Zin, too. A few Investors were standing outside his cell. They were looking across the aisle. They didn't pay attention to Danny quickly getting dressed.

Two more Investors came inside with a stretcher. They placed it next to Sid. He was still lying flat on the floor. The Investors began to dress him. His eyes were open. His mouth, too.

"Let's go, Danny Boy." Mr. Jones reached for him. "There's nothing to watch."

Danny pulled his arm away. *Mr. Constantino.*

"Come along, son." Mr. Jones blocked the view into Sid's cell. "Why don't you get to your room and get some rest. This was a long round."

"What happened to Sid?" Danny said.

"He just progressed a little faster than expected, nothing to worry about, son. Come along."

Danny hurried into the aisle so that Mr. Jones wouldn't touch him. He went to his room alone and looked across the Yard. A flatbed cart emerged from the trees. Someone was lying on the back of it, covered with a sheet and his Investor riding next to him. They went around the dormitory. Toward the Chimney.

You can stay here.

Lucinda pulled him into Foreverland, like she ripped his identity from his body.

Where was he now?

It didn't matter.

A satellite would soon be punching a crater in the Mansion.

LAST ROUND

Foster Parents Arrested for Neglect and Abuse

CHICAGO, Illinois. – Cynthia and John Halner were arrested for neglect and physical abuse of twelve foster children living in their home. The Department of Child and Family Services investigated claims of children complaining at school about being punished with belt buckles, bamboo sticks and screwdrivers.

Eleven of the children have been placed in the custody of other families. The oldest child, Eric Zinder, 16, was reported missing. Cynthia and John Halner claimed he had run away several months earlier and failed to report it, although they continued to receive support for his care.

44

It felt like his brains got pulled out of his head.

The Director had to yank the needle out. His hands were still shaking. He lay in the chair, his breathing shallow, staring at the needle in his forehead for too long. Foreverland had closed but he was afraid to reach for it. Each time he did, his hand quivered violently. It would be dangerous if the needle shook inside the stent and scrambled his frontal lobe like a lobotomy knife. He took a deep breath and ripped it out like a loose tooth.

It was several minutes before he stopped seeing double.

She shook Foreverland.

He'd never seen anything like it.

The boys were gathered around the sundial where the Director could see them very clearly. He didn't even sense her nearing, she just appeared out of nowhere. Before he could act, she struck the sundial and let loose tremors that never ended. They were still inside his head.

The Director threw the needle on the floor.

He put his feet down. He needed some water, maybe something to settle his stomach. He'd already been on the recliner far too long. The room felt like it was turning ten times as fast as it should've been. He was imagining it.

He stood slowly, hand on the armrest. He let go, took a step and another, quickly leaning over. The floor felt tilted. The Director went several more steps and crashed into the telescope. He rolled to his back, swallowed back bile bitterly surging upward.

Relax, you idiot. This will pass.

Foreverland needed to be shut down for awhile. He had to admit, that would be the best thing after what he saw. It was getting too risky. He'd never become paralyzed inside the needle. Not only had he lost track of Danny and the girl, he didn't see anything after she belted the sundial. He didn't know where they went or what they were doing. He was half-baked until the day finally ended and he returned to the chair.

But he couldn't shut things down. That would require starting everything over. He'd lose the confidence of the Investors. He might not get it back up and running. Besides, the girl… she was out in the open.

She was getting too strong. For that reason, Foreverland needed to continue, full speed ahead.

The Director decided right there – staring at the ceiling, swallowing foul gulps of saliva – he would follow Danny into the next round and put an end to this madness once and for all. He'd set a trap for the little bitch and be done with it. He had to do something. Soon.

But who's trapping who?

"Director?" the intercom called. "Is everything all right?"

"Yes." He rolled to his side and spent some time on his hands and knees. He decided to sit on the floor a bit longer. "I want Jones and Smith up here."

"They are with the boys right now."

"Well, send for them."

"I think we have bigger problems, Director."

Oh, you have no idea. "What would that be?"

"You'll need to come down to the network floor. I think we need to consider suspending the program until we can—"

"No."

The Director pulled himself up. He saw the cart driving away from the Haystack with someone lying in the back. He assumed the boy Zin had finally crossed over for graduation and was being transferred to the Chimney.

"What would you like to do?" the intercom spoke.

"Right now, I want Smith and Jones in my office." He filled a glass with water and drank. "Afterwards, I want to see what Danny Boy was up to."

"I'm not comfortable with the risk you're suggesting."

"Life is a risk."

"You're risking everything."

The world settled around the Director. He smoothed the front of his floral-designed shirt, brushing away the fear that, seconds earlier, churned inside him. He poured Scotch over the water.

"Get Smith and Jones up here. Now."

45

Danny woke in his bed.

His room was lit up. He pulled open the curtain. The sun was high enough to be noon. The Yard was active. Dozens of campers were playing soccer. Others were hanging out at the tables.

Something is wrong.

When the sleep-fog cleared, he remembered. The satellite!

It should have landed. The impact would've been like a bomb. There wouldn't be much of the Mansion left and there sure as hell wouldn't be a soccer game. Unless it was off the mark, landing a mile or two in the water. That was possible.

Maybe the Trojan horses were quarantined. Possible, sure. There was always a chance a security scan picked them up while they lay dormant. Still, they would find him. Eventually. One day.

He cursed.

Stupid. Stupid, stupid, STUPID. He should've pulled the trigger while he was there, sent them all hurtling toward the island. That way, at least, he could battle off security snoopers and if they caught him they would trace him back to the island.

Stupid.

He needed to get dressed, get over to the Mansion and see if anything had landed. Maybe there would be some debris that would indicate an off-target crash. Even if the satellite was fifty miles off, the military would cruise by the island. There was still going to be an investigation.

He threw on some clothes and noticed someone sitting at the card table. The camp wasn't down there throwing cards like usual. It was just one person. One he didn't expect.

Zin was lying on the table, hands folded over his stomach. Taking in the sun.

"Zin?" Danny approached, warily. "Is that you?"

Stupid question. But after seeing Parker not recognizing them, he worried that Zin would be absent. But then he turned his head and smiled. His eyes were bright and focused.

"Danny Boy," he said.

Danny wanted to hug him. They slapped hands, instead. Zin sat up, stretched. "Man, the sun never felt so good."

"What the hell happened?"

"I woke up in the Haystack before you did. You should've seen the look on my Investor's face! He looked like he dropped a ten pound load in his trousers when I stood up and hugged him while I was still full on naked. The old man was speechless. I wanted to wait until you woke up but the old men were running everyone out of the Haystack."

"I don't get it. What happened?"

Zin rubbed his face, looked out to the Yard, thinking. "I don't really remember anything about the last… week, I guess. I mean, I don't even remember going inside the needle. It just felt like I was… floating, I suppose. Like, I was out in the Nowhere just floating around and coming apart."

He stalled.

"It's weird, I don't know how to describe it. I just felt like I was being pulled in a hundred directions, like I was being stretched. It didn't hurt, really. It was all rather numb. And I just didn't care."

Zin looked good. He was more present. Healthy, somehow.

"The weird thing? I remember everything, Danny Boy. You know how we remember more when we go inside the needle? I'm Eric Zinder. My parents died when I was little and I ended up in foster care. I ran away and lived on the streets. I was homeless, dude. I was some street rat jacking cars and… and… no good, man."

He looked sick.

"I was no good."

Zin recalled robbing some tourists on their way to the theater, some old man and a woman way too young. He remembered getting hauled into a van and a sack over his head. Something over his mouth and vapors in his head.

And then he woke up in the Chimney.

But the weird thing was, Danny was remembering, too. He didn't know his whole life, not like Zin was reciting. But he remembered the stuff he knew inside Foreverland. He forgot things when he came out before, but now he was remembering it.

"She did it," Zin said.

"Who?" Danny said. "Your girlfriend?"

"A girl with this…" He chopped at his ears. "She had long red hair, these big eyes. She sent me back."

"Lucinda?"

Zin shook his head. "She didn't say her name, she just came out of the fog and then she was standing in front of me."

He put his hand on Danny's shoulder and bowed his head.

"'You don't belong here' she said to me, Danny Boy. And then I felt all pulled back together. The fog lifted and I woke up in the cell."

She sent him back. Zin was fading from his body, he was heading for Foreverland and she had the power to send him back. Of course, she did. And maybe that's what she did to Danny, gave him the ability to remember in the flesh. She did the opposite to—

"Sid!" Danny said. "What happened to him?"

"You didn't hear?" Zin threw his arm over Danny's shoulders. "Our man Sid set the record for smoking out, brother. He went into that round all normal and came out empty. The Investors were more baffled by Sid then they were watching me walk out of there. I think the rest of our camp thinks I'm possessed, they think maybe I did something. They're not talking to me."

They had to know it wasn't Zin. They saw Lucinda come out of the ground and hammer the sundial, stick her arm in Sid's chest. Right? Or did they not see any of that? Maybe they didn't even see her.

The sky was nothing but blue. No clouds or streaks or smoke. Untouched.

There was no point going to the Mansion. Nothing was coming. The good guys would never arrive. They were truly alone, now. The Director would figure out what he did in the last round, there was no way they were letting him inside the needle again. Maybe they already knew.

"What's going on, Danny Boy?" Zin calmly said. "You expecting someone to parachute into the Yard?"

Danny shook his head.

"None of this was supposed to happen," Zin said. "I shouldn't be here and Sid shouldn't be wherever he is. Did you do something?"

"No. Not really."

"Well, what did you do?"

Danny sat down, rested his elbows on the tabletop. All the dorm windows were open except Reed's. The curtains were drawn. He was probably curled up in the dark recovering from God-knows-what they did to him. And now Danny had to tell him that he had another round to go.

"I blew it, man."

"Ah, yes. You've got the world by the balls here on the island. You can do whatever you want, as long as you go to the Haystack and let them drill your head. Yeah, how could you blow that?"

"You really want to know?"

"I'm all about knowing." He held out his hands and smiled, typical Zin fashion.

Danny sat nodding and thinking. He got up, walked around. The sundial was fifty feet away. It was the center of Foreverland. Maybe it meant nothing in the real world, but he didn't like being that close to it, not when he was about to tell Zin everything.

"Let's go see Reed," he said.

46

The Director draped his floral shirt over the back of a chair and buttoned up a beige long sleeved one. He had not been for a walk on his island for quite some time. Lately, it had been all work, work, work.

When he first arrived on the island some thirty years earlier, he hiked every day. He could also see his abs. Now he couldn't see what color flip-flops he was wearing. It was the price of intelligence, he often told himself. That, and becoming a lazy slob.

It was an abandoned resort when he first arrived. Most of the buildings were in severe disrepair. The jungle was taking them back. It wasn't worth much. So he bought it.

He didn't know why he was so hasty. At the time, he just wanted to escape the world. He'd seen his share of heartbreak (his fiancé was having an affair) and disappointment (his business partner died of a stroke at the age of 41) and wanted to heed the advice of a famous philosopher, one Henry David Thoreau.

Simplify.

He planned on living out his life on that island. But nothing stays the same. That was the only guarantee life gave you: things change.

Yes, they do.

He needed to get out. He was nearing the most critical point of the program, of his life, and he needed to be thinking with a clear head. He had just returned from the fourth floor and had seen what Danny had done.

He spent some time contemplating it, but his penthouse was suddenly suffocating. Now he was lacing up snake boots to get outside for awhile. He shirked the flip-flops and shorts. He wasn't opposed to risk, just not when there wasn't a payoff. And what he'd seen on the fourth floor was a risk, indeed.

But the payoff was worth it.

The boy became data.

The fourth floor analyst, Mr. Jackson, advised him to remove Danny from the program. When boys went inside the needle, they needed a digital body. Once that was gone, the identity would scatter into the Nowhere, bodiless. Lost. Nothing.

But Danny didn't need a body. He became data, floating through the system like a ghost. He had done something no one had done before. Something the Director didn't know was possible. He had no idea what kind of power he had. It came too easy.

He could bring everything down the next time.

Danny had sensed the trap. The Director made it obvious, rigged it so that Danny would suspect it was too easy. He knew the boy was brilliant, and with brilliance comes patience. He wasn't hasty. He would look for another way to escape the island's network to get into the outside world, and the only other way was to infiltrate the heart of the Chimney.

Right where they wanted him.

Danny moved inside the Loop Program: a digital environment that simulated the outside world. There was a chance he would recognize it was a mock-up, but he didn't. Danny thought he had escaped again and went right through the United States military firewall like it was a video game.

His infiltration of Milstar was all inside the network of computers on the fourth floor. If he had actually been in the real world, there would be a satellite-filled crater somewhere on the island.

Brilliant.

Mr. Jackson suggested Danny be removed from the program permanently. *What if he knew it was the Looping Program and slipped out?*

Well, he didn't.

Mr. Jackson didn't understand what the Director saw. He didn't see the potential. He knew that Lucinda was an anomaly that escaped from Reed's mind and haunted Foreverland. He knew that she was getting stronger and more troublesome. But he wasn't looking in the other direction.

They were on the threshold of mankind's next great discovery. Freedom from the body. *Enlightenment through technology.*

The Director would go down in history ahead of Edison, Einstein and Jobs.

He would become the 21st century Buddha.

When the Director was young – in his 20s – he travelled to Third World countries, places like Ethiopia and Rwanda. He went there to help people with suffering. He brought them medicine and food; he worked with government officials to curb corruption. He educated them. But there was nowhere to go. And the more he helped, the more he saw their suffering.

It wasn't just the physical suffering. It was the suffering of the mind.

He decided, after only two years of service, the world needed a revolutionary way of healing the mind. If the mind operated clearly, physical suffering could be tolerated, even avoided. Nothing in the last thousand years brought relief to the mind. People weren't going to the mountain tops to meditate for twenty years, they were plugging in smartphones and tablets. They needed easier access to real freedom. The record number of prescriptions for depression was proof we were doing something wrong.

Life is suffering.

The Director came to the island to save humanity because God wasn't helping. He meditated on the cliffs and explored the wild. He rebuilt the island, renovated the buildings and created a paradise that would heal the body and nurture the soul. His father – just before his death – had developed alternate reality and the Director used it to rewrite corrupt minds and correct bad habits. He would do what the Buddha failed to do: bring enlightenment to the masses.

Such an endeavor wasn't free. He would need money. Lots.

But the Investors would need a reason to spend that kind of money. They weren't interested in altruistic endeavors like the Director; they needed a return on their investment that would be worth the risk. The Director gave them one. He gave the old and dying Investors what they desired most. He gave them the only thing their money couldn't buy.

More life.

The Director holstered a machete to cut through the overgrown paths. He carried a sitting cushion to the elevator. He decided that he would sit meditation on the cliff to further contemplate the future of the program. His thirty years had culminated at this very moment. He did not want to be rash.

Mr. Clark waited in a golf cart outside the front doors of the Chimney.

"Director," he said, "the Investors would like a word."

"I see." The Director started around the cart. "I will hike first, Mr. Clark."

"They request your presence immediately."

"Mr. Clark, I am not prepared for a meeting. I have a schedule. Presently, they're not on it. But I'll make room later today."

The Director started around again and Mr. Clark bumped the cart in front of him. "I think now, Director, would be an appropriate time to alter your schedule. Impatience can fester, you see. I suggest you come along."

"I see." The Director balanced the tip of the machete on the front of the cart. "Mr. Clark, what is it that cannot wait an hour?"

"Your future, Director."

He laughed. "I don't attend those meetings."

"Today, you do." Mr. Clark patted the seat. "We're all in this together. And we don't care how silly you look."

The Director didn't mind the insult to his hiking gear. He didn't like meeting on their terms. And certainly not on their grounds. But he slid onto the seat. Without the Investors, there was no program. And he was so close.

They took the wider path, heading for the Mansion.

47

Danny stepped back into the cover of the trees. He had been hiding outside the Chimney, trying to figure out how to get around Mr. Clark and through the front doors. Danny assumed he was there to pick the Director up, but the minutes dragged on.

The Director looked like he was going on safari. Danny had never seen the man in person. There was a picture of him in the cafeteria posing with a bunch of happy boys like they'd just won the lottery. He was smaller in person and sported a pot belly. He was wearing long sleeves and rugged pants with boots laced up to his knees.

He wasn't happy to see Mr. Clark, the way he jabbed the machete into the cart. After a few words, he got on the cart and they started in the direction of the Mansion.

Danny went to the front door but it was locked. He wasn't sure what he was going to do if he got inside. He just figured it was time to talk with someone in charge.

He had gone to Reed's room earlier that day. He began to open the door—

"Son!" Mr. Smith shouted. "Don't go in there."

Danny backed away. Mr. Smith walk-limped as fast as he could. He was carrying a lunch bag.

"I just wanted to say hello," Danny said.

"He's in no shape to talk with anyone." Mr. Smith huffed.

"Yeah, I wonder why."

"Don't take that tone, my boy. Have some respect when you talk—"

"What did you do to him this time? Did you poke sticks in his ears or rip his fingernails off? Did you break him in half? What was it this time, Mr. Smith?"

Zin pulled him back. "Danny Boy, come on. Let's come back another time."

"No, he needs to answer me!"

"Now, relax a second, son." Mr. Smith stopped Danny with a hand on his chest. "None of the treatments are permanently damaging. He'll recover just fine, he's just a little uncomfortable. It's for his own good. All of this is for his own good."

"Treatments? You're torturing him, admit it!"

"I'm going to call Mr. Jones."

"I don't care if you call God."

Danny pushed open the door.

The room was dark. Reed was curled up on the bed. He tried to roll over but convulsions shook him like he'd been struck by lightning.

Mr. Smith reached inside his pocket and then Danny went down. Everything went black.

He woke up on his bed with Mr. Jones.

It took several moments to realize Mr. Smith hit his tracker. *Mr. Smith. That wasn't his real name.*

When Mr. Jones finally left, Danny snuck out. And now that he saw where the Director was going, he could find plenty of trouble.

All the bastards will be together.

48

Mr. Clark dropped the Director off at the front steps of the Mansion and took the golf cart through the slowly opening garage door, closing just as slowly behind him. The Director stroked the flat side of the machete, contemplating the front doors and brass knobs. He despised going inside their fortress. It smelled old. Smelled like dying.

The Mansion was built upon the remnants of the resort's hotel. He had no input of how the original Investors would build it, only that it needed to keep the boys out. He envisioned a fence, but the Investors and their mountains of cash built a damn fortress that dissected the southern tip in gaudy, institutionalized fashion. There was enough square footage to hide a small village.

He stopped at the top step and knocked with the backside of the blade. He stepped inside the foyer, patting the machete in his open palm for all the old codgers to see. He thought it might be over the top, but it wasn't. They were on the veranda waiting for him. He saw them through the glass wall. Beyond their gray and balding heads, he could see the ocean.

All forty of them were in attendance.

They had pulled chairs onto the expansive veranda that jutted out from the back of the building. A few of them had canes leaning against their knees; others had oxygen tanks parked next to them. It looked like the Board of Directors for the AARP.

A podium was set in the center. In front of that, facing the committee of Investors, was a lone chair. Ceiling fans blew down on the Director as he stepped out to greet them, still handling the machete.

"You may shield your weapon, Director." Mr. Black, a fat Arabian with a checkered headdress, stepped to the podium. "Threats are not necessary."

"What, this? It's for brush cutting. You thought I was going to chop you up?"

These old bastards, so used to their former lives as CEOs and business titans with their formal rules and procedures, had to have a freaking podium just to talk. Now the Director regretted not changing back into his flip-flops.

"Please." Mr. Black aimed his best glare at him; a glare that worked well with employees.

The Director sheathed the blade with a flurry of sword-fighting moves. "I'm not sitting, gentlemen. This will be a short meeting. You've all signed contracts agreeing to the terms of the island and I have final authority of how to proceed. The fact I'm even here is a modern day miracle, so make it quick."

"I speak for everyone in attendance," Mr. Black said. "And we have had enough."

The Director rolled his eyes.

"We have sacrificed much, Director. But we are powerful men and we do not take risks without contingency. We will replace you if changes are not made."

The Director rumbled with laugher.

"Mr. Black, with all due respect to you and your gang," he cleared his throat, "I AM THE PROGRAM! You can't replace me, gentlemen, I am every reason you are here today. I brought you here because I have proved, over and over, this program works. You didn't risk everything because I made a promise, you did it because I deliver. I am the way, gentlemen. I am the Alpha and the Omega. Without me," he tapped his forehead, "there is no program, I suggest you understand that."

The men did not stir.

"Be that as it may," Mr. Black said, "there are reasons for concern. Eric Zinder has fully recovered from his progress with his memories intact. At the same time, Sidney Hayward has become completely unresponsive. And now we are hearing reports that Danny Forrester has circumvented security."

"Where'd you hear that?"

"We are not ignorant, nor will we sit back and be taken advantage of, Director. You are taking unnecessary risks that could impact all of us."

"You're not qualified to judge the program." He fingered the hilt of the machete. "None of you know what it takes to run this island, to do what I do. It cannot be done, it cannot be understood by anyone else but me, gentlemen. You should not speak where matters do not concern you."

"On the contrary, they do concern us. And, despite what you believe, *we* are the program, Director. We fund this operation. Without us, you are nothing. You are playing a game that you won't win. I suggest you listen."

The Director nodded along with the accusations. He let go of the chair, meandered around the Investors and leaned against the railing. The ocean breeze was warm but cooled his face as it filtered through his beard that was becoming itchy with perspiration.

"Director, please come back to the chair. Some of the Investors cannot see you."

"And what game would that be, Mr. Black?"

Chairs scuffled.

"Director, please."

"What game, Mr. Black? What game am I playing? The game that extends your lives another 80 years, is that the one you're referring to?"

"We are not barbarians, Director. You are torturing one of the boys. We did not agree to the inhumane treatment of them, that was in the contract. Perhaps you should review it, yourself."

"I see." The Director didn't want to leave the edge of the balcony, took his time doing so. He returned to the chair that was on trial and sat this time. Mr. Smith was sitting on the far left side of the semi-circle, arms crossed and tight-lipped.

"Gentlemen," the Director said, loudly and slowly, "you bought these boys. You arranged for them to be delivered to the island. You're not barbarians? What is it do you think we're doing to them that is not barbaric?"

"We agreed to discomfort, not torture."

"We have to make adjustments for abnormality. Mr. Smith has invested as much as the rest of you, I believe he has every right to collect on that investment. As would the rest of you."

"The boy is in agony."

"He won't be for long."

"You're not being honest, Director. These are more than minor incidents."

"Every science has its wrinkles, Mr. Black. We have to adjust. I assure you, the program is well. We are analyzing the current state of these abnormalities and will act accordingly."

Quiet settled, interrupted by the hiss of an oxygen tank.

"Now, if we're finished—"

"We want to suspend Daniel Forrester, Reed Johnston, and Eric Zinder," Mr. Black stated.

Mr. Smith stood up. "That was not what we discussed!"

In-fighting broke out.

The Director sat back, twirling the curly whiskers on his chin. Let them tear each other apart. They had no alternative, they knew it. They were all accustomed to having control and that rarely made for good teamwork. Especially when you add the desperation of impending death. They were all dying and that would tend to make anyone impatient, especially power-hungry old men.

THUD!

The front door cracked loud enough that almost all of them heard it on the veranda. The Director turned to listen while the argument began to lose steam. When the second one hit—

THUD!

—he was the first one to the door. He opened it, saw the fist-sized dents about eye level. Carefully, he looked outside.

49

Danny was halfway to the Mansion when he picked up the first rock. He didn't know why, but then he picked up another. He held the bottom of his shirt and cradled them like a hammock.

He launched the first one as he arrived at the bottom step. A direct hit, head-high. It went bang off the metal door like a gunshot. The stone skipped down the steps. He grabbed another one from his stash, yearning to hear that satisfaction again. He reached back—

Felt it ripped from his hand.

"What the hell you doing?" Zin tossed the rock into the trees. "You want to get killed?"

"They're already doing that, Zin."

Zin knocked his hand off his shirt and the cache of stones crashed on the bottom step. He grabbed Danny by the shirt. "Come on, before someone comes out."

He let Zin drag him a couple steps and pulled. "No."

The second rock sunk a dent as deep as the first and not more than six inches to the left. He was reaching for a third when Zin knocked him down.

"I'm not letting you commit suicide."

Zin was on his knees, chucking the rocks into the underbrush. They were going to get caught, but two rocks looked a lot different if there wasn't ten more waiting to be fired. He had just enough time to grab the two that rebounded off the door. The last one rolled out of sight just as the door opened.

The Director appeared in the doorway, wearing some kind of desert scouting outfit. His left hand rested on the hilt of a small sword. A fat old man pushed past him, followed by more.

"JUST KILL HIM!" Danny screamed. "He's not going to take the needle, so just go ahead and kill him, already! Put us all out of misery!"

Danny started up the steps. Zin caught him on the third one. He wasn't going to slip away again.

"I know what you're doing to us," Danny shouted. "You're a bunch of fat, selfish bastards!"

"What are you doing?" Zin hissed in his ear.

"If you don't want to just kill us, I will! I'll throw all of the boys over the cliffs." Danny jabbed at them. "We're all going over, anyway. We'll do it on our own!"

"DANNY BOY!" Mr. Jones stumbled down the steps. "Stop this foolishness, right this second. What has gotten into you?"

Another ten Investors were out the door, exchanging knowing glances. The Director's steely gaze never wavered.

"I'll tell you what got into me, go see Reed. Mr. Smith knows, he's doing it to him. He's breaking him. He doesn't want to take the needle, all right? Are you so desperate that you're going to kill him slowly for it?"

"He's just trying to help him, Danny Boy." Mr. Jones helped Zin restrain him. "You don't understand what's happening, you must trust us."

"Trust you?" Danny turned on Mr. Jones. *Constantino* was on the tip of his tongue. *Acquired,* too. He was about to spit them like darts. Had he, it would've changed everything. The Investors would've known their privacy had been breached. They would've condemned the Director without question. The program would have failed. Nobody would escape, ever.

But the Director's hand gently fell on Danny's shoulder.

"It's all right, son," he said.

Danny stopped struggling. Everyone said *son.* But the Director said it differently. It wasn't an expression, it meant something. And it fell quietly on Danny.

"Mr. Jones." The Director turned to him. "Let me have a word with Danny Boy."

All three of them – Zin, Mr. Jones and the Director – kept their hands on him, slowly letting go. Danny stared at the Director. He wanted to hate him, but there was calm in his expression.

"Gentlemen." The Director turned to the crowd inside the doorway. "We will proceed as usual. Remember why we've come together."

He turned to Danny.

"We're here to help," he said to the others. "Let's remember that."

No one moved.

The program teetered on that moment.

And then the Director led Danny away from the Mansion.

A man doesn't achieve that level of power without know how to handle pressure.

50

It was a narrow path. An overgrown one.

Danny trampled on leaves and fronds sheared cleanly by the Director's blade. The Director didn't turn around when Danny caught up to him. He was grabbing with the left hand and swinging the machete with the right. The jungle bent to his will as they made their way through it.

Sweat drenched the back of his shirt. Danny could hear his breathing between each swing. When they reach a small clearing where a tree had uprooted – its roots bare and dead. The Director wiped his head with a handkerchief and leaned against the massive trunk.

"Whew!" he said. "This trail hasn't been used in awhile, wouldn't you say, Danny Boy?"

Danny kept a healthy ten feet between them.

"It reminds me of the time I first discovered this place. Nothing but trees in this part of the island, nature taking back what mankind put in its way. Can you believe that was 30 years ago?" The Director looked up, shaking his head. "Goes by in a flash, Danny Boy. Cherish that youth, my boy, while you can. One day you're going to be fat and out of shape like me, son."

The Director pulled a drink from the canteen on his hip. He wiped his mouth with his sleeve and offered it to Danny. He didn't even bother shaking his head. He just stared.

The Director screwed the lid back in place and smacked his lips.

"Yes, sir," he said. "Thirty years ago, this was a dying resort for the super wealthy when I got here. I was going to resurrect it, turn it into an extreme vacation island resort with hiking and meditation and snorkeling. Maybe import some animals so it had a real jungle feel." He slowly moved his hand as if reading a banner. "Discover Your Inner Tarzan."

He laughed.

"Wouldn't have worked, Danny Boy. Stupid idea. The rich don't want anything to do with Tarzan and that's when I heard a higher calling. That's when I decided to help the world, to heal it one person at a time. This is a revolutionary program, Danny Boy. We're on the verge of taking mankind to another level in its evolution…"

He stared at Danny.

"But you've heard the pitch, I'm sure. I don't need to tell you. Right?"

The Director wiped his whole face, again, tucked the handkerchief in the upper pocket of his shirt. He leaned back and waited.

"That's hard to believe," Danny finally said, "after what you've done to Reed."

"I see." The Director nodded, thinking.

Danny clearly didn't understand what was going on. He was a kid. He needed an adult to explain the world to him.

"The brain operates like a computer, wouldn't you say?" the Director said. "It's got connections and information that form concepts and ideas. And computers are susceptible to corruption, like malicious code. Something that will disrupt its ability to operate normally."

"I've never fixed a computer with torture, Director."

"No, but you have reformatted one. Am I right? Of course, I am. You are a computer genius, there's no denying that, Danny Boy. You know that when an operating system is corrupt, sometimes it needs to be erased and reprogrammed from the beginning. It needs to relearn the right way to operate."

"There's nothing wrong with me."

"You don't know that, Danny Boy. You can't change and stay the same. In order to heal, you have to be willing to let go of the past. Be willing to let go of the programming that corrupted your soul to begin with. All you boys have a chance to be new again."

"Reed's almost crippled. He's broken. You're destroying him."

"Some are more damaged than others. I can only offer him salvation, Danny Boy. Only offer the healing, he has to take it."

"So you torture him?"

"It sometimes takes a strong hand to get people to let go of their past. People aren't willing to give up what tortures them. Every time Reed goes to the Haystack, he has the power to heal himself but refuses. I can't make him, I can only encourage him. He's got to trust what I'm doing for him, you see. Trust, Danny Boy."

"I don't trust you, Director. I don't know you."

"How do you know?" He raised his eyebrows, questioningly. "I could be the father you need to forget."

"No one on this island trusts." Danny tapped the back of his neck. "That's why everyone has a tracker, just in case. Including you."

"We're dealing with the human condition here, Danny Boy. Corruption, sin. People cheat if given the opportunity. These little things in the neck take that away. Makes everyone feel a little better. Good thing Sid had one, wouldn't you say?"

The Director smiled.

They walked for a long time, in silence. Their path was serpentine. The Director seemed to go out of his way to cut giant leaves when he could've just ducked under them. Eventually, the trees began to thin out. The soil turned to stone. A breeze howled down the path, rustling the leaves above them.

They stepped onto the barren ledge of a cliff. The ground was gray with granite and green with lichens growing in the cracks like whiskers and fuzz. It was the highest Danny had ever been on the island. None of the paths led to this spot. He figured if they continued to the right, they would eventually descend until they reached the beach on the north end.

The horizon was flat in both directions. The water deep, dark and blue. The Director wedged his hands on his hips and closed his eyes. He inhaled the ocean's scent.

"Don't you wish you could just be that, Danny Boy?"

He inhaled, again.

"The ocean, my boy. The smell, the sight… the life it contains. All of it, don't you want to be that?"

"How would I know?"

"What do you want, Danny Boy? If you could have anything in the world, what would you ask for?"

"I'd start with knowing who I am, but you took that away."

"I didn't take anything away, you didn't have it."

"Only I would know that."

The Director stepped closer to the edge. A half-step forward and he'd go a hundred feet to the bottom. He walked along the edge to a boulder that jutted up from the ground – flat like a table.

"This is where I had the epiphany, Danny Boy. I would come up here to sit every morning and this is where I received the calling. I knew what mankind needed. We needed to harness the power of the mind, the most powerful weapon a man possesses. If we can control the mind, Danny Boy, we get what we want. That's your answer, son. If you could have anything in the world, it should be the power of the mind."

The mind is a weapon.

"How can you torture us and call that healing?"

"Your body is a prison, my boy. You need to understand that through experiencing its misery. The Haystack is the best teacher you'll ever have. It forces you to face the body's desire, and the suffering that results. You take the needle, you see the freedom of the mind. That's all we're doing, son. Setting you free."

Danny wanted to flee. Everything about the island was wrong, but in the presence of the Director, it all made sense. The body was a prison. The mind was freedom. When he was inside the needle, there was nothing he couldn't do. Why was that less real than his flesh? He was still Danny Boy.

The Director picked up a handful of rocks and pitched them one at a time over the edge. "You went out into the Nowhere with the girl. She's been teaching you to be bad, Danny Boy. She gave you access to our mainframe and you escaped."

He peeked back.

"Didn't you, son?"

Danny didn't answer. There was no need to make it any worse. Now for the punishment.

"You're a true pioneer, Danny Boy." He threw the last rock as far as he could, grunting. "I tell all the boys they're a pioneer, but you are true-blue, Danny Boy. Amazing."

The Director smiled and laughed.

"You did something I never knew possible. You transformed yourself into pure mind. You became data without losing your identity. You were still Danny Boy. And I never thought that was possible, son. Always, I believed, the mind was rooted in the brain, it needed the physical body or it dispersed into random thoughts."

"The Nowhere. Is that what became of the boys before me?"

"Some of them. But you, Danny Boy. You went into the Nowhere and remained Danny Boy. She knew, didn't she? She knew you'd survive being out there, and once you did, you embraced it. You became it. And you were set free."

"How do you know her?"

"I know everything." He nodded, slowly. "Everything."

Danny walked back to the scrawny shade of trees and leaned against one, bending it with his weight. The waves crashed far below.

It's over.

"Is that why you brought me here? To throw me over the edge? Is that what you do with people like me and Reed, throw them in the ocean?"

Laughter. "Son, you don't understand what you've done. You've created an inner reality beyond the needle. Until now, all the boys were limited to Foreverland. Danny Boy, you created a new reality. A new dimension. I want to follow you out of the flesh. I want you to lead us to a new dimension of existence. Show us Nirvana, son. Bring us to the world of pure mind."

"You're wrong," Danny said. "I'm just a hacker. I just created an illusion, no different than a video game."

"We make our own reality." The Director touched his head. "With our minds."

"The reality you create with your mind, Director… that's the definition of delusion."

The Director shook the handkerchief out of his pocket and wiped his forehead, wiped his mouth. He went back to the ledge and put his hands on hips, losing himself in the view.

The cloudless blue sky.

Deep blue water.

Violent collisions on the boulders.

"They want you out, Danny Boy." The Director didn't turn around but said it loud enough for him to hear it. "You, Reed and Zin… you know what that means, don't you?"

Danny didn't want to answer. A lump swelled in his throat. Despite the anger burning his spine, fear had the trump card when it came to survival.

"The program is a delicate thing, Danny Boy. It has balance. When a candidate is rebellious, it tips the scales. These men have a lot invested in you boys. A lot of time, a lot of money. They don't want to see the program come down, a lot of people will get hurt. And sometimes it makes sense to sacrifice a few to save many."

Danny was sure that he had thrown people from the cliff. There was no doubt. It was neat and clean to crush them on the rocks and let the fish destroy the evidence. Not that anyone would find a body even if it was staked to the side of the cliff. This was the Director's island. He was judge and jury.

The Director strode away from the ledge in a meandering sort of way, head down with his fingers buried in his beard, scratching the hidden chin. He knelt at the edge of the trees and broke off a branch, twirled it.

"But I see something in you and Reed." He looked up. "Something this program needs, Danny Boy."

He walked over, looked down.

"I need you to show us what it can become."

The stem spun between his fingers like a helicopter stick with green blades. He plucked one of the leaves and crushed it in his palm, cupped it over his nose and inhaled with his eyes closed, savoring the fragrance.

"Take this." He put the leaves in Danny's hand and closed it. "Steep it in hot water for five minutes and give it to Reed. It'll relieve his suffering. He'll find peace."

"How do I know it won't kill him?"

The Director bit the tip off one of the leaves and chewed. "If I wanted him dead, I wouldn't send you to do it."

Danny put the leaves in his pocket.

The Director went back to the tabletop stone where he had his epiphany and leaped up. He stretched back with his hands on his hips, once again gazing at the view.

"This is your last chance to get Reed inside the needle, Danny Boy. The Investors are powerful men. I can only do so much."

He sat down and crossed his legs into a pretzel. His back was straight, his hands in his lap, he closed his eyes. Breathing, in and out.

Danny left him there so he could become one with the view. He had some tea to make.

51

Danny sat at the picnic table. A plastic cup was in front of him. The water had turned light green with shredded foliage floating on top. He fished them out – one by one – with a stick, steam wafting out. Occasionally, he'd look at the door at the end of the dormitory where an empty golf cart was parked parallel with the building.

The tea smelled like diluted turpentine. He put the cup to his lips, not too hot to drink. The aroma made his eyes water. He didn't sip. He wanted to save all of it.

The dormitory door opened. Mr. Smith limped to his cart and slid on the seat. Danny waited a few minutes before going inside, taking the cup with him.

The door was locked.

He should've known it. Mr. Smith knew he was coming back. Danny tried the door knob again, turning it with both hands, then put his shoulder into it. There was nothing in the hall, nothing like a fire extinguisher or a baseball bat to bash the knob off.

He went back to his room, looking for something heavy. The only thing was the sink. He could get that off the wall and drive a hole through the door big enough to crawl through. But that was only going to make things worse. Reed would be locked away in vault. Danny would never see him again. Maybe a rock on the doorknob could get it open without too much notice. There would be something at the beach.

He left his room—

Zin was on his knees, poking wires into the lock. It clicked. The door swung open.

"I told you I remembered everything," he said.

The room smelled like dirty socks rolled in bacon. The lights were out. There was a lump on the bed.

At least it wasn't convulsing.

Danny closed the door, quietly. He knelt next to the bed and put his hand on the lump.

"Reed." He shook him. "I need you to drink this."

No response. He shook him harder. Maybe he was finally sleeping and Danny was messing him all up. But he shook, anyway.

"Come on, man. Wake up."

On the fourth try – one more and he would quit – Reed rolled over. His hair, matted to the side of his face. His face, caved beneath the cheekbones.

"It's Danny Boy," Danny said. "Drink this, man. It'll make you feel better."

The tea was still warm. Reed tried to lift his head.

Danny reached under the pillow and picked his head up. Reed's hands were somewhere under the blankets. Danny lifted the cup to his lips. Reed was on the edge of convulsions. He winced and tried to pull away. Danny wouldn't let him, pouring the astringent water into his parted lips. It spilled down his chin but he swallowed – against his will – until it was all gone.

He dropped back down, breathing heavy. His eyes closed.

Danny could've stopped this from happening to Reed if he just called for help. It was his fault they were still on the island. His fault they might never leave. Reed could be in a proper hospital with medicine and doctors, not sunk into a sweaty mattress. He'd die on the next round.

If he makes it that long.

He sat there a while longer. Reed slept.

"Hey, come on." Zin stuck his head in the room. "Let's go already."

Danny left. He looked back. There was no more quivering.

Danny followed the path out to the tabletop cliff for more leaves, then remained there until the end of the day. He snuck into the cafeteria late at night and stocked up on food, eating in his room. He was back out to the tabletop cliff before the sun was up, watching the water catch fire beneath the sun's burning rise.

He returned with more tea. Reed didn't shake as much. He lifted his head on his own, drank more than he spilled. The room still smelled like a corpse. Reed still looked like one.

It was the third day he brought tea that Reed was sitting up.

"Get me out of here."

Zin and Danny walked across the Yard. Reed was between them, a hand on each shoulder. His shirt fluttered like a sheet thrown over bones. His skin was something like the yellow of old parchment.

People stopped what they were doing to watch.

"Mind your own business," Danny shouted. That only made it worse.

It was a relief to reach the beach. Reed was exhausted. He sat back, the sun on his face.

"Give me some time," he said.

So they did. When they came back to get him, he was still in the same spot. They walked back to the dormitory. He draped his arms over them, dragging his feet. They carried him to his room. The window was open. The stink still lingered. They carried him over to Danny's room so he didn't have to sleep in the smell. It had sunk into his clothes.

Mr. Jones was inside. "Where have you been, Danny Boy?"

"Helping Reed." They dropped him on the bed. Zin picked his legs up, put them on the bed.

"This is not appropriate. Mr. Smith will want him in his own room."

"The bed is ruined. He needs some rest before they kill him."

Danny arranged the pillow so Reed's head wasn't at an odd angle. Zin pulled the sheet over him. Mr. Jones watched them close the curtain.

"I'll be in Zin's room," Danny called.

Mr. Jones followed them out, stopped them from closing Zin's door. "Danny Boy, I don't like what's going on."

"Yeah, neither do I."

"Is there something you want to tell me?" Mr. Jones said.

"You go first." Danny held onto to the doorknob, waiting. Mr. Jones had the sense that someone much older than a thirteen year old boy was looking back. "I'll see you when the next round starts," Danny said.

The door closed.

Mr. Jones suppressed the urge to pound on the door. The insolence. The disrespect.

He tried to have compassion for these boys' plight. They were confused and distressed. They needed space to process everything. But something was going on and he didn't like it. He felt the need to slap Danny, knock some sense into him. But he didn't want to upset the program. Any more stress and it would only slow things down. Besides, there were signs Danny was wearing down. Soon, he'd come close to graduating.

He just had to be patient.

Reed was different.

Perhaps he needed to consult with Mr. Smith. He'd been here longer than Mr. Jones. He'd know what to expect from Danny. Besides, he should know what they were doing with Reed.

52

Mr. Jones lived on the west wing. His penthouse was an apartment with enough square footage for a family of four. Even so, he only lived in a small portion of it to cut down on cleaning and cooking.

He walked down the empty hallway, rounding the corner in the foyer onto the veranda. The chairs were still arranged in a half-circle from their meeting with the Director. There would be another soon, he believed.

Mr. Smith paddled on top a floating board in the swimming pool. Mr. Jones went to the end of the pool. Mr. Smith grabbed the ledge and looked up.

"I would like a word," Mr. Jones said. "I don't trust what's going on. The Director, the boys… they have things on their mind."

"You believe they're planning an escape?"

Mr. Jones shook his head. "I think we should cancel the next round and call another meeting. Maybe the boys need to be reset."

"Everything is back on track. They have Sid ready to graduate. Besides, I don't have time to start over, Mr. Jones. The clock is ticking for this old man. It's now or never."

Cancer is an impatient foe.

"Have you seen Reed?" Mr. Jones said. "You might live longer than him."

"He's young, Mr. Jones." He floated on his back, spitting water. "His body can recover once he gives it up. There's nothing I can do about this body."

He drew a long breath and went underwater. He frog-kicked to the steps and pulled himself out. Mr. Jones handed him the towel. Mr. Smith dried off and collapsed into a lounge chair.

"Do you ever feel guilty?" Mr. Jones asked. "What we're doing to them."

Mr. Smith draped the towel over his neck. “They had their chance at life, Mr. Jones. The mind is a terrible thing to waste. And so is a perfectly good body.”

He put on sunglasses and laid his head back. Mr. Jones watched him. He was lightly snoring within a minute.

Mr. Jones left him.

He’s right. They had their chance.

53

Danny went out to the tabletop cliff with a bag of food.

He wouldn't return to the dormitory. He had enough food to sustain him until the next round started. Reed had enough leaves, too. He could make all the tea he needed. Danny just wanted to be alone. He needed to think. He needed a plan. One that would make it their last round, ever.

There were rumors that Foreverland was getting smaller. It still worked, but they couldn't get out to the water or fly as high into the sky without running into the Nowhere. Lucinda had something to do with it. Danny knew it. And the Director did, too.

There was only one way to stop him. Only way to be sure. They couldn't wait for someone to save them.

Danny knew what he had to do.

The trees rustled behind him.

Danny was sitting on the tabletop, legs crossed, practicing his breathing when Zin emerged from the forest.

"It's almost time," Zin said.

Danny unfolded his legs. "Where's Reed?"

"He's on the beach."

They started back down the path. Danny looked back at the view.

It would be the last time he would see it.

Reed was sitting on the sand dune.

He wanted to get up, walk the beach. His body began to ache again. He reached into his waistband and pulled out a long leaf. He stopped bothering with tea. He chewed the leaf, instead, spitting out the coarse fibers and swallowing back the acrid flavors that stuck in the back of his throat.

The healing compounds surged into his blood. His muscles let go. Nerves relaxed. A mellow cloud drifted through him and he tingled with pleasurable numbness. The ocean seemed to surge through him, each wave pulsing in his groin. He sat there, smiling.

Life is beautiful.

He wanted to try the water, feel it on his ankles. One more time. He might be flying high, but he was lucid enough to know this could be the last time he'd ever get a chance. They would come for him, take him to the Haystack again.

He wouldn't be leaving it.

He rolled onto his hands and knees. He would straighten his legs first then try to throw himself upright. He started with the right leg—

"It won't work."

She was there, to his left.

Her hair glowing fire.

Reed blinked, shook his head. But she was still there, her butt planted in the sand. Her hair fluttering.

"You can't do it, Reed," Lucinda said. "You don't have the strength. You don't have much of anything. It's just about over."

He collapsed back to the ground. A pile of mashed leaves was between his legs. *How many did I eat?*

"I think it's time you went inside the needle," she said. "You've waited long enough."

He closed his eyes and covered his ears. His heart thumped inside his head.

But she was still there.

"I'm serious." Her eyes were big and green. "There's nothing to lose now. May as well come to me, Reed."

"I thought…" he started. No. He wasn't going to talk to her. She wasn't sitting there. He was alone on the beach. She was in his dreams. She was in Foreverland. She couldn't be sitting there next to him. He wasn't going to acknowledge it.

"I agree." Another Lucinda said on the other side of him. There were two of them. "You should come inside, Reed. You're not leaving the Haystack. You may as well come to Foreverland."

"But…" He dropped his head into his hands. *No. No, no, no…*

"I know about the dreams," the first Lucinda said. "I know we told you to stay here, but now that's over. The end is here, baby. I think it's time you come inside."

"No." He clamped his hands over his ears, eyes tightly closed. "This isn't happening."

"We've waited long enough." He could still hear her.

"I'm not going." He shook his head. "I'm going—"

She touched his arm.

He fell back, pushing away from her—

"Reed." Danny stood over him, his hand out. "You all right?"

He looked around. The Lucindas were gone. Danny and Zin were there. That was it.

"I think…" he said. "Yeah, I'm all right."

He relaxed, melting into the warm fuzzy euphoria of the leaf juice.

He wanted another.

Danny and Zin heard him talking.

They thought he'd fallen asleep sitting up, but he was shaking his head. He jumped back like he'd seen a ghost. Green flecks stuck to his chin. Half-chewed leaves were scattered at his feet. *Good.*

They helped him stand. "Can we walk to the water?" Reed asked.

His legs were sticks. They stopped just where the foam skidded over the firm, black sand, splashing over his bare feet. He smiled a strange smile, a dreamy one. Closing his eyes.

"I'm going to miss this," he said.

"Not me," Danny said.

"I'm with Danny," Zin added.

Reed hummed to himself, wiggling his toes into the sand. Danny and Zin let their shoes become soaked, propping Reed up as he began to slouch.

"She wants me to go inside the needle," he said, slurring. "After all this, she said I should come inside."

"You can't," Danny said. "That's what the Director wants you to do."

"You said she was alone."

That was before I knew she was a memory.

"Reed," Danny started, "I was wrong. She's not…"

He stopped. It was better not to tell him.

"Listen, I'm taking the island down. I'm going inside the needle first and stopping everything. The Director has to be stopped. I'll bring down the power and ignite all the trackers. It's all coming to a stop, we're going to hijack the island. It'll all be over. Foreverland is going to disappear and everyone has to be out of it when I do it."

Reed nodded. A moment of clarity. "You're right."

"You won't suffer anymore." Danny tucked a handful of leaves into his waist. "Eat these, man. Zin and I will go inside the needle and be out before they can do anything to you."

"Are you sending for help?"

"If I can send for help, I will."

Reed wasn't going to recover no matter. Danny would send for help, but it wouldn't get to the island in time to save him.

The Haystack bell sounded.

Reed began chewing another leaf. Danny thought about telling him the truth about Lucinda. She *was* real Reed. And she *loved* you.

But she's gone.

54

The Director opened the cage. The birds squawked. They were rarely let out. On occasion, he would reach in and let one perch on his arm. If he set it down, he'd leash its foot to a stand. This time, he carried them both to an open window. He set them on the ledge and walked away. They turned around, watched him pull the floral shirt off and drop it on the floor.

He scratched at the curly brown and gray hairs on his chest, stepped out of his flip-flops, then his shorts. Naked, he went to the bar.

A Bloody Mary for the road.

It felt so good to be free of clothes. It would feel even better when he was free of the skin.

Today was the day he transformed. Today was the day he shed his flesh and soared to higher planes. It had been thirty years in the making, and now it was here. He swirled the tomato juice into half a glass of vodka. It would be the last time he would need a drink. From that day forward, euphoria would be on tap.

"Director," the intercom called. "We're ready down here."

"Very well, continue. I'll be down after the round is complete."

He lied. They could get started, but they'd never finish.

His plans were carefully laid out. He wouldn't need them anymore. Wouldn't need anyone.

The Haystack bell rang.

The Director finished his drink while the group walked toward their final round. He waited until a trio of boys crossed the Yard – one propped in the middle of the other two. Once they entered the path leading to the Haystack, he placed the drink on a table and slid onto the chair. The material stuck to his skin but was soft and warm. The rollers whirred beneath his buttocks. He sunk into the cushions.

The needle was greased and ready.

It entered his brain.

Here I come, world. Ready or not.

55

Reed's head bobbled.

Danny and Zin walked sideways to get down the narrow path. Reed was throwing a lazy step for every two steps they were taking. They were almost carrying him by the time they reached the Haystack.

Mr. Smith was standing at the entrance. Reed's lips were tinted green. He wouldn't feel a thing. Danny wanted to give the sadistic old bastard the finger, standing there with his hands behind his back, waiting patiently for Reed.

Danny and Zin began turning to walk Reed through the door. "Stop there, boys."

"He can't walk." Danny cleared his throat, tried to take the venom out of his tone. "Mr. Smith, he can't walk on his own. He's messed up, as you know."

"You won't be going inside." Mr. Smith didn't hide the smirk.

"What are you talking about?" Danny said. "The Director told me we were all going to do this round, you can ask him."

"I don't need to, son. He changed his mind. You and Zin will be sitting out this round."

The other boys were going to their cells. Reed's chin was touching his chest.

"I don't believe you," Danny said.

"I don't care." Mr. Smith put his hand in his pocket. "You can ask the Director, but right now you're going to let go of Reed. If you don't, I'll drop you on the ground. You're familiar with that feeling, aren't you, son?"

Smile.

Danny pulled Reed back. The old bastard would have to zap him, if that's what he wanted. He wasn't giving him up. Zin got between him and Mr. Smith, like that would stop the tracker. The old man smiled bigger. He was going to enjoy this.

"Danny Boy." Mr. Jones came out of the Haystack. "It's true, son. The Director gave us new orders to postpone your round until this one is over. It's only temporary, my boy. I promise."

He reached out, but Danny jerked away.

Mr. Smith took a step forward, reached deeper in his pocket. Mr. Jones put up his hand to stop him. He looked sad. Remorseful. Pleading with Danny to stop the foolishness. Mr. Smith would drop him if he didn't.

Danny took Reed's arm off his shoulders. Mr. Smith ducked under it and took Reed's weight. He needed Mr. Jones to help with the other side. Together, they walked into the Haystack.

Reed's feet were dragging.

Just before the door closed, Mr. Clark could be heard announcing from inside. "Clothes on, gentlemen. The Director has granted you reprieve."

"Something's not right." Danny paced outside the door. "None of it makes sense. No suffering, clothes on. Something's not right, Zin."

He looked at the closed door.

"He knows."

"Who?" Zin said.

"The Director. He knows I was going to blow up the island. He locked us out and now something big is going down. I got a bad feeling, Zin. I got a bad feeling Reed isn't going to hold out. He's going inside the needle."

Zin took a knee at the door, inspected the lock. He could pick it. They could go get Reed as soon as the Investors were gone. But that would only delay the inevitable. And make it worse. The Director would toss them over the cliff for sure.

There were no needles anywhere except the Haystack. Even if they could find them, they wouldn't work. Putting a needle in his brain wouldn't automatically take him to Foreverland. There had to another way to access the island, another way to hack into the system.

"I got it."

Zin turned around. “What?”

“We got to get to the classrooms.”

Zin didn’t know what he was thinking, but he didn’t bother asking. They were running across the Yard.

56

"Stand up, son." Mr. Smith sagged under Reed's weight. "You're not helpless."

Reed's feet flopped behind him. Mr. Smith and Mr. Jones struggled to get him in the cell and lower him to the floor. His arm slipped from Mr. Smith's grasp and his face kissed the concrete.

"Goddamnit." Mr. Smith put his hands on his hips, huffing. He looked around the cell, deciding how to make it work. "Let's push him against the cell door and then we can hold him from the outside."

Mr. Jones helped pick up Reed. It was difficult. He flopped against the bars, knees buckling. They maneuvered around him. Mr. Jones went to the aisle first, holding Reed under the armpits. Mr. Smith quickly jumped out next, catching Reed as he slid down. They were able to hold him up and close the door.

"Go on." Mr. Smith pushed Mr. Jones out of the way, harnessing Reed by wedging his arms beneath the armpits and grabbing the bars. "I'll hold him until the round starts."

"You sure?"

"Yes, yes! Now go, I'll be out in a moment."

The boys in the other cells watched the spectacle silently, fully dressed and waiting. Mr. Smith looked at the empty cells next to his. There were two of them.

Danny Boy and Zin are gone. The Director made the right decision, those boys would be a distraction. They'd be trying to keep Reed from the lucid gear. This has gone on too long.

Mr. Smith met with the Director the day before. The slob stood over his damn telescope sipping whiskey while Mr. Smith – for the thousandth time – made suggestions.

"It's now or never," the Director said. "Let's make it happen now."

Mr. Smith, if he was honest, was shocked. The Director agreed to everything Mr. Smith asked to do. He'd leave Reed in that cell until he either took the lucid gear or died.

And that was fine with Mr. Smith. He had grown weary.

Sweat ran on both sides of his face. When Mr. Jones closed the door, the skylights went dark and the lucid gear dropped. The boys quietly pulled their gear to the floor and slid it over their heads. In moments, the only sound was Mr. Smith's labored breathing.

Then the cell walls began to click.

The back wall continued moving until it pressed against Reed's back. Mr. Smith heaved him up one more time before removing his arms to avoid being pinned. The wall pressed him tighter. Tighter. And tighter.

Reed let out a groan. His eyes opened.

Something popped in his chest before the pressure eased.

"Last chance, Reed."

57

The floor wasn't stable.

It was like walking on a platform that was balanced on the end of a pole. No matter which way Reed leaned, it was too far. He tried to compensate but couldn't find the tipping point.

When the old men got him to his cell, he crashed.

He tasted blood and the acrid tang of green leaves. His chin was numb.

"He's a pig. He wants you to die."

She was in the next cell. Her hair was long. Red. He couldn't make out the features, his eyes too swollen, but he recognized Lucinda's voice.

She squatted so she was eye-level. Grabbed the bars.

"Disgusting pigs."

Hands grabbed him, again. Heaved him against the cold bars. His knees refused to lock. His arms, noodles. Old breath was in his ear.

Door slammed.

Lights out.

And then the clicking of the cell. And the squeezing. The pressure.

The pain.

It cut through the leaf-induced fog.

A rib popped.

He couldn't breathe. His breath burned in his chest. And the cell squeezed. It would crush him.

And then it relaxed.

Reed sucked in air that sliced inside his broken chest. He tried to stop, but he had to breathe. And each one hurt so bad.

The cage remained tight enough to hold him up.

Mr. Smith, his old spotted face, was inches away. His eyes relaxed, limp and uncaring. He told Reed *last chance*. This was his last chance. Reed knew what that meant. He knew he would die in the Haystack this time.

Grateful it would finally end.

"Don't let them win." Lucinda was behind Mr. Smith. "They want to keep us apart. If you die, they win. This old, rotten bastard… wins."

Reed tried to speak, but there was only enough space inside his chest for a ragged breath before he needed another.

"Don't fight it," Mr. Smith said. "There is peace inside Foreverland, Reed. There is no need to suffer."

A breath.

Pop.

"I…" Reed ran out of wind.

Mr. Smith was unsympathetic. Unmoved. Eyes of grey, uncaring.

"I hate you." Reed whined with the next breath that cut deeply into his rib cage. His eyes streamed tears. Not sadness. *Hatred.*

"I want…"

"Stop, son. I didn't do this to you. You have steadfastly refused to help yourself. You have no one else to blame. You can put a stop to it right now. Let's end it, my boy."

Mr. Smith put his hand on Reed's cheek. Meant to comfort, it was stiff and cold.

Reed quivered. Head convulsing. He kept his breath shallow and braced for the pain.

He spit in Mr. Smith's face.

"Get… out." He squeaked. "Get out."

Mr. Smith stepped back. He wiped the pink saliva off his face, unable to control the stern anger that pinched his brows and hid his eyes in shadows. Stiffly, he marched away, pulling his dead leg along.

Lucinda remained in the aisle. Smiling.

Reed closed his eyes. A sob escaped. He tried to control it. It only hurt inside. But when she reached out, when she touched his face, it was warm and loving and kind.

His tears grew hotter.

58

The Director was not surprised to see that the sky had been consumed by the Nowhere. He felt it getting smaller. Foreverland was disappearing into chaos. It wouldn't be long, but he wasn't too late.

He assumed a body that, for all intents and purposes, looked like the one lying on the chair at the top floor of the Chimney. Minus the belly and wrinkles, he looked like the Director in the flesh. Perhaps a little more youthful and glowing. A body worthy of an immortal.

He walked across Foreverland's Yard. It had not changed much since the first day he had visualized it. In the very beginning, he decided that his alternate reality environment would look like the island. It didn't really matter what it looked like. When he invited the boys into it, they didn't seem to care since they could do anything and be anything.

After this trip, he would escape the confines of Foreverland and burst into the universe like the Big Bang. He would be much bigger than his own little mind. He reached the edge of the Yard and leaned against a tree. Then melted into it. He became the tree. He waited patiently for the boys to arrive. And one at a time, they did. Until they were all there. Just about all of them.

The Director had a change of heart.

After much thought, he decided Danny was, indeed, too dangerous to let free inside Foreverland. He had progressed much too quickly. It was too much of a risk that he would control everything this time. And if he got control of Foreverland, he would control the Director. There was a chance he might even crossover into the Director's body and abandon him in the Nowhere, lost in his own mind.

All would be lost.

The Director formed a thought-command. He learned that from watching Danny. He willed all the boys in the Yard to disperse. He willed them into the Nowhere. He felt their identities loosen, watched them scatter like molecules set free. They drifted like vapor into the gray fog where their identities would unravel never to be what they were before that. Their bodies would remain vacant in the Haystack. Some might call it murder.

When the Yard was clear, he waited.

And when the time was right, he willed himself into another body, this one in the likeness of a red-headed boy with freckled cheeks. And, next to the sundial, he appeared as if Danny Boy had returned. The Director walked around and looked surprised.

The girl fell from the sky like the Goddess of the Nowhere.

She meant to snag Danny and pull him into the Nowhere. Instead, Danny grabbed her.

She had taken the bait.

Danny turned into a bearded man. He smiled at her.

"At last, we meet."

She squirmed but it did no good. The Director wrapped his mind around her and squeezed.

The first of many screams rattled in her throat.

59

Danny and Zin took the steps three at a time and threw the door open.

The library was quiet and empty. Lights hung from the vaulted ceiling, softly illuminating the rows of bookshelves.

The main desk was to the right. Mr. Campbell – one of the oldest looking and slowest moving men on the island – was straightening a pile of papers. He looked up with a stiff neck.

"Hello, boys," his voice rasped. "I'm closing the library. It'll be open tonight sometime."

"Mr. Campbell." Zin took a second to catch his breath. "We just need to get a book for a… for a report that's due… soon."

"Well, you'll have to come back tonight when we open."

"Please, sir. We've fallen behind on our studies and just want to make sure we do things right this time. We're serious about our studies, sir. We'd like to better ourselves, our minds and bodies. We'd—"

Danny elbowed him. "Just five minutes, Mr. Campbell. And then we're out of here."

Mr. Campbell carried the papers to the shelves behind him. It took so long they thought he might have forgotten they were there.

"Five minutes, boys."

Danny and Zin took off.

"And no running," Mr. Campbell said, forcefully. "This is still a library."

"Laying it on a little thick back there, don't you think?" Danny said. "We just want to check out a book, not rewrite the Constitution."

They turned down an aisle, the shelves towering over their heads.

"You know these geezers, they love it when we do our best."

They turned right at the end of the aisle, moving along the wall with the classrooms along it. Danny stopped at the one in the corner. He could see the cabinet in the corner of the classroom.

"That's the one. Do your dirty work."

Zin took a knee, pulled wires from his pocket and inserted them into the lock. Danny walked away, looking down the aisles. He could hear Mr. Campbell sorting books at the front desk. The wires were clicking in the doorknob.

"What's taking so long?" Danny whispered.

"I can't get it."

"I thought you were an expert."

"I never said that."

Zin dropped the wires and went to the nearest aisle, looking quickly through the books.

"What are you doing?" Danny ran back to the door. "We don't have time…"

Zin reached to the top shelf and pulled a thin, spiral-bound book down. He slowly ripped the plastic cover off the front and pushed Danny out of his way. The cover was flimsy but stiff. Zin inserted the corner between the door and doorjamb. He moved it up and turned the knob.

It clicked open.

"I take that back." Zin stepped out of the way. "I am an expert."

Danny quietly closed the door. Zin stood outside. He moved through the room, plowing into one of the desks up front. He stopped, moved more slowly this time.

The box of tablets was on the bottom shelf.

He grabbed one and moved to the wall next to the door so no one could see him. He turned it on.

His hands were shaking.

This is it.

If he screwed this up, they were all dead. He had to hack the Chimney's security system, find the power grid to shut down the island and the trackers to knock everyone out. He had two minutes.

Maybe three.

60

Mr. Jones waited patiently outside the Haystack.

He heard groaning inside.

It was the sound of a tortured young man.

When Mr. Smith opened the door, he was followed by hoarse cursing. Mr. Smith was told that he could go to hell and burn forever. He closed the door behind him. His eyes were dead.

He shook his head.

"I'm sorry," Mr. Jones said. "Is this really necessary?"

"It is his end. He has a choice."

Mr. Jones did not reply. He did not care to think too deeply on the subject. He had agreed to come to the island. He knew what they did and he agreed to be part of it. He could not judge.

Not now.

"Mr. Williams is prepping Sid to crossover," Mr. Smith said. "We should go witness. Perhaps we will be next."

"Your method may destroy your investment, Mr. Smith." Mr. Jones couldn't stop himself. "What good will he be to you then?"

"Bones can heal, Mr. Jones." He looked away. "Much quicker than mine."

They climbed onto a golf cart and cruised down the path. As they crossed the Yard, they both noticed the white parrots flying out of the top floor of the Chimney.

They stopped the golf cart next to all the others.

The Investors had all arrived at the Chimney to watch Sid's graduation and crossing over. If they were lucky, they wouldn't have to wait for the Director to finish the round. Sometimes the crossover took place without him, when there were no issues. They needed to have very few problems. They needed to be assured everything was on course, that when it came their turn to cross over it would happen without a problem. Mr. Jones didn't like the way things had changed.

He didn't like a lot of things.

They stepped onto the elevator and held the door for late-arriving Investors. They arrived at the fourth floor. There was only one hallway. Halfway down, there was a door on the left, another on the right. The one on the right was the network computer room. Mr. Jones had never been in that room. There was no need, he knew very little about that part of the program.

He followed the others to the one on the left.

They passed Sid lying motionless on a bed, a needle protruding from his forehead. A cable was attached to the needle, plugging into the equipment that was beside the bed. The technician, Mr. Jackson, pulled the curtain across to hide Sid's Investor, Mr. Williams, lying on a bed parallel to Sid's. A needle protruding from his head as well. Eyes closed.

Mr. Jones averted his stare.

He did not like thinking of the needle. He imagined it would feel like a cold, steel nail when it came to his turn. He hoped it would be quick and numb, that he wouldn't remember it. That when it came his turn for the crossover, he wouldn't remember any of this. That he could leave all the memories in the past, start a new life.

He followed the Investors into the side room where they would watch the progress. It would be quite boring. Many of them resented being forced to sit in the waiting room like outsiders. Mr. Jones didn't mind it so much. He could sit in a way that he didn't see the needle sticking from the boy's head. And he didn't have to smell the antiseptic that clung to the back of his throat.

He got comfortable in one of the chairs at the back, happy to let the others sit in the front row. Besides, the air vents were on the ceiling and aimed at the back wall. It was a relief to have fresh air on his face. The room was so stuffy.

He leaned back and folded his hands over his belly. He thought, maybe, he might take a short nap. It could be hours before there was any progress. It was like waiting for a baby to be born. It was like that in more ways than one. And sometimes, when the crossover was slow, they went back to the Mansion.

You never knew when the delivery would take place. You just hoped you didn't miss it.

His eyelids became heavy.

61

"Okay, my boy." Mr. Campbell's voice was muffled outside the door. "It's time to lock up. I hope you boys found your books because I have a meeting to attend."

Danny's hands were slick with perspiration.

He stopped to take a breath in order to steady his hand. It quivered over the scrolling text and he needed to be touching with accuracy. He had circumvented the security without setting it off and located the power grid. It would be simple to overload the power distribution and cause a blackout but he needed to find the tracker net before he did that or he wouldn't be able to activate them and there would be a horde of old men looking for them.

"Yes, sir," Zin answered. "We got them, thank you for letting us find them. You know, we don't want to waste any more of your time, but you know how important it is that we do well in our studies. They say that a brain that is active in studies is one that will be stronger and healthier. In fact, research has shown that higher brain activity increases the—"

"Where's Danny Boy?"

"I'm sorry?"

"Son, you're playing games. Where is Danny Boy?"

Found it.

The tracker net wasn't difficult to open. He had gotten past the hardest part of the security system, but the database of trackers was large. He did a quick search for names, located his own tracker. Now he need to find Zin… Zin…

Brain cramp. He couldn't remember Zin's real name.

"He had to take a dump, sir," Zin said. "He ate some spicy food at the cafeteria an hour ago, I think it was a bad burrito or something. Anyway, he was—"

A shadow passed in front of the window. Danny moved down the wall, all the way to the corner, squatted behind the last desk. He did a global search for…

The cabinet is open!

Keys jingled outside. “Son, you better locate Danny Boy in the next five seconds.”

Metal connected with metal as the key slid inside the lock.

The knob turned.

Danny crouched down as low as he could, inputting a global search for *Zin*. Dozens of names scrolled over the interface. He went down the list. Everything with a Z was showing up. No time for another search. He went through the names.

The light went on.

Cameron. Nicholas. David.

Mr. Campbell stepped inside. Shuffled over to the cabinet.

Anthony. Benjamin. Theodore.

Closed the door. Looked around.

Hayden. Dane—

He saw him, stooped in the corner. Cheeks flushed, Mr. Campbell moved his hand quicker than Danny thought possible.

ERIC ZINDER!

Mr. Campbell’s hand reached inside his pocket—

Danny punched the tablet.

The classroom went dark.

Desks slid and tumbled. Mr. Campbell fell into a heap of overturned chairs. He lay motionless, hand buried in his pocket.

Eric Zinder was still highlighted on the tablet.

“Cut that sort of close.” Zin leaned inside the room.

62

He had drifted away – how long, he couldn't say – when the rattle of the air handler went quiet.

The air stopped blowing.

The lights went out.

The room was pitch black.

"What the hell is going on?" someone said.

Mr. Jones felt a tingle on the back of his neck. He had never had the sensation before. He was told that the tracker was installed for his own protection, that everyone had one in case something went wrong. Even the Director had one. But, he was assured, no Investor ever had experienced the unconsciousness brought about by the tracker voltage that shocked the nervous system and overloaded the senses.

But they all felt it.

It was sudden. Like a hot wire spiking the back the head.

The old men dropped like sacks of meat.

Mr. Jones's foot twitched in the dark. He would never experience pain that intense again. He would never feel anything again.

None of them would.

His last thought. *We deserve this.*

63

The Director walked around the sundial, taking his time to let the grass slip between his toes. The gray Nowhere had blotted out the blue sky, descending like a plague of locusts.

She thought she could take his world.

Not anymore.

The girl was on her hands and knees inside a circle of dirt. She wouldn't escape the ring where the Director focused all his attention. He willed her to experience her flesh curling off her bones, willed her to sense the smell of fried hair and boiling bones. None of it actually happened to her.

But she felt it.

He took a knee. Her red hair hung over her face, shimmering as she convulsed. He lifted her chin. Her face contorted. Eyes filled with tears.

"It's all over, *Lucinda.*"

She lunged, snapping her teeth at his hand. He pulled back, laughing.

She cried out, curling into a ball.

Now that she was out of the Nowhere and into the open, he knew everything about her. *Everything*.

"You know what you are, don't you?" he said. "You're just a thought. A memory. You're nothing different than data. You are a reflection, a shadow, of a girl that once lived. A girl that is now dead. Your body has long since fed the worms. How does that make you feel?"

He waited.

Her skin fluttered in waves. Her nervous system fired uncontrollably. It appeared her flesh was trying to strip itself from her body.

"I am Foreverland, Lucinda. This whole existence," he stood up, waving his arms, turning in a circle, "that you've been trying to destroy is me. It is my mind that creates this. That's why I'm a little bitter you've been pissing on it."

He wiped the hair from her face so she could see him.

"You're one dimensional, darling. You can't understand what I've done to help people. You don't know what I've sacrificed to give them a new life. I pulled their memories from their damaged minds to heal them.

"At first, Foreverland was just a computer program but it didn't work. It was too scripted, too artificial. Their identities didn't survive and they turned into vegetables. I discovered they needed an alternate reality that's organic. I became that, Lucinda. They plug the needle into their brains and transfer their identity into my mind where they can live their fantasies. Where they can heal their lives. I am the beautiful mind that heals them. I am the new dimension of existence."

He leaned closer.

"And you tried to take that away. Shame on you."

Another wave of pain. She shook, bouncing on the ground. This made the Director smile. He began pacing around the circle, observing the trees barely visible in the gray fog.

"I gave you life when I pulled you from Reed's mind, Lucinda."

He breathed the sweet air.

"You're dead, but I made you live, again. And how do you repay me? A thank you? Maybe a kiss on the cheek?"

He looked down on her trembling body.

"You're an ungrateful little bitch. But not for long."

She was inferior. He could control her, but he couldn't destroy her. And as long as she was inside Foreverland – inside his mind – she would be a distraction. But any moment now, his solution would arrive and absorb her, take her out of Foreverland—

"I know what… you are." Her words scratched her throat. "I know… what you hide… from yourself."

Something vibrated in the Nowhere.

"Your true memories…" she said. "The ones… you want… to forget… I know what you are."

Something buzzed around the Director.

He closed his eyes, but a thought still entered him. A boy's voice, pleading. It came from above.

No! No, please, please don't! Please! PLEASE!

"You are not who you believe. You try to forget…" She sat up. "What you've done."

The thought he heard was more than a voice. It was a vision. A young boy, his African skin was black. His arms skinny.

His eyes, empty.

A needle in his head.

Stop. Stop, stop, stop… STOP!

The Director spun and pointed. "WITCH!"

Lucinda was lifted by invisible hands. A stake emerged in the ground, her hands bound behind her back. Kindling at her feet.

"You will poison me, no more," he said.

He refocused his efforts, pushed away the thoughts of dead and dying children, willed them back into the Nowhere. Pushed them far away until he forgot them, until he was strong again. Sure of who he was. He was a man that brought healing to the world.

The 21st century Buddha.

A body began to form near the sundial. Translucent and fetal.

The Director smiled. He released the girl from the witch's stake. She collapsed in a pile. *Pathetic.*

"Your end has arrived."

64

Reed tried to count a breath. Tried to be with the pain.

He could not.

The bars were crushing him; his chest had no room to inflate. His breaths were shallow, quick and stabbing. When he supported some of his weight, the bars would relax. He had more room to breathe. But that brought more pain. And there wasn't much feeling left in his legs.

The lucid gear brushed the top of his head.

"They want to keep us apart." Lucinda stepped out of the dark aisle. "They'll win."

"They—" He grimaced, took a dozen tiny breaths. "They want me to take the needle."

He went limp. The bars squeezed. He whined.

"Why do you think they brought you to the island?" She reached out.

The room was darker.

Reed couldn't see the ceiling. Or the fan.

But he could see her. Like she was in a spotlight. Her fingernails candy red. Like her hair.

She reached for him.

"They want to keep you away from me. They don't want us together."

Her fingers touched his ribs. Cold numbness spread across his ribcage. She traced up his side, to his arm, numbing a path as she went. It was cold and freezing and pleasurable.

He took an easy breath. It came out smooth.

Her hand was on his shoulder.

Touched his collarbone.

Erasing the pain.

"I can't," he said. "I won't—"

"You die. They win."

A black tunnel closed around him, ate up the cells across the aisle. Closed in behind Lucinda as she leaned closer. Her lips were full. They touched his ear.

"Bastards," she whispered.

The pleasurable numbness spread across his face.

Down his neck.

"I miss you," she said.

Her fingertips touched his lips. His upper lip frosted over.

"I miss you, Reed."

His lips fluttered.

"Tell me," she said. "Tell me."

"I…"

She hooked her finger beneath his chin. Sensation left his bottom teeth.

"I miss you." He closed his eyes.

Let her lift his chin.

Let her lift the crown of his head into the lucid gear.

The strap tightened around his scalp. The knob snugged up to his forehead. He was losing feeling in his head, but could feel the coldness of the needle searching for the hole that had healed long ago. It sensed the stent embedded in his skull and centered over it.

Lucinda's lips hovered over his.

The needle shot through.

Cracking the skin. Piercing the frontal lobe.

His head snapped back. He saw a bright light. His body stiffened against the bars. Crackled. Then let loose.

He went inside the needle with his eyes open. Head cocked to the side.

Body, limp.

He went to Foreverland.

65

Danny and Zin left Mr. Campbell in the classroom. They didn't bother to check his pulse.

They stood outside the entrance of the building. The sun was up. The sky was blue. It was like any other day, except for the four bodies in the Yard.

"How long did you put them out?" Zin asked.

"I don't know. I just activated every tracker in the system, besides ours." He looked at the tablet. "I think I hit them pretty hard. And I crashed all the solar and hydrogen power systems, so everything's off. Well, everything except the building with a backup generator."

"Which one is that?"

"Guess."

The Chimney was pouring smoke.

"We can stop him," Danny said. "This is our chance. Maybe our only one."

"What about Reed?"

Danny looked at the tablet. There was no telling how much time the trackers would keep the Investors unconscious. He could always zap them again, assuming the system didn't lock him out this time.

They sprinted toward the Haystack.

The Haystack smelled like sewage and piss.

Maybe that was how it always smelled during a round, they weren't used to it. But it was stronger, more pungent. Danny's eyes watered when they entered. It took a few moments to adjust to the darkness. They went down the aisle, past their empty cells—

Reed was crushed.

"Oh, no." Danny got there first. "Oh, no, no, NO!"

Zin was on his knees, working the lock. Danny could tell, even in the dim light, that Reed's face was blue. His tongue swelled in his mouth.

"HURRY, ZIN!"

Zin fumbled with the lock, but it was taking too long. Danny reached for the lucid gear—

"Don't take that off!" Zin shouted. "It's too soon, he might be in there and won't be able to come back if you take it off."

"It doesn't matter." His hand brushed Reed's cheek. It was cold. "He doesn't… he shouldn't have died like this."

Danny slid the black strap off his head. The needle was wedged firmly in his forehead. It came out like a cork. Watery fluid leaked from the hole.

The lock clicked.

Reed's dead weight threw the door open. Danny caught him before he hit the ground. Zin helped lay him down and started to arrange his hands in a dignified manner.

"Not in here," Danny said. "I don't want him staying in here anymore."

His body was limp, but not as difficult to carry as it should've been for someone his age. He weighed less than Danny. They stopped outside the door.

"Let's take him to the beach," Danny said.

Zin shaded his eyes, looked at the sun. "We don't have time."

Danny retrieved the tablet. He was right. There was no telling when someone would recover. Once the island was back to full power, there would be nowhere to hide.

They left Reed's body outside the Haystack, hands folded over his chest.

Eyes closed.

Dozens of golf carts were parked around the Chimney.

Danny and Zin hid in the trees, just in case someone was watching. No one was in sight, awake or unconscious. Danny started out first. Zin made a lot of noise.

He was holding a stick the size of a bat. "Just in case."

Together, they crept to the front door. Still no one. Nothing.

Danny took a deep breath. "We're in deep, man. There's no going back, now."

"So what are we waiting for?"

Zin started to inspect the lock. Danny yanked the handle and the door opened. No jokes, this time. They moved cautiously inside. The ground floor was open floor space with bunches of comfortable furniture and tables for informal meetings. Large monitors were mounted on the large cylinder elevator, showing an overhead tour of the island on a continuous loop. It looked like an area to entertain company or tourists. Or potential clients.

They stepped inside the elevator. There were four buttons.

"Where's the fifth floor?" Zin asked.

"Fifth floor is the Director. No one goes there, he brings them."

"Where then?"

Danny dragged his finger over the tablet, rearranging data and tapping commands. He searched the Chimney for clues. "Most of the power consumption is on the fourth floor."

Zin pushed number four. "We have a winner."

The doors closed slowly. The floor shifted. The elevator began a slow ascent, the numbers ticking off above the doors.

Second floor, we have the doctor.

Third floor, where we wake up.

The elevator eased to a stop. Number four appeared. The doors jerked a bit, then began to slide open. Zin cocked the stick. Danny stood off to the side. They waited.

The hallway was reflected on the back silver wall. Empty.

Tentatively, they looked out.

One hall. Nothing branching out, just one long hall. Near the end, there was a door on the right, one on the left.

Someone was on the floor, halfway inside the left door. Legs in the hall.

"It's Mr. Lee."

Zin gently rolled the old Asian man onto his back. He felt cold. Zin put his fingers on his throat, looking for a pulse. He didn't really know how to do that, so he put his ear next to Mr. Lee's mouth and listened.

"I think he's dead."

"Oh, man." Danny looked at the tablet like it would tell him what happened. But he knew. "Oh, man."

"It's not your fault, Danny Boy. You weren't trying to kill him."

Danny shook his head. He didn't want to hurt anyone, despite what the old bastards had been doing. He just wanted off the island. He wanted his life back.

"What the hell?" Zin went inside the room. "Is that Sid?"

Danny followed.

There was a hospital bed with white sheets and a curtain next to it. Sid was on his back, hands folded over his chest and a needle poking from the center of his forehead. Danny approached with the tablet at his side. Zin cocked the stick back, ready to swing.

Sid looked skinnier than usual. Sort of gray. His mouth was open, breathing. At least he was alive. Danny followed the wire from the end of the needle to a machine next to the curtain.

"What the hell is going on?" he said. "I thought he already graduated."

Maybe that was the last step, one last trip to Foreverland where they download the rest of the memories, all reprogrammed for a better, more efficient mind.

Danny reached for the curtain—

"Take a look at this, Danny Boy."

Zin was looking inside a large window with the stick at his side. It looked like a waiting room. Danny could see the old men piled on the floor as he stepped up to the glass. They must have been standing there, watching, when Danny ignited their trackers. Some of them had knots on their heads where they hit the floor.

Mr. Jones was in the back, laid back on a lounge chair. His fingers laced over his belly. He couldn't tell if he was breathing.

Zin tried the door. "Want me to pick it?"

"No."

He didn't want to find out if he killed all of them. Especially Mr. Jones. The guy cared about Danny in his weird way. He didn't want to live with the thought that he accidentally murdered him. Even if Mr. Jones did *acquire* him.

Even if his name was really Constantino.

"What's over there?" Zin asked.

It appeared that the room was fairly large, separated by the curtain. Zin snuck up to it with the stick ready for action. Danny grabbed a handful of the fabric and yanked it to the side—

A flash of silver.

Zin wasn't fast enough to stop the aluminum table leg from cracking Danny's hand. The tablet hit the floor, the glass screen spiderwebbed. The old man jumped back, table leg back and ready for another swing. Danny got behind Zin, his hand already tingling.

"You all right?" Zin asked, faking a swing at the attacker.

"What the hell you kids doing up here?" the old man said.

"None of your business!" Zin shouted. "What the hell you still doing awake?"

The old man huffed, his eyes darting around. "You did this? You knocked out the power and killed the Investors? You did this?"

He shook his head.

"You boys are done, you hear me? You're done, out of the program. You had your chance but you're finished now. The Director will be down any second."

"Why is he still awake?" Zin muttered back to Danny.

"I don't know. Maybe he wasn't on the tracker net."

"And neither is the Director," the old man said. "You can say goodbye any second now. Any second."

He stepped behind the hospital bed that was on the other side of the curtain, this one parallel to Sid's. An old man was on it, same position as Sid and a needle in his head that was attached to the same machine. They had never seen an Investor with a hole. They never went to Foreverland.

"Isn't that Mr. Williams?" Zin asked.

Yeah, thought Danny. *Sid's Investor.*

Side by side, same machine. Needles in their head.

That's how Parker graduated. And when he was done, they never saw his Investor again.

After that, Parker began parting his hair on the left.

"What the hell is going on?" Zin said.

"I think I know."

66

Reed felt nothing.

Saw nothing.

And liked it.

He'd been trapped in a broken body for too long. He couldn't remember the last time he was without pain. *If this is death, then it is sweeter than imagined.*

But it wasn't death.

He drifted in the black nothingness, his identity drawn inside the needle, drifting toward Foreverland. He only knew the sweet release.

But another body formed around him. This one firm and pain-free. Curled up. Fetal.

He clutched at tufts of grass with his eyes tightly closed. There was wind in his ears. Light on his face. There was sound—

"Reed."

Her voice. It was feeble. It was near.

It was not a dream.

He blinked. A blurry layer of fluid smeared over his eyes. But he could see her. She was out of reach. She was on the ground, curled up like he was. Her head turned so that she could see him.

Blink. Blink, blink, blink.

Her lips quivered. Her body shook. She was in pain.

He tried to move his hand, tried to reach for her, but he couldn't feel his body enough to control it. Barely felt the ground below him. But his heart ached. He couldn't reach her. Couldn't help her.

Couldn't save her. Again.

She managed to crawl out of the circle scratched from the grass. She pulled her body over the ground, dragging her legs behind her. Her breath was labored. Tears in her eyes. She stopped to gather her strength, then pulled herself closer. One handful of grass at a time.

Until her breath was on his face.

"Where am I?" he asked.

"You're with me, my love."

Her hand, convulsing, reached out. Gently cradled his cheek. Warm and soft.

And he remembered.

Lucy.

He knew her when he was very young. He stopped a boy on the playground from pulling her hair when they were seven. She watched him in church, leaning forward and smiling at him from the end of the pew. He watched her at basketball games, with her friends.

They held hands in the back of a friend's truck on the way home from a concert. Their fingers interlaced like broken pieces that belonged together.

Their first kiss was on the couch when her family was gone.

He remembered her smell.

The memories returned, and filled him. All the joy. All the pain.

She put her arms around him. In a full embrace, they merged. His body became light. It became sweet.

He was home.

The bitch is a liar.

She manipulated the memories in the Nowhere to fool the Director, to make him forget who he was. He was not those things. He was not a murderer, he was a savior.

He felt Reed arrive near the sundial. His body appearing like a full grown baby, naked and curled up. So helpless.

And the Director felt such happiness.

He's here.

The air shifted. Suddenly, it was not so heavy. The gray seemed lighter.

Reed couldn't move. He was lucky to open his eyes, to see his memory – the bitch – in front of him. The Director released her from the confining circle so that she could crawl to him like a wounded animal.

Specks of gray flitted from the sky, penetrating them like tiny bullets the closer she got. And when she touched his cheek, it rained gray pellets. They had become a magnet the Nowhere could not resist. When they embraced, they absorbed the lost identities that filled the Nowhere.

And in a burst of light—

An explosion—

A thunderous clap—

Foreverland expanded into infinity.

The Director closed his eyes, shielded his face from the burst. And when he opened them, they were gone.

Not a hole in the ground, not a depression, no sign they ever existed.

And the blue sky reached into the heavens.

And the ocean reached the horizon.

In that moment, he realized how puny Foreverland had become. Now it was all existence. He was free. For the first time in his life, he was free.

Enlightened.

He was these things. He created them. He was a god, after all.

And it was finally time to act like one.

To stretch out, let the world know who hears their prayers.

He reached out, feeling a connection with all of Foreverland. His body, back in the Chimney, was of no use to him now. He was free to be his mind, to be whatever he wanted. He dissolved into the air, his identity drifting like vapor, like the data Danny Boy had demonstrated.

The Director moved his identity into the Chimney's network where he would slip out into the world, melt into the vast web of data that inhabited homes and businesses and governments. He would know everything. He would be everywhere.

I'm God.

The computers bent to his will, the network did what it was told. And as he streamed through the Chimney network, as he passed through his last portal, just before he graced the world with his omnipresence, a room formed around him. He didn't recall this avenue.

It was a large room. There were shelves all around, filled with books.

A pedestal in front of him.

A book slid off one of the shelves near the ceiling, floating like an invisible hand had pulled it and brought it to the pedestal. There was a name on the front.

Harold Ballard.

He willed the book to be gone, for the room to disappear. He was ready to leave. But none of that happened. The book remained. And it opened.

And the Director witnessed Harold Ballard's past.

Foreverland faded into sunbleached colors.

First the sky turned lighter blue, then white. Then the ocean followed. Whiteness crept over the trees. It was a different kind of nothingness, not filled with random memories of lost identities but the void of non-existence.

Foreverland was ending.

Reed walked out of the trees just before they evaporated.

He crossed the Yard with the white void nipping away the ground behind him. He went to the sundial. Put his hand on it. Just like she told him.

And he was absorbed by it.

He left Foreverland as it ended.

Forever.

67

Why didn't we see this before?

It seemed so obvious, now that the answer was lying in a pair of parallel beds. An old man and a young kid, their brains wired to the same machine.

"Don't you see, Zin? They kept us physically fit and exercised our brains. They let us doing anything we wanted so that we were happy. The put our memories inside the needle and made us go after them. You said it yourself, you just wanted to leave. You belong inside Foreverland."

Zin was squeezing the stick with both hands. His face relaxed but his hands didn't.

"It's a body farm," he said.

"Every Investor has a kid," Danny said. "And when the kid graduates, we never see the Investor again, do we?"

Zin stepped toward the old man. "Oh, we saw one of the Investors. We saw one inside Parker's body."

"How are we doing so far?" Danny asked the old man.

He backed into the door, slid all the way into the corner, the table leg held in front of him like a four-sided long sword.

After Danny went inside the needle the very first time, the old men were telling Mr. Jones that *he got a good one.* Yeah, he got a kid that would graduate soon. A smart one. And Mr. Smith was so desperate because Reed refused to cooperate. The amount of money it took for them to *acquire* one of them had to be a lot. These were billionaires from all over the world that refused to die. The Director showed them a way that they could live another 70 years. All they needed was a kid that no one cared about and bring him to the island so they could lure him out of his body, scatter his identity into the Nowhere until his body was empty.

So they could take it.

"The rich old bastards?" Danny said. "None of them are using their real names. It's all regular names like Jones and Smith. None of them really want to know who each other are. They aren't helping us, Zin. They're just kidnapping kids that no one will miss, kids with a troubled past and no connections. Like you and me, Zin. No one's looking for us. No one will notice when our bodies return to the outside world. Without us in them."

"You're done," the old man said. "You'll go right in the oven for this."

Danny grabbed the back of Zin's shirt before he charged. The table leg was shaking in the old man's hands. Zin tried to get loose.

"WHY ISN'T HE KNOCKED OUT?" Zin shouted.

Danny shook his head. "Doesn't matter. Tie his ass up, we'll figure it out later."

"Don't come near me." The old man reached behind him while holding his table leg in the other hand. He scattered the items off the table, swung his arm around with a syringe in his hand. He pulled the rubber cover off with his teeth.

"There's enough in here to kill one of you," he said. "Come after me, and one of you dies."

"If someone has to do, then I vote for you." Zin raised the club over his head.

Danny stopped him, again. "Don't hurt him."

"Are you kidding me?" Zin didn't drop the stick. "Weren't you listening to your own story? He's one of them… he's some rich old bastard that's going to kill one of those kids out there and steal his body. If we ace this old bastard, we save the kid. Eye for an eye, Danny Boy."

He poked the stick at him. The old man hit it like they were dueling.

"Who's your kid?" Zin asked. "Which one of us were you going to steal, you sick bastard, huh? Did you import a nice little Kenyan for your next life?"

The old man's head was shaking as bad as the table leg. Danny's grip loosened. Zin stepped closer.

"A Kenyan too dark?" Zin said. "How about a Canadian, they got nice white skin, you might like that better, you know with racism and everything. It might make things easier."

The old man pointed the needle at Zin, then Danny. Back to Zin. His eyes darted back and forth with the needle.

"We didn't hurt you boys," he said. "No one got hurt."

"Oh, no. That Haystack was a blast," Zin said. "We loved freezing our balls off."

"But you didn't get hurt, we just make you uncomfortable so… so…"

"So you could what?" Zin said. "So you could kill us with kindness. You're demented. You're the ones sick in the head. You're the ones that deserve to die."

"You wasted your lives!" The old man dropped the table leg and held the syringe with two hands like he was going to squirt it at them. "Maybe it wasn't your faults, but it didn't matter. You were going nowhere, your lives were a waste of time, you didn't need your bodies to continue a life of misery. Trust me, you were heading for a lot more suffering than that Haystack. You would've ended up in jail or killing someone or something worse. The Investors have lived good lives, they've helped a lot of people, and they deserve your bodies a lot more than you."

"It's murder, and you know it," Danny said. "I don't care what you say."

"You choose to leave your body," the old man said. "You reached for the needle, you went inside it. We didn't make you, it doesn't work that way. You have to want to leave your body. All we did was make it uncomfortable and you did the rest."

Danny thought about the two splotchy purple lines down the front of Reed's chest where the bars had crushed him. He wouldn't cooperate. So they killed him.

Danny pulled Zin back and shoved the corner of the bed against the back wall, pinning the old man in the corner. "Knock the needle out of his hands, Zin. Just don't hurt him. Not yet."

"Are you kidding, I'm going to knock the brain out of his head."

"No, don't. I want him tied up and alive. He doesn't deserve to die, not yet. I want him alive when the authorities get here—"

The old man genuinely laughed. "Stupid kids. No one's going to find this place. It's been operating for over thirty years, you think a couple rogue teenagers are going to bring it down? There are trillions of dollars that protect it. The rich stay rich, son. And they stay alive."

Zin swiped at the needle, narrowly missing. The old man tried to back up further but continued to smile. They couldn't charge him with that needle and they'd wasted enough time. Danny wheeled the bed back a few feet, put his weight into it and shoved it like a battering ram into the old man's gut. He picked his leg up to absorb the blow at the same time Zin took a full swing. He caught the old man on the hand, knocking the syringe into the wall. It skittered across the floor.

Danny pulled the bed out. "Grab some of those wires, Zin. We'll lace his ass to the bed—"

"That's enough, boys."

It was the one voice that could freeze them.

The Director stood in the doorway with his hand in his pocket.

68

"I need you boys to step over to the booth." The Director pointed to the observation window. "Just do as I say."

Danny didn't move. Zin was fingering the stick like he was deciding if the next pitch would be a strike.

"Boys, you realize I'll knock you into next week." He wiggled the hand in his pocket. "And it won't be any kinder than what you've done to the Investors. Now step away from the bed and plant your backs to the wall. Do it, now."

The Director stared them down.

The man had exceptional skills, some sort of hypnotic spell he cast just by looking. It didn't matter if it was a rich, power-hungry oil baron or a juvenile delinquent, he knew how to get people to do what he wanted them to do. And the boys did just that.

Zin lowered the stick and followed Danny. Neither one of them turned their back on the Director. It wouldn't matter, all the power he needed was in his pocket, the miniature controller that activated trackers. And the boys knew it.

"Are you all right, Mr. Jackson?"

Was he all right? The island was filled with troubled youth. An occasional uprising wasn't surprising, but when half the Investors drop dead and two little maniacs show up with a stick to knock his brains out his ear? No, Mr. Jackson was a little less than all right.

But the Director had arrived. He would put things back in order. He always did. You don't run an island like that for thirty years without ironing out a few wrinkles.

"We've had some problems, Mr. Jackson. I'd like to start in the network room."

Mr. Jackson cradled his hand against his chest. It was probably broke. The Director moved the bed out of his way. He wasn't concerned about the Investors or the aborted crossover lying in the bed.

"Problems," Mr. Jackson said. "Yeah, I think we need to start in the observation booth, Director. Some of the Investors don't have a pulse."

"Yes, we'll get to that. First thing's first. Let's have a look at the network room."

The boys watched them cross the room. Mr. Jackson kept his distance. *Why doesn't he just knock them out?*

The Director was barefoot. He let Mr. Jackson lead the way. They stepped over Mr. Lee – spread-eagle in the doorway – and crossed the hall to the only other door on the fourth floor.

There were endless racks of servers in the network room that went up to the ceiling in aisles that paralleled the curvature of the building. The network room took up half of the fourth floor. Midway around the semi-circular room was a large monitor with continuously scrolling data.

Mr. Jackson sat down. His left hand took the majority of Zin's stick. He couldn't move his fingers. *Broke, for sure*. He placed it gently on his lap and worked the mouse with his right.

"What the hell happened?" he asked. "Power is out on the entire island. The Chimney only has about three hours of charge left in the backup generators. And the Investors…" He looked back. "How could this happen?"

The Director stood behind him, arms crossed, staring at the monitor.

"Something unexpected happened, Mr. Jackson." He fiercely scratched his beard. "Call up the Looping Program, please."

"Looping…? That's not active. We shut that down after Danny Boy hacked into it and thought it was the outside world."

"Humor me."

The Director was acting weird. He was an odd-ball, but none of this seemed all that alarming. Things went wrong, but never at this magnitude. And now he was concerned about some insignificant computer program.

"All right, well, let's see." Mr. Jackson executed a few commands, the screen went blank. More data came up. He leaned closer and squinted. "That's strange. It's been activated. How did you…"

"What's in there? Tell me what you see."

Mr. Jackson wasn't aware that the Director couldn't decipher the data.

He used his good hand to peck out a few more commands to interpret what he was seeing. It didn't seem possible, but there was an identity inside the Looping Program that was often used to mimic the illusion of Foreverland, but they didn't use it that often. An identity could be damaged if it spent too much time solely in the artificial circuits of the network. That was why the Director had become the interface between the boys and the network, serving as an organic "computer" that became Foreverland.

But now there was someone in there. Someone got left behind. Everyone should be out of the Haystack.

Mr. Jackson leaned closer. He could see just fine, the monitor was six feet wide. He leaned closer because he couldn't believe what he was seeing. Couldn't believe who it was that was inside the Looping Program.

"Tell me what you see," the Director said. "Tell me."

Mr. Jackson turned slowly. His lips were moving, finally uttered, "Password, Director. Give me the password."

The Director stared back.

Mr. Jackson waited.

And waited.

He knew what he had seen inside the Looping Program. He saw the identity that was trapped inside it.

And then he saw the Director put his hand inside his pocket.

Mr. Jackson didn't flinch. Didn't try to escape. He just waited for the darkness of unconsciousness to arrive.

It was painless, when it did.

Mr. Jackson crumpled in the chair, falling to the floor in a heap.

He didn't see the Director watching him. Didn't see the Director look at the meaningless data on the monitor. The

Director couldn't interpret it, but Mr. Jackson's expression told him everything he needed to know. Asking him for the crossover password to confirm who the identity was inside the Director's body.

Mr. Jackson also didn't see the Director go to the window and begin to weep.

69

"Something's not right," Zin said. "That guy has no mercy and he tells us to just hang out after we just brought the whole island down? No sense, Danny Boy. It makes no sense."

They leaned against the wall like they were told. They looked through the window at the Investors, still motionless. Some of them were breathing. Occasionally, they'd twitch like the tracker was still hitting them with a low dose of voltage to keep them out. Danny didn't feel so sad about Mr. Jones, not after putting it all together. Maybe he did care about Danny, maybe he did want the best for him while he was here. It didn't matter. In the end, the old bastard brought him here to steal his body.

And that could not be forgotten.

Zin was hunched over Sid, looking closely at his open eyes. Danny walked around the bed toward the back wall.

"Where you going?" he asked.

"I'm not waiting around to get zapped." Danny put his hand on the doorknob.

"Hell, if you're going to do that, let's just get out of here."

"And go where? We can't outrun this." Danny smacked the back of his neck. "Let's see what else these old bastards are up to."

Zin thought for a second. He was right behind Danny.

The room was fairly dark, lit only by a few backlights beaming up the wall near some of the desks and the faint glow of tiny lights flashing on computers and various machines.

The room was dominated by a large stainless steel table in the center with a big lamp hanging from the ceiling. A number of shelves and steel carts held more computers or medical equipment.

"Think they did surgery in here?" Zin asked.

"I don't know."

It didn't look like surgery. There was just the one table and too many computers. If anything, it was an autopsy room.

There were nine doors on the wall to the right arranged in three stacks of three. Like a tic-tac-toe board. The doors were only three feet by three feet. Danny had seen doors like that on TV. They were used to store bodies. Pull the handle and the bed would slide out just like a filing cabinet with a plastic bag and a body inside.

He touched the handle on the one in the center. *Did they deep freeze a new candidate until they were ready to suck out his memory and scramble his mind with random ones? It would be so claustrophobic inside. And what if they woke up?*

He yanked the handle. An empty slab rolled out with a cloud of frosty air. It was a freezer. They were storing bodies in sub-zero temperatures. Nobody would survive that. *Did they just hold the old men in these things after they crossed over into the candidate's body?*

He had his hand on another handle—

"Danny Boy."

Danny jumped. Zin scared the hell out of him.

"Come here." He had his hands around a small window on the other wall. "You need to see this."

Zin stepped aside to let Danny have a look. The window was on a heavy-duty door. There was a slab inside but it wasn't like the freezers on the opposite wall.

"Watch this." Zin punched a button next to the door.

The interior lit up with blue flames. The room flickered with an eerie glow.

"A crematorium," Danny said. "They burn bodies in there."

"You thinking what I am?"

Danny nodded.

Once the Investor crossed over, their body was empty. They had no use for it. So they cremated it. That's why the Chimney smoked whenever someone graduated. It was the Investor's body they were destroying.

"Boys."

They jumped back. The crematorium's blue light illuminated the Director standing in the doorway. His eyes flickered with strangeness. Danny and Zin backed up.

"I need to show you something." He turned around and left.

Danny and Zin waited for him to come back. After a minute or two, they found him across the hall in the network room. He offered the chair in front of a large monitor to Danny. They moved slowly, suspiciously. The Director stood several feet away from them, but distance didn't matter. Not with the controller in his pocket.

Danny sat down. The Director told him to tell them what he saw on the monitor.

It took Danny a few minutes to understand what he was seeing. He was able to interpret the information and it became apparent who was standing next to him. The Director was inside the Looping Program, even though his body was standing next to him—

"It's me, Danny Boy." The Director held out his arms, displaying his new body. Tears brimmed on his eyes. "I made it out."

Zin was a little shocked to watch Danny hug the Director.

70

Harold Ballard's mother was a beautiful woman. She was tall and slender and – given the right breaks in life – could have had a career as a model. Instead, she was committed to a psychiatric hospital. She received electric shock therapy on three separate occasions. Each time she returned home, things were better before they got worse.

Harold's father was a genius. He was an unassuming fellow with glasses that sat crooked on his nose. He was nothing close to model-quality. Seeing him with his wife at a party, one would guess he had tons of money.

He did.

He was recruited by every computer manufacturer's research and development department. He was, arguably, the most sought after man in the computer industry; that is, until he was fired for unethical practices. His crimes were never made public, but the word behind the scenes had tainted his reputation enough to make him untouchable.

No matter. He didn't need to make money, not with the number of patents that belonged to him. His basement had become his laboratory.

Harold was their only son. He was not pretty, not ugly. Not brilliant, not stupid. What he lacked in looks and raw intelligence, he made up for in cunning.

He was never allowed in the basement. Instead, he spent his nights looking at the stars through his telescope. But during the day, he shot squirrels with a pellet gun. He'd put birdseed on a plate in the middle of the yard and hide in the bushes. He'd lie there sometimes for an hour, pretending the enemy was coming over the fence, and then he'd plug the first squirrel that dared to grab a sunflower seed right through the eyes. Sometimes he'd nail them to a tree, put them in poses of the crucifix. The yard stunk like death, but his parents never went back there.

He was a loner at school. He was the weird kid with weird parents. His mom was crazy and his dad a nerd. The jocks put rotten food in his locker and the burnouts tripped him in the hallway. At the bus stop, Blake Masterson got on his hands and knees behind Harold and John Lively pushed him over. They laughed, all of them. Even the girls.

That night, Harold climbed on the roof with his pellet gun and a high-powered scope. He was up there until his fingertips were numb from the cold. When John Lively – who lived two doors down – walked outside, Harold put a pellet in his left eye. It was an amazing shot.

The doctors saved his eye. No one ever found out who did it. But John knew. Off the record, everyone knew.

They caught him getting off the bus.

Even though Harold wasn't physically fit, he got away by swinging his book bag and losing his jacket when they grabbed it. He bound up the steps of his house and through the safety of the back door. But John and Blake didn't stop there. They went inside after him. Harold threw the kitchen chair at them and ran through the basement door.

He stumbled down the steps, falling all the way to the bottom. There was a sharp pain in his wrist. He rolled into the corner and watched John and Blake stalk him. But, halfway down the steps, they stopped.

Across the room, there were two bodies lying side by side. One was his mother. The other, his father.

Needles sticking out of their foreheads.

Harold's father was arrested after John and Blake told their parents what they saw and the FBI showed up with search warrants three days later. The computers were confiscated. The needles, too. Harold went to live with his grandparents. He rarely saw his parents after that.

But he picked up where his father left off.

Computer-Assisted Alternate Reality (CAAR) had been banned from all developed nations as cruel and destructive to all forms of life. No animal would be subjected to the debilitating effects that plagued the users of such technology, invented by his father.

But a dictator will look the other way when the bribe is big enough.

Harold used his trust fund to begin CAAR research. He set up labs in Mexico, Ethiopia, and Somalia. He went through thousands of unwilling subjects. None of them were healed in any way. They all died. All destroyed. Sometimes, tragically. Sometimes, horrifically.

The body continued to live, even though the person – the identity – was destroyed.

While some would view his research as a failure, as a crime against God, life and humanity, Harold saw it as an opportunity. The world was run by a small percentage of very wealthy people. The only thing these powerful men and women could not purchase was more life. Death was non-negotiable.

Not any more.

Harold found the island. He found the money.

And he continued destroying.

Eventually, he used his own technology to rewrite his life, erasing all his memories and the atrocities he'd committed. He came to know himself as a good-natured man that served the best interests of humanity. A man of God.

He even shed his name.

And became known as the Director.

The Director knocked the book from the pedestal.

His rage burst out like a telekinetic tidal wave, wrenching all the books from the walls and ripping out their pages and setting them on fire. The room shook and cracks opened on the ceiling, raining bits of concrete on the marble floor. He searched for an escape, a way to dissolve back into data and escape the library, to slip back into the network and find a way back into the world. He might even go back to his body and DESTROY THE BITCH THAT DID THIS TO HIM!

But then he found himself standing in the library, again, the shelves reassembled, the cracks repaired, the books back in order.

And a pedestal in the center with Harold Ballard's book opening to play out his history.

He experienced it again.

And again.

And again.

71

Lucinda laid the trap.

The Director was right, she was getting smarter. His only mistake, he had no clue just how much she knew. In the end, she knew everything.

When Danny was caught in the Looping Program, she knew he was not in the real world. But it gave her access to all of the Chimney's data. Danny was only able to see a few of the records – his and Reed's – before he returned to the Nowhere. But Lucinda absorbed it. She knew the real purpose of the island, she knew all the Investors, and she knew the Director's true past.

She knew everything.

She also knew that the Director would eventually get Reed to go inside the needle. And when he did, she would cease to exist. She would return to being a memory. She was not sad about that. After all, it was her true identity. In fact, she yearned for it. Being away from Reed had been… difficult.

But what she couldn't accept was the future of Foreverland and all the boys it would continue to destroy to satisfy the gluttony of men.

While the Director ruled Foreverland – he *was* Foreverland – Lucinda ruled the Nowhere. She knew all the random thoughts, all the lost boys. She knew, also, the Director's thoughts and his desire to be free. She knew the Looping Program was a dead-end, a virtual cul-de-sac with only one way in, one way out.

She laid the trap.

He attempted to leave the island through the only data conduit to the outside world and, like Danny, mistook the path into the Looping Program as the way out. Before he recognized his mistake, the door closed behind him, trapping him inside. Lucinda had programmed the loop with the data of all the island's records, most importantly that of Harold Ballard. He would see his true identity, his authentic past. He would exist in the loop until he knew what he had done. As long as there was power on the island, the Director would live in the hell he created.

Lucinda also knew that Reed's body was beyond repair, that he would likely be physically dead. With the Director's identity in the Looping Program, his body would be abandoned and vacant. When they embraced, he absorbed her. No longer conscious, she was part of him. Her thoughts and memories of her time in the Nowhere became part of Reed.

He knew everything, too.

Including her best laid plans.

When the Director exited Foreverland, Reed couldn't go back to his dead body. But he made his exit, as well. And entered the Director's body at the top of the Chimney.

My body, now.

72

Danny was on one end of the bag. Zin on the other.

They let it rest on the floor of the elevator until they reached ground level. Zin was blowing on his hands to warm them up. Ice crystals had formed on the bag.

They managed to get it outside without dropping it. They slid it onto the bed of a cart. They both began blowing on their hands. Zin took the wheel. They drove away from the Chimney.

The Yard was bustling.

It was another day in paradise and all the boys were outside, playing cards, throwing discs and everything else. Not an Investor in sight.

Danny checked the tablet. A few strokes of the finger told him the old men were all exactly where they were supposed to be. The Mansion.

About half of them survived the prolonged blackout. Mr. Jones was not one of them. Most of their bodies were sick with disease or just broken down with age. They didn't tolerate the voltage. They relocated the survivors to the Mansion and left them a note that the island was under new management and they would be staying inside the Mansion until further notice. Then they locked the doors from the outside and had not heard from them since. Danny occasionally checked the location of their trackers, just to be sure.

The only indication of the old men that was outside the Mansion was concentrated inside the Chimney. The Investors that died were put inside the freezers, some stacked two high. They could have cremated the bodies but it made sense to preserve as much evidence as possible. Someone would have to sort through everything.

They drove the cart through the Yard. No one paid much attention to the body bag. The boys were told that the Haystack was closed until further notice. Until then, it was unlimited game room and no suffering.

No one argued.

They drove over the sand dune.

A man was in a hole about waist deep, shoveling a pile of sand next to him. He had a round belly and shoulders red from the sun. His face was clean shaven.

"Slow down there, old timer." Zin pulled up behind the man. "You're not a teenager anymore, you know that."

Reed tossed a shovel full of wet sand off to the side and leaned on the handle. He was breathing hard. His cheeks red with exhaustion.

"Got to get this fat ass in shape," he said.

"You can't do it in one week, son."

Reed rubbed his smooth chin. The beard was the first thing to go. It was smelly and itchy. How they hell the Director walked around with those long, curly hairs around his mouth Reed couldn't understand.

Danny and Zin pulled the body bag off the cart and dropped it next to the hole. Reed climbed out and pulled the zipper down. His former body was inside. Frost had accumulated on the eyelashes. The lips purple. He pulled the zipper to the bottom. The chest was bruised and bony.

"You sure you want to bury yourself on the island?" Danny asked. "Not a lot of good times here."

"That's not me," Reed said.

It made sense to put it on the beach. That's where he spent most of his time while he was on the island. The body should remain part of it.

They rolled the stiff body into the hole.

It was strange to throw sand on the face. It was hardly recognizable, but it was the only thing Reed had known until a week ago. He was breathing harder with each shovelful of sand. It wasn't so much the exertion anymore. *That's not me,* he kept telling himself. *That's not me.*

But he didn't resist when Danny took the shovel from him. Reed went to the water while he and Zin finished the job. He listened to them pack the sand over the body's final resting place.

Finally, it was at peace.

The sun dropped below the horizon. The sky was a myriad of purples and reds and oranges. They stood on the hardpacked sand, the water wrapping around their ankles. Home was out there. The outside world was within reach.

For the first time, Reed embraced hope.

Zin leaned on the shovel. "You know, they were right, the old men. There's not much for us to go back to. I don't know about you guys, but I got nothing out there. I'm not saying I want to stay here, but there's nothing great waiting for me in the real world. My life sucked. I got no parents, no home… I got nothing."

"That's why we're not going back there, Zin." Danny put his arm over his shoulder. "We're starting a new life."

Slowly, the sky went dark.

They left the golf cart on the beach and walked back. They crossed the Yard and went around the dormitory. For the first time ever, the Chimney was dark. They passed it on their way toward the Mansion.

Danny was on the back of a yacht.

The foamy water rippled in deep-cut waves as the ship's motors churned the water. He held onto the railing and watched the island recede into the night. A few lights twinkled on the back of the Mansion. Danny informed the old men that he would be passing through and they needed to be in their rooms. He reminded them that he had control of their trackers and that he would put them to sleep on sight.

They were old and harmless. Still, the three of them walked cautiously through the building and across the back yard to the yacht. He saw them watching from their windows. They would see the Director with them (without the beard) and would want to talk to him, to find out why he was keeping them imprisoned after they paid a fortune. They would want to tell him that he would not get away with this. But they wouldn't get the chance.

They would never have the chance.

The Director, as they knew him, was no more.

Reed had shut down the Looping Program, ending the identity known as the Director.

Even if the old men knew the Director had passed, there was nothing they could do. There was no communication with the outside world. That was the terms of their contract. They signed their life over to the Director. They had purchased a younger body when they acquired a young man, but had to sell their soul in order to do so.

Once they were on the yacht, Reed took the helm. Zin stayed up front to watch the way to the other island. The rest of the boys were back on the island and would never know they were gone. They would keep playing games, find food in the cafeteria and sleep in the dormitory. They probably wouldn't even know something was wrong.

Until help arrived.

"There it is!" Zin called. "Straight ahead!"

Reed waved from the helm. Danny joined Zin at the bow. The water was black and the island invisible in the dark except for a single light at the end of the dock. There would be someone waiting to help them tie off the yacht. Reed had called ahead, telling them to prepare the plane. He would be bringing the boat over soon.

They sounded surprised. The Director, flying?

Of course, he told him. *Vacation is long over due.*

It took some research, but Danny discovered the Director was a billionaire many times over. He had so much money that if they split it three ways, they would all still be billionaires. For the time being, they were going to stay together. The Director had an estate in Italy.

That seemed like a good place to start a new life.

Missing Satellite Uncovers Human Trafficking Ring

ASSOCIATED PRESS. – The Military Strategic and Tactical Relay (MILSTAR) reported the sudden crash landing of one of their satellites in the South Atlantic when their network was infected with a malicious virus. The virus will likely cost the government millions of dollars to recover and reestablish communication.

However, the recovery of the downed satellite was near a remote island previously thought to be unoccupied. Authorities of the United States have reported a sophisticated human trafficking ring. Preliminary reports have identified wide-spread use of banned technology called Computer-Assisted Alternate Reality (CAAR), though it is unclear how the organization was using the technology.

In addition, dozens of previously reported dead or missing people were being held captive in a resort located on the island. All the people are male and worth billions of dollars. None have agreed to cooperate with the investigation until they have consulted their legal counsel.

However, many have admitted the leader and creator of the island's society was missing. Currently, his name has not been discovered but he went by the nickname, The Director.

Enjoy Foreverland?
Please review on Amazon and Goodreads.

Get more of Tony Bertauski's writing
http://bertauski.com

<u>Novels by Tony Bertauski</u>
Claus: Legend of the Fat Man
The Discovery of Socket Greeny
The Training of Socket Greeny
The Legend of Socket Greeny

<u>Novellas by Tony Bertauski</u>
Drayton (The Taker)
Bearing the Cross (Drayton #2)
Swift is the Current (Drayton #3)
Yellow (Drayton #4)

<u>Short Story</u>
4-Letter Words
(South Carolina Fiction Open Winner, 2008)

<u>Columnist</u>
Post and Courier Gardening
http://www.postandcourier.com/section/featurescolumnists

Interview with Tony Bertauski

When did you start writing?

I always wanted to write creatively. I just wasn't good at it. I didn't have a writer's muscle, either: that ability to spend hours at the keyboard. I was a technical writer before fiction. I did a Master's thesis and wrote several articles for trade magazines before completing two textbooks on landscape design. After that, I figured fiction would be cake. Turns out, the craft of fiction – *good fiction* – is a hell of lot harder than I thought.

My first effort started with Socket Greeny. It was a story I started for my son because he hated to read. He still hates to read, but this character – Socket – took root. It was the first time I felt possessed by a character with a story to tell. It took me 5 years and countless rewrites to get it right. I thought I had the Golden Ticket, that I just needed to pick a publisher to mail me a giant check. I even estimated how many years it would take for the movie.

Turns out publishing fiction is harder than writing it.

If you can't make money, why write fiction?

I didn't say you can't make money. There are a lot of people out there with a book; I'm just a minnow in a crowded pond. It took a good deal of networking and research to realize just how hard it is.

Thanks to epublishing, I can still get books out. That frees me up to write what inspires me. Writing is the true love. It'd be great to make a living from it, but for now it's just a hobby and money is just a bonus. There's something deeply satisfying to have characters come to life and watch their stories unfold. It's a deeper experience than reading someone else's story.

What do you want readers to get from your stories?
I've always been inspired by fearless writing that asked poignant questions; questions like *who am I* and *what is the universe?* Things that made me look at life slightly different; books that exposed a layer of reality. Writing in the young adult genre appealed to me most because that's the age I really craved those questions and answers.

When someone reads my stuff, I want them to see the world slightly different.

Who is your favorite character?
I love a bad, bad antagonist that you can't entirely hate. There's some smidgeon of redemption you feel inside this demented, sorry character. Heath Ledger's *Joker* is a good example, a despicable character that didn't deserve an ounce of pity, but, for some reason, I didn't hate him as much as I should have. It's that character I find most intriguing.

How do you come up with stories?
After I finished the Socket Greeny trilogy, I thought I was done with fiction. I'd written three novels, developed the covers and interior, edited and queried until I was spent. The Socket Greeny story just unfolded and (to bludgeon a cliché to death) I was the conduit. I didn't feel anymore stories. I didn't traditionally publish but felt like I'd accomplished something special.

Six months later, a seedling germinated. Don't know how, don't know why, and can't even remember what it was, but in one night I'd scratched out the rough outline for what would become *The Annihilation of Foreverland.* It took three months to write. The writer-muscle was developing.

Once *Foreverland* was complete, I was empty again. And then, while visiting relatives during the holidays, my nephew was talking about Santa's invisible ninja elves. I felt it, this time. I knew the moment my next novel had arrived. *Claus: Legend of the Fat Man* was finished four months later.

After that, I don't know. Something will probably come up. I'll know when it does.

What is your writing process?

I'm not a "blank page" writer, one that lets the story just go. I need to know where it's going, to some extent. A lot of times, I'll sit down and let a few chapters just unfold in my imagination, like I'm watching a movie. I quickly write down keywords so I have the direction and then, when I have time, I can get them on the computer. My writing muscle is up to 2 or 3 chapters in one sitting, but that's still only 3 or 4 hours of writing. Writing champs, like Stephen King, can go all day, uninterrupted. I don't have the stamina. Although, once I got in the zone and my wife and daughter left for the grocery store. They walked right back in the house. *I thought you were going to the store?*

They did.

CPSIA information can be obtained at www.ICGtesting.com
Printed in the USA
LVOW07s1950230615

443535LV00008B/1044/P

9 780982 845288